"A fast-paced and thought-provoking story. Dynamic characters in *Blue Moon* will leave you with no doubt that you are reading something special . . . the beginning of an exciting new series." —*Enchanted in Romance*

"This book has everything—excellent writing, fascinating characters, suspense, comical one-liners, and best of all, a super-good romance." —*The Best Reviews*

"An incredible werewolf story with a twist . . . full of sass and with a delightful, sarcastic sense of humor." —*Paranormal Romances*

"The action is fast-paced, the plot is gripping, the characters are realistic, and I absolutely positively cannot wait for the next book in this series." —*Fallen Angel Reviews*

"A dry wit that shines . . . Everything about this book is wonderful: the sizzling sexiness, the three-dimensional characters, and the sense of danger." —*Romance Junkies*

"Great intensity, danger, drama, captivation, and stellar writing." —*The Road to Romance*, Reviewer's Choice Award

"Lori Handeland makes a superlative debut in the world of paranormal romance with *Blue Moon*, first in an enticing new *Moon* trilogy. *Blue Moon* is simply not to be missed." —*BookLoons Reviews*

"If you enjoy werewolves that are linked to folklore with characters that seem to be in every town, whether it is small or big, then pick up a copy of *Blue Moon*. You will not be disappointed." —*A Romance Review*

"A captivating novel that draws readers in from the first page." —*Romance Reviews Today*

ST. MARTIN'S PAPERBACKS TITLES
BY LORI HANDELAND

Hidden Moon

Rising Moon

Midnight Moon

Crescent Moon

Dark Moon

Hunter's Moon

Blue Moon

MORE . . .

"Smart and often amusing dialogue, brisk pacing, plenty of action and a generous helping of 'spooki-ness' add just the right tone . . . an engaging and enjoy-able paranormal romance."   —*BookLoons Reviews*

"A fantastic tale starring two strong likable protago-nists . . . action-packed . . . a howling success."
—*Midwest Book Review*

"Handeland writes some of the most fascinating, creepy, and macabre stories I have ever read . . . exciting plot twists . . . new revelations, more emo-tional themes, and spiritual awakenings are prevalent here."   —*Romance Reader at Heart*

HUNTER'S MOON

"Another fast-paced, action-packed story of sacrifice and love in the shape-shifting realm . . . a terrific sec-ond book in her werewolf series."   —*The Best Reviews*

"A continuation of the perfection that is a fascinating series the author started in her novel *Blue Moon* . . . fantastic and way too hard to put down."
—*Romance Reader at Heart*

"Handeland has more than proved herself a worthy author in the increasingly popular world of paranormal romance with these slick and highly engrossing tales and has become an author whose works will always be greatly anticipated."   —*The Road to Romance*

"An absorbing, fast-paced story that will keep read-ers enthralled from start to finish . . . a paranormal delight . . . once you read this, you won't be able to help going back and reading the first [novel]."
—*Fallen Angel Reviews*

HIDDEN MOON

LORI HANDELAND

St. Martin's Paperbacks

This is a work of fiction. All of the characters, organizations, and events portrayed in this novel are either products of the author's imagination or are used fictitiously.

HIDDEN MOON

Copyright © 2007 by Lori Handeland.

Cover photo © Shirley Green

ISBN: 0-312-94917-0
EAN: 978-0-312-94917-4

Printed in the United States of America

St. Martin's Paperbacks edition / August 2007

St. Martin's Paperbacks are published by St. Martin's Press, 175 Fifth Avenue, New York, NY 10010.

10 9 8 7 6 5 4 3 2 1

ACKNOWLEDGMENTS

Though an author's life is solitary, it is also full of people who help us to do what we do the best we can.

My husband, who might not understand what I do, but is always the first one to tell me I have to keep doing it

My sons, who've never known a life without a mother who writes and therefore think I'm normal

My agent, Irene Goodman, an honest woman whose opinion I value

My editor, Jen Enderlin, still the best in the business today

Everyone at St. Martin's Press, who make it such a great place to work

My publicist, Nancy Berland, and her staff

Vickie Denney, the computer whiz behind my *Howls* newsletter

I couldn't do any of this without you.

HIDDEN
MOON

1

I CAME HOME to escape one hell and stepped straight into another. I guess I deserved it. I had walked out at eighteen and never looked back.

The Cherokee call the mountains where I was born Sah-ka-na-ga, or the Great Blue Hills of God. I'd always thought the phrase an exaggeration; now I wasn't so sure. In my present state of mind, the Blue Ridge Mountains did seem a little bit like heaven.

"But then, a lake of fire looks good compared to this," I muttered, scowling at the mess that nearly obscured the top of my desk.

"Have you ever seen a lake of fire? It isn't pretty."

To my surprise, Grace McDaniel stood in the doorway.

We'd been best friends in high school. Then I'd gone to college and taken a job at a television station in the big, bad city of Atlanta, while she'd stayed behind.

Grace was now the sheriff in Lake Bluff, and I was the mayor. Talk about the sins of the fathers. . . .

Phones rang in the outer office. My assistant had informed me I had three people waiting, before she'd taken off to God knows where to do Lord knows what.

Everyone said Joyce Flaherty had been the assistant to the mayor since there'd been a mayor in Lake Bluff, Georgia. Considering the town had been settled by the Scotch-Irish well before the Revolution, that would make Joyce downright supernatural. If the statement had been true.

In reality, Joyce had been my father's right hand during the thirty-plus years he'd been in charge here and now she was mine. The woman had an annoying habit of doing my job, then telling me about it later. But she knew the job so much better than I did.

"Problem?" I asked.

Grace didn't often show up at my office; she called, left a message, sent a report. We'd been friends, but now . . . Well, Grace seemed a little pissed at me, and I wasn't sure why.

"You might say that," she murmured in a slow, smooth southern accent. I hadn't realized how much I'd missed the cadence—one I'd trained out of my own voice years ago—until I'd come home.

Grace glanced over her shoulder, then stepped into my office and shut the door. I waved at an empty seat, but she shook her head and began to pace, her nervous energy crackling in the small, enclosed space.

Grace was the least likely small-town cop you'd ever come across. Tall and strong, like the Scottish ancestors we both shared, she also possessed the high cheekbones and stick-straight ink black hair of the Cherokee who'd roamed these mountains for centuries before they'd been dragged west during the embarrassment we've all come to know as the Trail of Tears.

The slightly smoky shade of her perfect skin also hinted at the intermingling with a slave or two somewhere on that family tree. A common enough occurrence in these parts, since the Cherokee had once owned African-American slaves, too.

Grace could have been a fashion model, but she was as unaware of her beauty as I was unaware of how to be the mayor. And she loved Lake Bluff more than she loved anything or anyone; she'd never leave it like I had.

Suddenly she stopped pacing and rested her palms on the front of my desk. "You need to come with me."

A thinker and doer, Grace made a decision and then she executed that decision. Sometimes—hell, most times—I wondered why *she* wasn't the mayor. Except in Lake Bluff, people followed the path of their parents, and if they didn't want to, they got out of town.

"There's a caravan of Gypsies camped at the lake," Grace said.

I blinked. "I'm sorry. I thought you said 'caravan of Gypsies.'"

Her lips curved. "Nothing wrong with your hearing."

The way she said it made me think there was something wrong with other parts of me. There was, but Grace didn't know that. No one did.

"Claire." Grace sighed. "What happened to you in Atlanta? You used to understand sarcasm, give as good as you got. You used to be fun."

"Now I'm the mayor," I muttered.

"There you go." My eyes met hers and she winked. "We'll have you back to yourself in no time."

I'd never be the self I'd been before I'd left, but maybe I could at least stop jumping at shadows now that I was home.

The shrill *brrrring* of the phone made me start up from my chair, heart pounding.

Or not.

Grace made an impatient sound. Had she ever been afraid of anything in her life?

"Don't answer it," Grace ordered. I lifted a brow. "You'll only have to deal with some bum-fuck nonsense, and I need you to come with me."

"Bum-fuck nonsense?" God I'd missed her.

Grace shrugged. "You know how it is around here. Jamie's cow got into Harold's corn. Lucy's cat beat up Carol's dog. Some dumb-ass kid got his head stuck between the bars of the jungle gym and screamed bloody murder for an hour."

"That sounds more like your bum-fuck nonsense than mine." I stood, relieved when my phone stopped ringing at last and went to voice mail.

"Fine." Grace opened the door. "Then you won't have to listen to someone whine about their property lines, their taxes, or the unfairness of the city bylaws."

That would be my bum-fuck nonsense all right.

Pausing at Joyce's desk, I scribbled a note, checked my cell phone to make certain it was on, and jerked a thumb toward the rear exit.

We'd almost reached the back door when someone called, "Mayor?" I began to turn, and Grace shoved me between the shoulder blades.

I stumbled in my off-white pumps, the perfect complement to my pale peach summer suit, then nearly fell on my face when the back door burst open, spilling us into the summer sun.

"Ah." Grace cast an amused glance around the parking lot. "Remember when we smoked pot out here in high school?"

"Grace!"

"What?" She slid dark sunglasses over her light green eyes.

"Someone might hear you."

"So what if they did? It's not like we got high yesterday. We were sixteen."

"It would leave a bad impression," I said stiffly. "You're supposed to be the law around here."

"You want me to arrest myself for something I did ten years ago? Sorry, but the statute of limitations on that crime is over."

Grace set off, her long, lithe legs eating up the distance more quickly than mine ever could. Not that I was short, just shorter, three inches shy of Grace's five-ten. And I wasn't lithe by any means; I was more . . . round. Not fat—at least not yet. But I had to work at it—low-fat yogurt, low-fat dressing, dessert only on very special occasions, like the Second Coming.

Grace reached the squad car and slid behind the wheel. I clambered into the passenger seat, snagging my hose on the door and cursing.

"If you didn't wear the stupid things," Grace muttered, "you wouldn't ruin them. This isn't Atlanta."

I glanced at Grace's tan slacks and equally tan blouse, complete with a stylish Lake Bluff Sheriff's Department patch.

"Don't say it," she warned.

"Say what?"

"That someone in an outfit like this has no business giving fashion advice."

"Okay." I faced front. "I won't say it."

Grace gave me a long look over the top of her sunglasses; then she just drove.

I'd returned to Lake Bluff three weeks ago for my father's funeral. He'd only been fifty-five, and while he'd never watched his weight, or his intake of cigarettes and whiskey, his death had still been a shock. That I'd agreed to remain and fulfill the rest of his term as mayor had been an even bigger shock, yet here I was.

I stared out the window as we left town and headed onto the highway that led to Lunar Lake. The present incarnation of the town had sprouted on a hill a few miles from the lake—hence its name. No matter where you stood in Lake Bluff, the view was incandescent.

The majority of the population—just under five thousand souls—made their living in the shops, restaurants, and small, quaint hostels that lined the main streets. A goodly portion of that living came to us during our yearly Full Moon Festival.

People traveled from miles around to enjoy the weeklong celebration, which culminated on the day and night of August's full moon with a parade, picnic, and fireworks. We were expecting a huge turnout this year, since a rare total lunar eclipse would take place that night.

Each year two to four lunar eclipses occurred, but only during a small percentage of them would the Earth totally cut off the sun's light from the moon.

As far as I knew, the Full Moon Festival had never coincided with such an event. Therefore not only would we be hosting the usual summer tourists, but also stargazers—amateur and professional—would arrive to observe nature's performance. Since many of the scheduled events took place at the lake, I understood Grace's concern about the Gypsies.

We wound down the two-lane highway—paved with asphalt, surrounded by gravel—into the valley where Lunar Lake gleamed.

In between the rich evergreen of the trees, the sun sparked golden shards off the clear surface. On the other side of the valley, the mountains rose toward a sky the same shade as the lake.

"So"—I turned away from the sight—"do you get a lot of Gypsy caravans through here these days?"

Grace pulled onto the hard-packed dirt trail that led to the lake. "Not a one."

"Are there any Gypsies left?"

"I think they went extinct about the same time as the Indians."

"More sarcasm," I said. "Goody."

Her lips twitched, but she didn't crack a smile. She so rarely did. "Gypsies are everywhere, Claire. Most people just don't notice them."

We came around the curve in the road, and Grace slammed on the brakes. For an instant I thought we'd traveled back in time—Romania in the 1700s perhaps?

I don't know what I'd expected to find. Tents? Hippie throwbacks? A homeless convention? I had definitely not expected to see a jumble of horse-drawn wagons and a crowd of brightly dressed . . . Gypsies.

"Well, you *said* there were still Gypsies," I murmured.

Grace glared at me, or at least I thought she glared. I couldn't see her eyes past the tough-cop sunglasses.

As soon as we'd come into view, everyone stilled. When Grace and I climbed out of the squad car, they stared at us as keenly as we stared at them.

They appeared as if they'd escaped from the Disney version of *Hunchback of Notre Dame*. The men wore black pants and colorful blousy shirts; the women, long rainbow-hued skirts and white peasant-style blouses with scarves covering their heads. Gold bracelets, beaded chains, and hoop earrings sparkled everywhere.

Several wagons were fitted with bars, and animals paced inside, though the conveyances were too far away, the forest too thick and shadowed, to determine any species. The horses that drew the wagons were huge—Clydesdales maybe, though they didn't resemble the Budweiser crew, except in size. These were dappled gray instead of brown and upon closer inspection possessed broader chests and stockier rumps.

"Lake Bluff Sheriff's Department." Grace removed her sunglasses, hooking the earpiece in her shirt before striding forward with her hand on the butt of her gun.

Those nearest to her shrank back. The babble of another language rose from the ones behind them.

"Bull in a china shop," I muttered. I might have changed, but she hadn't.

Putting on my best CNN anchor smile, I moved up beside her. "I'm Claire Kennedy, mayor of Lake Bluff. Can I ask what you're doing here?"

The babbling slowed to a trickle, although everyone continued to stare. A few actually made the sign of the cross, or near enough. If I didn't know better, I'd think they were afraid of me. Or maybe they were just afraid of Grace.

"Take your hand off your gun," I whispered.

"Not."

"You're scaring them."

"Scared of the sheriff is a healthy thing to be."

I pressed my lips together. At my change in expression the indecipherable babble started up again. I raised my voice. "Is there anyone in charge?"

"Someone who speaks English?" Grace added.

"That would be me."

A ripple began near the back—sound, movement,

an aura of deference as they bowed their heads. The crowd parted and a man appeared.

"Holy shit," Grace murmured.

I choked, not just at her words but also at the sight of him. "Holy shit" about summed it up.

He wore the black pants common to the other men and shiny knee-high black boots, but his chest was bare and shimmering with sweat or lake water, hard to tell without a taste.

I blinked at the thought, a type I hadn't had for a very long time.

Smooth, bronzed skin flowed over lean muscles and a ridged abdomen. A breeze blew in from the mountains and he tensed, biceps flexing, at the sudden chill in the air.

But it wasn't just his body that left me speechless. With eyes like blood beneath the moon and a face that was all sharp edges at the cheeks, chin, and nose, how could I be faulted for staring?

Someone handed him a towel, and he rubbed the cloth over his chest, the movement both efficient and suggestive. My stomach skittered, and I had to force myself not to look away from his suddenly amused gaze and follow the path of his hands.

He lifted the towel to his slightly curling ebony hair, just long enough to brush the spike of his collarbone. When he scrubbed at it, droplets flew, and the strands played peekaboo with the silver cross dangling from his left ear.

He threw the cloth behind him as if expecting someone to catch it, which they did, before handing him an impossibly white shirt. While he drew it over his head, I glanced at Grace, who rolled her eyes.

"Sheriff," he greeted, with an accent so Irish I smelled

clover. "Mayor Kennedy. I'm Malachi Cartwright." He bent slightly at the waist. "Call me Mal."

"No need to get chummy," Grace said. "You won't be staying."

Cartwright's eyebrows lifted, along with one corner of his mouth. "Won't we now?" he murmured.

2

GRACE STEPPED FORWARD again, fingers tightening on the butt of her gun. I threw my arm out, smacking her in the chest. She growled.

"Stop that," I ordered. "I'll handle this."

My father always said you catch more flies with honey than vinegar, and I'd found it to be true. Of course Grace's dad had been of the opinion that might is always right, and he'd made certain that was true. Grace was more a chip off the old block than I was.

She ignored my words and shouldered her way in front of me, leaving her hand on the gun. "You can't just camp here. We've got a festival starting in a few days."

"Which is exactly why we've come, darlin'."

Cartwright stretched out his arm and a sheaf of papers appeared in his palm. I knew the stack hadn't just appeared, but whoever was giving him things was damned quick about it.

He presented the sheets with a flourish. "We've been hired to entertain you."

The way he said "entertain" caused heat to flare in my stomach. I had no doubt that his idea of entertainment and mine were a whole lot different—or maybe, considering the direction of my thoughts, just the same.

Grace glanced at me with a scowl.

"Wasn't me." I held up my hands in surrender.

After snatching the papers from Cartwright, she peered at the first page, then lifted her gaze to mine.

"Joyce," we said at the same time. Grace passed me the contract.

Sure enough, my assistant had hired the caravan to entertain during the week of the Full Moon Festival.

The festival planning had begun long before I'd returned, and since those who'd been planning it had done so for years, I'd let them continue. I probably should have paid more attention.

I didn't think the people of Lake Bluff were going to be all that happy to discover itinerant Gypsies camped at the lake. From the way Grace was eyeing them, she wasn't wild about the idea, either.

Unfortunately, they'd been paid a good chunk of our treasury already, and it was too late to hire someone else to entertain now, even if we had the money for it. The festival was our cash cow. Without it, Lake Bluff wouldn't survive.

"Is everything in order?" Cartwright asked.

I glanced up and found myself captured again by his dark, dark eyes. I was disturbed, not only by their strange color but also by their intense expression. What was it about me that interested him?

Perhaps it was just the novelty. I wasn't the only blue-eyed redhead in Lake Bluff, but I was the only one *here,* and no one in the immediate vicinity wore a business suit and heels. Smart of them. My Dior jacket had me baking in the sun, and my Kenneth Cole pumps were coated with dust, the heels sinking into the gravel with every step, no doubt scratching the surface beyond repair.

"Everything appears to be fine," I said, and returned the contract.

His fingers brushed mine as he accepted the papers. I jerked away, nearly tearing it in my haste to retreat.

The Gypsies murmured. Cartwright's smile froze. Grace shot me an exasperated look.

The reaction was rude, as if I didn't want him to touch me. I didn't. Not because of who he was, but because of *what* he was.

A man. They frightened me.

"I guess you can stay," Grace allowed. "But you'll need to keep your people under wraps."

Cartwright's eyes narrowed. "What exactly is your meaning, Sheriff?"

"My meaning is this—everyone in Lake Bluff has a gun and no one is afraid to use it. Sneaking around after dark where you don't belong is an invitation to get shot."

"You think we'll be stealin' then, perhaps kidnapping a few of your wee ones?"

Cartwright let his gaze scan Grace from top to bottom. His perusal was not complimentary—probably the first time in the history of Grace.

"You should know better than to believe everything you hear. All Gypsies aren't thieves and baby stealers any more than all Indians are lazy drunks."

Grace's cheeks darkened. "Point taken. I apologize."

My eyes widened. Another first.

"But the warning still stands. Others in Lake Bluff might not be as enlightened as I am."

Cartwright's mouth twitched. "Of course not."

He said something to his people in their language, and they shuffled and murmured and stared.

"What did you tell them?" I asked.

"To stay in camp after dark."

"Does anyone else speak English?"

"Some. But we prefer to speak Romani, the language of the Rom. The Gypsies," he clarified. "We don't want to lose our heritage."

"Understandable," Grace murmured.

When we were kids, Grace had spent a lot of time studying the old ways with her Cherokee medicine woman great-grandmother who'd insisted the ancient knowledge should not be lost.

Now that Grace was a public servant, I wondered how much of her background she flaunted. The Lake Bluff sheriff was elected, and while the residents were used to seeing Native American descendants in their town, that didn't mean they wanted their head cop performing a rain dance beneath the light of the moon. If the Cherokee even had a rain dance.

I turned to Cartwright. "What type of entertainment are we talking about?"

For all I knew, *they* might have come here to do naked rain dances, which would not be the kind of show we wanted for our family festival.

"Human sacrifice and the like."

I gaped; so did Grace. A few of the Gypsies began to laugh.

"Sorry." Cartwright spread his hands. "I couldn't resist."

When neither Grace nor I cracked a smile, he said a few short words in their language and his people dispersed, then he returned his attention to us.

"We perform like our ancestors did. As you can see"—Cartwright swept an arm out to indicate the wagons, the animals, the gaily dressed people—"we endeavor to bring the flavor of the Old World to the new one. The Rom have long been travelers."

"Why is that?" Grace asked.

"The easier to avoid arrest for our stealing and kidnapping."

Beginning to get his humor, I laughed; Grace didn't.

"Seriously," she said. "What's up with your blast-of-the-past show?"

"People enjoy it." He shrugged. "We're different, and that'll keep you workin' week after week."

"When you say different—"

"Fortune-telling, animal acts, trinkets."

"Big whoop," Grace muttered. "Been there, done that, a hundred times before."

"Not like this." He turned to me as if I'd been the one questioning him. "If you'd like to come by another time, Mayor Kennedy, I'd enjoy showing you just what makes us so special."

3

"HE'S GOT THE hots for you," Grace said as we drove away.

I glanced back. Malachi Cartwright stared after us, his dark gaze boring into mine. I quickly faced forward. "No, he doesn't."

"'Come on by, Mayor Kennedy,'" she mocked, sounding like the love child of Scarlett O'Hara and the Lucky Charms leprechaun. "'Preferably alone. Without that nasty old sheriff. I'll show you my etchings. I keep them in my pants.'"

"Grace," I protested, barely able to speak past the laughter. "He was just trying to be friendly, and since you were doing your Godzilla-stomps-on-all-the-little-people act—"

"He couldn't keep his eyes off you," she interrupted. "Barely looked in my direction the entire time we were there."

"And I bet you aren't used to that."

"No," she agreed. "But I didn't really want him to look at me. His eyes are . . ." Her voice faded.

"What?"

"Pure black. Like a demon or something."

"A demon? Have you been hitting the peace pipe again?"

"No one's eyes are pure black," she insisted.

"And neither were his. They were dark brown. It was just a trick of the light."

"Sure it was," she muttered.

I didn't bother to argue with her. Arguing with Grace was never worth the headache that followed.

We reached the town hall, and she let the car idle out front. "You're not coming in?" I asked.

"Nope. Places to go, people to arrest." I got out but leaned back in the window when Grace called my name. "I appreciate your coming along," she said.

"Why'd you ask me?" Her brows lifted above her sunglasses. "It's not like I'd be of any help in a sticky situation." I waved my hand at my suit and heels, which were pretty much ruined after the trek to the lake.

"You might not carry a gun or have much in the way of balls," Grace began.

"Wow, Sheriff McDaniel, you're so PC sometimes, you scare me."

"*But*," she continued with a scowl, "you've got your father's gift of gab."

Jeremiah Kennedy had been the consummate politician. He'd known everyone's names, where they lived, their dogs, their children and grandchildren. He'd been good at this job in a way I doubted I could ever be.

I was starting to wonder if I was good at anything anymore. In high school I'd been not only a cheerleader but also captain of the debate team and a state champion forensics speaker. The rush I'd felt in front of a crowd had been seductive.

I'd taken my counselor's advice and gone into

broadcast journalism, dreaming of a career beneath the bright lights of CNN, only to discover I wasn't pretty enough, talented enough—hell, I wasn't anything "enough" to succeed.

"Except for today," Grace continued, bringing me back to the subject at hand. "That guy made you go all girlie."

"Did not."

Grace ignored me. "I'll run a check on them later. See what you can find out from Joyce."

"Sure." I straightened, and Grace pulled away from the curb.

Grace had never much cared for anything girlie, and that was understandable. She was the youngest of five and the only girl. Her mother had run off when Grace was three, right around the time mine had died on an icy mountain road she had no business being on.

Mama had been from Atlanta, and she'd missed it every day. She'd been a newspaper reporter, and in the late seventies Atlanta was a very exciting place. She'd met my father while doing a story on small-town mayors, and they'd fallen in love. She'd given up the job she adored to come to Lake Bluff, then spent the next four years trying to get away as often as she could—or so I'd heard in whispered snatches of gossip throughout my childhood.

Grace and I had been thrown together, both motherless, both largely ignored by fathers who were devoted to something larger than us.

I'd been as fascinated with Grace's differences as she'd been with mine. Not that she hadn't teased me mercilessly about them, which had, in turn, led to me teasing her just as mercilessly. We'd been like sisters, and I wanted that closeness back more than I'd wanted anything for a long, long time.

Center Street bustled as everyone made last-minute preparations for the festival. Directly across from the town hall, Bobby Turnbaugh, owner of the Good Cookin' Café, hung a banner advertising *Blue Ridge Dining at Its Finest—Southern Chocolate Gravy and Biscuits*.

I made a face. Chocolate gravy and biscuits had never been my idea of fine dining, but my father had always enjoyed them for breakfast.

Bobby lifted a hand. I did the same. We'd dated our junior year, and he'd taught me a few things in the front seat of his daddy's pickup that I had remembered fondly for quite a few years.

Directly next to the café was a combination bookstore and souvenir shop, complete with Native American trinkets, Appalachian doodads, and Civil War paraphernalia. On the other side stood a beauty salon, then the Gun and Loan, where firearms could be bought and just about anything else could be borrowed, and a coffee shop that sold the fancy lattes and chai teas that had become so popular in big towns. No one had thought the Center Perk would take off, but a hundred thousand Starbucks couldn't be wrong.

Farther south, the Lake Bluff Hotel housed a fine-dining restaurant and a higher-class gift shop. Subsequent streets held several bed-and-breakfasts, candle and candy shops, plus various establishments that sold jewelry, knickknacks, and other bright and shiny things. It never ceased to amaze me the amount of junk people bought when they were on vacation.

I let my gaze wander over the quickly moving, industrious citizens, a stark contrast to the lazily milling tourists who had already begun to arrive. I should have asked Grace if she'd sufficiently fortified the local police force with rent-a-cops, but I was certain she knew her job and needed no help from me.

"Claire!"

Joyce's shrill voice hailed me the instant I entered the foyer, echoing throughout the high, domed ceiling.

Town hall had been constructed before the Civil War, back when they'd been able to afford building government offices out of stone and marble. The place was a monstrosity and would last until the end of time.

My assistant hustled to meet me. Nearly six feet tall in her bright white walking shoes, Joyce was as solid as an oak, in stature and temperament. Her hair was shorn close to her head and black as the day she'd been born, courtesy of a standing appointment with Miss Clairol. Joyce dressed like the lumberjack her father had been—jeans, flannel shirts, and boots in the fall and winter, khaki shorts, plaid, sleeveless shirts, and walking shoes in the spring and summer.

She'd started life as a high school phys ed teacher. But when kids became mouthier and a teacher's ability to kick their ass for it became nonexistent, Joyce came to work for the city. She'd never married, devoting herself to this job and my father to the exclusion of all else. There were times I'd wondered if they had a thing going on; I'd decided I didn't want to know.

"Everyone's left." Her mouth flattened in disapproval.

"Who's everyone?"

"I told you there were people waiting to see you, then you snuck out the back door."

Oops.

"I knew you and Grace would be up to your old tricks the minute my back was turned."

I stifled a grin at the memory of some of those old tricks. Although I doubted Grace and I would be sneaking a joint out back or getting sick on cheap wine anytime soon, you never could tell.

For the first time since I'd returned, I felt as if returning might have been a good choice and not the second stupidest thing I'd ever done.

"You have to be above reproach," Joyce said. "The whole town's watching you."

My urge to smile faded. "I know."

When I'd returned for my father's funeral, I hadn't planned to stay, although I hadn't had anywhere to go. I'd recently quit my job as the producer of one of the top Atlanta television stations.

I hadn't been all that broken up about it. I was an adequate producer but not outstanding. I was never going to go any further than I already had, and for the first time in a lifetime, Atlanta did not appeal. The gilded glow I'd placed over the city—because my mother had loved it so—had been tarnished.

"Balthazar was here," Joyce said.

"He's always here."

Balthazar Monahan was a recent transplant from the North. No one knew exactly where he was from; no one knew exactly why he'd come, unless it was to be elected the mayor. He'd been after the job from the day he'd arrived and had not been happy when it was offered to me for the taking.

He'd spent the past three weeks tallying every one of my mistakes, then trumpeting them far and wide, which was easy for him to do since he owned the *Lake Bluff Gazette*.

"What did he want this time?" I asked.

Joyce shrugged. "He came in as he always does; then when he found out you were gone, he started whispering to the people who were waiting to speak to you."

"Shit," I muttered.

"You can say that again."

"Shit."

Joyce chuckled. "Relax. People have to give you a chance to get used to the job. Being the mayor isn't easy."

"Tell it to Balthazar."

"Won't matter. Man was born to be a pain in the ass."

Joyce had him pegged, but she so often did. I don't know if it was her years as a teacher or her years at the desk in town hall, but she could read people in an instant. Good, bad, ugly—Joyce took one look and knew your heart. Which was why she was still working for me despite her tendency to bitch, moan, and mother.

"Speaking of a pain in the ass," I said, "where did you get the idea of hiring a caravan of traveling Gypsies?"

Her face brightened. "They're here?"

"Do you even read the notes I leave?"

"Sometimes."

I rubbed my forehead. "Why Gypsies?"

"They contacted me."

I let my hand drop back to my side. "They what?"

"The head guy . . ." Joyce pursed her lips. "A biblical name. It's on the tip of my tongue."

"Malachi Cartwright?"

"That's it. Last book in the Old Testament."

"I don't remember a Book of Cartwright."

"Hardy-har-har. You'd better watch that quick mouth of yours now that you're in politics."

She was right, as usual. My quick mouth had served me well in Atlanta, but here it might get me lynched, or at least recalled.

"Cartwright contacted me," Joyce continued. "Said he'd heard about our festival and wanted to perform. Then"—she jutted out her chin and did a horrible

Marlon Brando impersonation—"he made me an offer I couldn't refuse."

"What kind of offer?"

"They perform every night for the entire week and only charge us half the price of everyone else I talked to."

"Why?"

"Didn't ask. Gift horse and all that. You know how close the treasury is to empty."

I did. We needed to make a decent profit on this year's Full Moon Festival or things were going to go badly.

Sometimes I thought I should just turn the office over to Balthazar and let him have the headache since he wanted it so much. Then I remembered—without this job, I'd have nothing.

"Are they any good?" I asked.

"We'll find out."

"You didn't check their references?"

"References?" Joyce began to laugh. "They're Gypsies."

"I got that when I saw the earrings and the horse-drawn wagons, though they seem to be laying it on a little thick."

"Showmanship is the name of the game."

"They could be a traveling band of serial killers," I pointed out.

"Grace will run them through her computers."

"She will, but she could have done that before you hired them and saved everyone some stress."

"I forgot."

Which wasn't like Joyce, but I guess she had to start losing it sometime. Why did it have to be on my watch?

The rest of the day passed in a blur. Since the mayor

of Lake Bluff was in charge of pretty much everything municipal that wasn't handled by the sheriff's office, and my only staff was Joyce, I had a full plate.

Every week we had a town council meeting. I didn't think we needed a weekly meeting, but since the all-male, all-ancient membership had nothing better to do, and they'd been getting together every week since time began, I was outvoted.

In the time that I'd been here, the meetings followed the same pattern. They argued; I refereed. We rarely decided anything, and at 9:00 P.M. they adjourned to the American Legion Hall for two-dollar pitchers of Bud Light. They never invited me along. They'd always invited my dad.

Unfortunately for me, tonight was meeting night.

I heard them arguing before I reached the community room. I was tempted to turn right around and leave them to it. Would they even notice if I didn't show up?

"I say we need a new sidewalk in front of the elementary school."

"I say we don't."

"Maybe we should wait awhile and think on it some more. I can see both of your viewpoints."

"We need to lower taxes."

"We have to raise them."

"Now let's not be hasty. . . ."

I took a deep breath and walked in. The room went silent.

"Gentlemen."

"Claire."

Every one of them had known me since I wore diapers. I could hardly insist they call me Mayor Kennedy. That was what they'd called my dad.

My father had secretly referred to his council by the nicknames See No Evil, Hear No Evil, Speak No Evil, and Have No Fun. I hadn't needed to ask who was who. One meeting and I'd easily been able to assign the monikers myself.

"What's on the agenda this evening?" I asked.

"Sidewalks and taxes."

Why had I asked?

"Didn't we discuss sidewalks last week?"

"We didn't decide anything," said Wilbur Mcandless. He'd once owned the hardware store but had left it to his son and now spent his days worrying about sidewalks. I guess someone had to.

Wilbur couldn't make a decision; both sides of every coin always sounded fine to him. Dad probably should have named him Speak Nothing That Ever Helps, but that wouldn't have fitted in with the joke, so Wilbur was Speak No Evil.

"We haven't finished our discussion on taxes, either." This came from Hoyt Abernathy, former president of the Lake Bluff Bank. He liked to talk about money. Incessantly.

Rumor had it that on the day Hoyt had retired from the bank, he'd made a bonfire of every one of his dress shoes, which was why he now wore slippers. Everywhere. It wasn't a bad idea.

I'd identified Hoyt as Have No Fun—to him everything was a disaster of epic proportions. Personally I'd call him Eeyore for the whiny nature of his comments.

"We can't raise taxes!" shouted Malcolm Frasier, not so much because he was angry as because he was deaf. Hear No Evil—or anything else, for that matter.

"Why not?" Hoyt shouted back.

"Folks are hurtin' already. Higher taxes will make them leave Lake Bluff altogether."

"Why would anyone ever leave Lake Bluff?" asked Joe Cantrell, retired fire chief. "It's so wonderful here."

For Joe—or See No Evil—the world was always rosy, an odd outlook for a fire chief. However, there weren't that many fires in Lake Bluff, and the ones that we did have weren't serious. People lived too close together and minded one another's business too well for a fire to ever get out of hand.

The room went silent as all eyes turned to me.

"Oops," Joe murmured.

I wasn't sure what to say. I'd left because I had to. Needed to. Come back for the same reason. But I didn't want to discuss that with them.

I straightened. If I meant to be the mayor and not just play at it, I needed to *be* the mayor. Now was as good a time as any to begin.

"All right." I rapped my knuckle on the tabletop twice. "We've yapped enough."

"Aye?" Malcolm cupped his ear.

"No more talking!" I shouted. "We vote. Tonight. Make a decision. That's why you were elected."

"A vote?" Wilbur asked. "You sure? We usually just talk about stuff."

"Not anymore," I said. "Gentlemen, grab your pencils."

Fifteen minutes later the old business was settled. New sidewalks in front of the school, since the ones there had crumbled into a hazard, and slightly higher taxes to pay for them.

"That was fun," Joe said. "Let's do it again!"

Wilbur slouched in his chair. "I'm not sure we should have decided on anything so soon."

I ignored them both to ask, "New business?"

Everyone looked around, shrugged.

"We've been so busy worryin' about the old business, we forgot to think up new stuff," Wilbur admitted.

Thank God, although I was certain that wouldn't last. They didn't have much to do except think up stuff.

"Your father never made us vote," Hoyt grumbled.

"Maybe he should have."

All four of them gasped. I tensed, waiting for the lecture. I really had no business criticizing. Dad had done just fine for thirty years.

"We're adjourned," I said.

"What?" shouted Malcolm.

The other three made a beeline for the door, no doubt smelling the Bud already. Malcolm saw them going and took off, too. I glanced at my watch. The meeting had been completed in a half an hour. I was so damn proud of myself I nearly danced. Maybe I could do this job after all. It just might take a little time.

4

A s I shut and locked the front door of town hall behind me an hour later, dusk hovered on the horizon. Joyce had left at six, speed walking the mile and a half home as she did every day.

My own commute was considerably less than Joyce's. My father had left me the largest house in Lake Bluff—a white rambling two-story, with a veranda that encircled the first floor, jutting out into a deck that overlooked the backyard. All I had to do to get home was turn in the opposite direction of the Center Street shops and head uphill for three blocks.

The streetlights hadn't come on yet. The setting sun cast tendrils of shadow across the pavement.

My heels clicked, a lonely, somewhat creepy sound emphasizing my isolation, but I had nothing to fear. Crime was virtually nonexistent in Lake Bluff. The only time it did exist was during the festival and it could always be traced to outsiders. There hadn't been a murder here in decades.

So why did I suddenly get the shivers and increase my pace to a brisk power walk?

The mountains rose in the distance, huge and navy blue. Whatever happened, those hills would always be there. The sight of them calmed me.

The sun slipped below the horizon with a near-audible sigh, spreading the grayish haze of early evening over my world.

A pebble tumbled down an incline to my right. My gaze jerked in that direction, and a shadow flitted between the tree trunks. I hesitated, glancing at town hall, which was now farther away than my front door.

Determined, I faced forward and kept walking.

I'd been traveling this path twice a day for nearly three weeks, and I'd never been nervous about it. Of course I'd never felt the presence of anything out there until tonight.

Something howled, the sound sharp and unfamiliar. I'd heard a thousand coyotes in my lifetime, and none of them had ever sounded like that.

"Has to be a coyote," I murmured. Despite the acres of space and the plethora of trees, there hadn't been a wolf in these mountains for a very long time.

The shrill, mournful sound died away. I waited for an answer, but none came.

Strange. When I was a kid and the coyotes howled, there'd always been more than one.

A *scritch* against the pavement, and I whirled, a scream rising in my throat at the sight of a man only inches away.

"Balthazar." My breath rushed out. "What are you doing here?"

He crowded into my space; he always did. I'd never

been certain if he was a close talker or just a jerk who used his size to intimidate.

The man had to be six-five and weigh 270. His barrel chest spread in front of my eyes, covered with a black dress shirt. Several equally black chest hairs poked out between the straining buttons. Balthazar was not only big but extremely hairy.

I inched back, peering up into his large, flaring, also hairy nostrils. The streetlights came on with a tinny thunk, and their reflection gave his brown eyes a golden glow.

He smirked, and I knew in that instant he'd meant to scare me, probably been waiting in the trees for hours until I went home. I'd tried to keep my fear of men hidden, but in the way of wild animals Balthazar had sensed a weakness and exploited it.

"I wanted to get some information on the squatters at the lake."

I scowled. How had he found out so fast?

Just as he'd sensed my weakness, he seemed to sense my question, and answered it in a flat Yankee accent that grated on my nerves more than the mysterious howl had.

"One of my reporters saw you and the chief head thataway." He pointed toward the lake.

Being an equal-opportunity bigot—a racist and a sexist, as well as plenty of other "ists" I hadn't figured out yet—Balthazar had as much use for Grace as he had for me. He constantly referred to her as the police *chief,* as if the play on words were the funniest thing he'd ever heard. The guy needed to get out more. Way out. Like out of town.

"You were in such a hurry," Balthazar continued, "he decided to follow."

Sometimes Balthazar's reporters seemed more like spies.

"Imagine his surprise," Balthazar continued, "to find Gypsies."

"Imagine mine," I muttered.

His smile deepened, and I wanted to bite my tongue. I could easily see those words as tomorrow's headline.

"The caravan is the entertainment for the festival," I said. "If you want more info, talk to Joyce."

"I'd rather talk to you."

My teeth ground together, making an audible crunch in the suddenly silent night. What had happened to the . . . whatever had been howling?

I forced my attention back to the problem at hand. "They do old-time Gypsy entertainment—fortune-telling, that kind of stuff."

"If they're just the entertainment, then why did you and the redskin rush out there in the middle of a work-day?"

I winced at the term but didn't bother to correct him. Grace was going to kick his ass one day, and I was going to watch, maybe help. It *had* been a long time since we'd done anything fun together.

Since there was no way I was going to tell Balthazar that Joyce had hired the caravan without my knowledge and Grace had dragged me along to oust them, I lied: "We wanted to welcome the caravan to the neighborhood."

"You've got nothing better to do with your day?"

The entire length of the conversation, I'd been fighting my fear of being alone in the dark with a man. Now I got angry, which was usually how I got into trouble.

"It's nearly nine, and I just left an office I walked

into at the same time this morning. Why don't you put *that* in your paper?"

His mouth tightened, though it was hard to tell, considering the paper-thin line of his lips. His cheeks flushed, making an already ruddy complexion mottled. Fury flashed in his beady dark eyes, and I could have sworn he growled, just as he reached for me.

But before his fleshy fingers closed around my arms and he did whatever it was he planned to do, a howl burst from the trees. The combination of the volume and the proximity made me gasp as my heart threatened to leap out of my chest.

"What the hell is that?" Balthazar muttered.

"Sounds like a wolf." I stared at the thick, dark stand of trees, waiting for the beast to burst forth and end not only our curiosity but also our lives.

I expected Balthazar to scoff, to remind me that timber wolves had been hunted to extinction ages ago and the reintroduction of red wolves had been a failure. The only large wild animals in these mountains were bears and bobcats; neither one of them howled.

When he didn't speak, I risked removing my gaze from the shadows that had begun to swirl and dance with dizzying speed to look at him.

All I saw was his back as he hurried in the other direction. A wave of relief made me dizzier. I didn't even mind being left alone with . . . whatever—as long as Balthazar was gone.

"Nice doggy," I murmured, and began to inch in reverse. My house was up this hill and around the bend, but I didn't plan to take my eyes off the trees. If I was going to be ripped limb from limb by an animal that shouldn't be here, I planned to see it coming. Too many bad things in my life had blindsided me when my back was turned.

Slowly I crept toward safety, my shoes scuffling on the pavement, my breath harsh and fast in the silence.

The trees rustled. A shadow flitted.

The wind? Or something more substantial and deadly?

I could have sworn eyes stared at me from the depths. I blinked. I couldn't help it. I'd been working all day and half the night; I was tired. When I opened my eyes, the other set was gone.

I turned and smacked into Malachi Cartwright so hard my chest bounced off of his, and I stumbled.

He steadied me, the roughness of his palms scratching against my sleeves. My startled gaze lifted to his face, and the beauty of it captured me.

I'd spent a lot of time around beautiful men and women. Television was full of them. I'd learned quickly that the prettier people were, the less they felt they had to do because of it. Cartwright didn't seem of the same opinion.

With a face and body like his he could have been posing for *GQ* ads, at the least strutting a catwalk in his underwear. Instead he traveled the country in a wagon, working with animals until his hands were so hard, calluses scraped the fabric of my suit.

"Did you . . . ?" I paused as an idea flickered. "Is there a wolf in your menagerie?"

"Why do you ask?"

"I heard a howl."

His gaze moved to the trees. "Just now?"

"A few minutes ago. Didn't you hear it?"

He shook his head, but he continued to stare at the forest.

Strange.

"What are you doing here?" I asked.

"I came to see your lovely town."

"Sheriff McDaniel told you not to come at night."

His dark eyes returned to mine. "I don't take orders from Sheriff McDaniel."

I doubted he took orders from anyone. I recalled how whatever he'd wanted—towel, shirt, contract—had appeared in his hand that afternoon. To paraphrase the great prophet Mel Brooks: It must be good to be the king. I smiled at my own, secret wit.

"Do I amuse you then?" Cartwright asked.

Any amusement I'd felt fled. "No."

One thing he didn't do was amuse me. I didn't want to examine *what* it was he did, because the feelings I had whenever I saw him were almost as scary as the howl of the wolf that couldn't exist.

"You never answered my question," I pointed out.

"Which question was that, darlin'?"

I refused to be charmed by the accent and the casual endearment. "Do you or do you not have a wolf in one of those cages at the lake?"

"I do not."

He continued to stare at the trees as if searching for something, which brought to mind a better question—just in case he'd taken my query in completely literal terms: "Did your wolf get loose?"

"I do not keep a wolf. They're . . . troublesome."

"In what way?"

"Wolves don't make good show animals. They're too independent to train, and they spook the hell out of the horses."

"You seem to know an awful lot about them for not having one."

At last he stopped staring at the trees. "I'm an animal trainer. Knowing which ones are good and which are bad is what I do."

"I thought there were no good or bad animals, only good or bad masters."

He gave a snort of laughter but didn't elaborate.

"Who was that you were talking to?" he asked.

"Balthazar Monahan. Owns the local newspaper. He'll want to talk to you."

"He can want whatever he likes; that doesn't mean he'll be gettin' it. We prefer obscurity."

I eyed his flamboyant dress, long hair, and the crucifix swinging from one ear. "I can see that."

His full lips curved. "This costume is what people expect."

"How do you get any business without publicity?"

"We've never lacked for work. We choose when and where we perform—midsized venues in places we are interested in traveling to. Like your Full Moon Festival."

Which explained why he'd contacted Joyce. Must be nice to pick and choose when and where and how much you worked.

He lifted his face to the sky. Opening his mouth, he inhaled, as if drinking in the silver light of the moon. When he lowered his head, his eyes appeared again like bottomless black pools. I took an involuntary step back and the reflection shifted, making his eyes just brown once more.

"I'll walk you home," he said.

"Not necessary. I live—" I broke off. Did I really want him to know where I lived?

"Do you think I don't already know?"

Had he read my mind?

"Come along." He headed up the hill. "You shouldn't be out alone at night."

I fell into step beside him. "This is Lake Bluff."

"You believe you're safe here?"

I did. Or at least I *had*. Safety had been one of the main attractions when I'd said yes to my father's job. That and not having another.

"Do you do double duty as an animal trainer and a fortune-teller?" I asked.

"Only our women possess the sight. Or so they'd like us to believe."

We turned the corner, and my house rose up in front of us. Tall, stately, in the dark with the gibbous moon rising behind it, I could easily imagine it haunted. I shuddered.

"Cold?" Cartwright murmured.

I stared at his back. He hadn't even been looking at me when I'd shivered. I must have made a *brrr* sound and not been aware of it.

"I'm fine."

He pushed the front gate open with a polite dip of his head. "I'll be sayin' good night then."

"Since when are Gypsies Irish?" I blurted.

His teeth flashed. "Been waitin' all day to ask me that, have you?"

I shrugged.

"You're thinking I'm not a real Gypsy?"

"I wasn't thinking of you at all until you appeared out of nowhere."

Liar. I'd thought of him on and off since I'd met him. How could I not?

The deepening of his smile said he knew I'd lied, and he liked it. I suppose lying was an admirable trait to a Gypsy.

I rubbed my forehead. I was as bad as Balthazar. I knew nothing about Gypsies beyond what I'd seen in the movies and on television.

"We are known as the Rom," Cartwright said. "The

term 'Gypsy' came about because people believed we'd come from Egypt."

"You didn't?"

"India, they say, though no one really knows for certain."

"How did you end up in Ireland?"

"I lived in Ireland all my life until . . . recently. The Rom arrived long ago. When we left our homeland, we spread over the globe—Greece, Russia, Hungary, England, Scotland, and Ireland."

"What about Romania?"

"That would be the Ludar."

"Not Gypsies?"

"We prefer the name Rom. Those in Romania are known as the Ludar, just as the English are called Romnichels; the Serbs, Russians, and Hungarians, the Vlax."

"Are those tribes?"

"In a way. We were one once, but centuries of separation changed us."

I found myself fascinated by the information, as well as the silky roll of his voice. I should go inside, although the only things waiting for me there were my television and an ancient calico cat. I'd rather learn more about Gypsies.

"What are the Irish Gypsies called?"

"Travelers." The gaze he turned on my house was oddly wistful. "We do not like to stay in one place very long."

Grace would say that was because they were running from something or perhaps had something to hide. But maybe they just liked to see the world. It wasn't a crime.

The sharp *yip-yahoooo* of a coyote to the west was answered by several more to the east. We remained silent until the last vestige of sound died away.

"That wasn't a wolf," Cartwright murmured, "but a coyote."

"I've listened to a hundred coyotes sing to these hills. What I heard earlier was nothing I'd ever heard before."

"It could not have been a wolf," he insisted. "Wolves don't tolerate coyotes in their territory. Where you find one, you will not find the other." The coyotes began to yip again, much closer than before. "If there was a wolf anywhere near here, all the coyotes would flee."

"How do you know so much about them?" I repeated.

His smile was lazy, sexy, and when he reached out, I started so badly I banged my elbow on the fence.

But all he did was take my hand and brush his lips across the surface. Then he glanced into my face, his dark eyes even darker this far from the light.

"I know so much about so many things, Mayor Kennedy," he whispered, and put his mouth against me once more.

This time I felt the scrape of his teeth, the pull of his lips, the flick of his tongue, and a bolt of awareness ran the length of my arm, tightening my nipples and causing a tingle in places that hadn't tingled in a very long time.

5

HE RELEASED ME before I could pull away—*would*
I have pulled away?—then sketched a quick bow
and strolled back in the direction we'd come. In seconds he'd disappeared around the bend; I continued to
stand in the street staring after him like a fool.

You'd think I'd never been kissed before. Of course
I hadn't been kissed like this.

I lifted my hand, which glistened in the silvery
moonlight—moist from his tongue, a slight scrape
from his teeth, a darker mark where he'd pulled the
skin into his mouth and sucked. Before I knew what I
meant to do I put my own mouth where his had been,
my lips moving against my skin, capturing the damp-
ness he'd left behind.

A car went by, the harsh lights washing over me,
making me drop my arm and hurry through the gate to
the front door. I found my key and let myself in, moving through the front hall and into the kitchen without
bothering to turn on a light.

I'd lived in this house all of my life—excluding the

four years I'd spent at college and the four years I'd
lived in Atlanta. Dad had never changed a thing, leaving it exactly the same as it had been on the day my
mother died. If I stayed I was going to have to do
something—at least paint, perhaps gut the place.

Tossing my purse onto the counter, I stood in the
darkness and thought about dinner in an attempt to
keep myself from thinking about Malachi Cartwright.
I gave up on both. I wasn't hungry, and I couldn't stop
thinking about him.

What kind of man kisses a woman's hand? A gentleman in a historical romance novel.

What kind of gentleman uses his tongue and teeth
to arouse during such a kiss? None I'd ever read about.

Perhaps that was because life wasn't a romance
novel. I'd learned that the hard way in Atlanta. I
couldn't forget it just because I'd returned to Lake
Bluff.

Exhausted and deep down horribly lonely, I
climbed the steps to my room. I flicked on the light and
got an offended *meow* from the dappled cat that had
been sleeping on my pillow.

Oprah—who'd arrived one sunny Christmas morning during my talk-show-host phase—blinked at me in
disdain, then shot her back leg up and began to clean
her butt.

"Hey, not on my pillow." I crossed the room and
yanked the thing out from under her. She tumbled onto
the floor and walked away haughtily as if she'd meant
to do that.

The two of us shared the house, although sometimes I got the feeling she was only tolerating me until
someone better came along, then I'd be out on my ear.

Though I knew I should eat, watch television, read a

book, do something other than work and sleep or I'd be falling back into the same pattern that had contributed to the host of bad decisions I'd made in Atlanta, I threw off my clothes and tumbled into bed, not even bothering with pajamas.

I dreamed the moon became a mist and curled in through my window. Smooth and gray, it floated over me, settled upon me, and gave me peace.

In the depths of the night I sighed, felt the mist on my skin, a cool velvet rain bringing with it the scent of the midday sun beating on freshly turned earth and the moon shining across the water at midnight.

I rolled across the sheets and my body came alive. The hand where he'd kissed me throbbed; the ache that had begun at the touch of his mouth intensified. I was alone yet not alone, visited by both the mist and the moon.

I touched myself, drawing my fingertips across my belly, down my thighs, then up to my breasts. The chilly vapor followed, trailing moisture in its wake.

My nipples hardened; I writhed against the bed, wanting, needing, something more. The sensation I'd first experienced only hours ago—his mouth on my hand, his teeth, his lips—came again against my breast.

Glancing down, I watched as the mist took the shape of a man, lips locked to my nipple as he suckled. I could feel the heat of his mouth, the press of his tongue, the sharp, stinging sensation as he marked sensitive flesh with his teeth.

My moan of arousal drew me from the dream. My skin tingled; I could barely stand to have the sheets rub against it. I was perched on the edge of orgasm, so frustrated I wanted to sob. Why couldn't the dream have lasted just a little while longer?

The shade clacked against the window, and I turned my head. I could have sworn I saw mist disappearing over the sill.

Slowly I got out of bed, then walked across the room and glanced outside, expecting to see a light smoky dew shrouding the grass, the trees, the sky. Fog often rolled in over the mountains. But there was nothing.

I'd dreamed the mist, just as I'd dreamed the sex. No kidding.

I didn't sleep very well for the rest of the night—probably because I'd slammed shut the window and the room had become stuffy and uncomfortable even without my clothes. My father had never installed air-conditioning, believing it a vulgar waste of money, but I would have to.

By 6:00 A.M. I stood beneath a tepid shower, hoping the lack of warmth would put an end to the lingering throb of arousal I couldn't seem to shake.

I stepped out of the shower, dried off, then reached for the hair dryer. One glance into the mirror and I dropped the apparatus into the sink at the sight of the hickey on my breast. Then my eyes narrowed; I leaned in close and *tsk*ed. "Birthmark."

I'd had the thing since I was born—a small, brown-ish pink circle on the underside of my left breast, right where the mist that had become a man had suckled me.

"Bizarre," I murmured, and rubbed my thumb over the discoloration. At the first touch my breasts seemed to swell, the nipples tingling. I really needed to get laid; however, considering my recent issues with men, that wasn't going to happen.

Instead of drying my shoulder-length hair, I scraped it into a knot and secured it at the back of my head with pins. The style always made me look like an accountant or maybe a district attorney. But right now I needed to get out of this house where every breath I took reminded me of something that hadn't happened yet seemed so very real.

I grabbed another suit, a matching set of heels, then paused before putting them on. Just because my father had worn a suit every day of his life didn't mean I had to. In fact, it would be better to draw attention to the contrasts between him and me, lest people think they were getting the same mayor in a different package.

I pulled out khakis, a sky blue top, and boring but comfortable flats in the same shade as the pants and put them on.

Oprah squalled from the kitchen, reminding me of the second reason for her name—she never shut up—and I hurried downstairs where she circled an empty food bowl. I dumped dry cat food into it, the ping of the cereal-like Xs a cadence that harked back to high school.

Every morning I'd fed Oprah, grabbed my backpack, and raced out the front door to pick up Grace. Dad always let me drive the car to school, which was located a mile outside of town to accommodate the kids who lived in the nearby mountains.

He had walked to work—come rain or come shine—both to clear his head and to give people a chance to approach him on a more casual basis than an appointment at town hall. I'd tried to follow his lead, but so far no one had come to talk to me on my morning or evening jaunts, except Balthazar.

I filled Oprah's water bowl as I munched on a piece of dry toast. Though it was early yet, I headed for work. I had nothing better to do.

My job was time-consuming. I'd known that when I'd taken it. I'd lived with the mayor all my life, which meant I'd been pretty much on my own. The long hours, the nights my dad hadn't come home until I was asleep, the emergencies that had called him away, seemingly whenever I'd needed him.

As a teen I'd believed that everyone else was more important, that Lake Bluff held a place in his heart I never could, and with a childish resentment, I'd sneered at both the town and the office, refusing to entertain the idea of ever living here or sitting behind the mayor's desk.

The streets of Lake Bluff were a little busier today than yesterday, a trend that would continue for the next week. The drugstore on the corner—an old-fashioned pharmacy where the pharmacist knew everyone's ailments and dealt with the customers directly instead of through an assistant—was open.

In this family business, the pharmacist's wife ran the front register, his children the lunch counter, where people could buy tuna salad and a cherry soda, or hot-fudge sundaes and chocolate malts, made with real malt.

No superstore invasion in Lake Bluff, at least not yet. I hated to think what would happen then. There were far too many guns sprinkled throughout this town for it to be a peaceful transition. Folks in Georgia didn't take kindly to their livelihoods being undercut by anyone, let alone a big-money corporate conglomerate from far away.

I would have walked right past Lake Bluff Drug and Sundry as I did every morning, glancing in the window, waving to Mrs. Charlesdown and whichever one of her six children had drawn the short straw and wound up working the counter that day, except customers began to shoot out the door at an alarming rate.

Even that might not have made me do anything except question the leader of the pack but for the shrill scream that split the growing warmth of the sunny morning.

6

I DIVED FOR the entrance, struggling against the wave of locals and tourists headed in the opposite direction. The screams continued, their terrified cadence filling the air, preventing me from asking anyone what in hell was wrong.

I wanted to put my hands over my ears; the sound made my teeth ache. But I needed my hands to shove aside the last stragglers before I could burst into the store and, from the volume and nature of the screams, prevent bloody murder from continuing.

However, when I at last stood on the tile floor near the cash register, all I saw was a young Gypsy woman facing off with Mrs. Charlesdown, she of the earsplitting screams. Her husband the pharmacist, and her oldest son stood rooted a few feet away, staring at the Gypsy with wide eyes.

"What's the matter?" I shouted.

At least Mrs. Charlesdown stopped screaming. Mutely she pointed at the girl. I couldn't tell what was so terrifying about her. All I could see was her back.

Tall and willowy, she had long dark hair that reached over her white blouse to the waist of her colorful skirt. Her feet were bare, displaying golden rings on two of her toes; I didn't understand why that would make Mrs. Charlesdown lose her mind.

Then the Gypsy turned, and I saw what had. A cobra hung around her neck, undulating and sticking its tongue out in an age-old na-na-na-na-na gesture. I hadn't seen the thing because the girl's hair had masked the body looped around her neck. But from this angle, there was a whole lot of snake.

My gaze lifted to the Gypsy's face. She was perhaps twenty, with the olive skin common to the rest of her clan, though her eyes tended more toward hazel than brown. Strong nose, high cheekbones, there was nothing remarkable about her, except for the snake.

"She . . . she . . ." Mrs. Charlesdown continued to point.

"Relax," I soothed. "Miss?" The girl ducked her head so that her hair fell over her eyes. The cobra weaved back and forth as if dancing to a tune only it could hear. "You probably shouldn't come to town with your . . . pet."

Her lips curved, and she stroked the snake with one long-fingered hand. The golden bangles on her wrist clacked together, making Mrs. Charlesdown jump as if someone had goosed her. The involuntary movement brought back her voice.

"She was stealing."

Mrs. Charlesdown glanced toward her husband for support, but he'd already retreated behind the pharmacy counter and gotten back to work, as had her son.

"She *was*," Mrs. Charlesdown insisted.

The Gypsy's lips tilted downward, and she shook her head so vigorously her hair flew out of her face.

"Oh yes, you were," Mrs. Charlesdown insisted. "What's in your hand?"

The girl shoved the hand that wasn't stroking the cobra behind her back.

"See?" Mrs. Charlesdown said triumphantly.

"Just because she's got something in her hand doesn't mean she was stealing it," I pointed out. "You didn't give her a chance to pay."

"She was on her way out the door when I stopped her. Then that *thing* hissed at me."

This was really a job for Grace, but since I was here . . .

"Can we see what's in your hand?" I asked.

The Gypsy continued to shake her head; eyes wide, she reminded me of a horse, rearing and bucking and frothing at the mouth.

"I'm calling the sheriff." Mrs. Charlesdown picked up the phone.

The girl made a strangled sound of negation and shot her arm out.

"Put that down," I ordered, and Mrs. Charlesdown complied.

The fingers of the Gypsy were permanently curled inward, stiff, clawlike. What I could see of her palm was empty.

Mrs. Charlesdown's cheeks reddened, but her lips pressed together primly. "You can't blame me. Everyone knows Gypsies steal."

"Just as we kidnap children."

Malachi Cartwright stood in the doorway, the bright summer sun casting a halo around his head and throwing his face into shadow. His tone had been light, as if joking, but the way he held his body, tense, ready, revealed he was not at all amused.

"Sabina," he murmured. "I told you not to be coming into town alone."

The girl hurried out, head down, completely chastised or perhaps terrified. But of whom?

"We had a misunderstanding," I began.

"Which happens often enough with narrow-minded people." Cartwright stepped into the store, his bland expression somehow more accusing than a glare would be.

"If the child had just spoken up, there wouldn't have been a problem," Mrs. Charlesdown said.

"Except she doesn't speak, any more than she uses her right hand."

"Oh." Mrs. Charlesdown became flustered. "That's too bad."

"She does well enough with her snake," Cartwright continued. "They understand each other without the words."

"Was that a cobra?" I asked, though I knew that it was.

He dipped his chin.

"Aren't they poisonous?"

Mrs. Charlesdown gasped. "Poisonous? Are you insane, allowing that addled child to wander about with a poisonous snake?"

"She isn't addled, nor is she a child, and the snake's fangs were removed long ago. Sabina is a gifted charmer, but it's best to be safe rather than sorry."

"Snake charmer?" Mrs. Charlesdown repeated, in a voice that was more of a shout. "Next you'll be telling us you have a fat lady, two dwarfs, and a tattooed man."

"If you're wantin' a traveling circus, then you hired the wrong people." He shifted his gaze from the older woman to me. "I told you we performed like the Gypsy caravans of old."

"I'm afraid we're fresh out of old-time Gypsy caravans. You're our first."

"Your first?" His smile was so suggestive my face flushed.

Mrs. Charlesdown snorted, and I indicated with a jerk of my thumb that Cartwright should join me outside. A group of customers remained huddled on the sidewalk.

"All's clear now," I announced, and they filed back in, casting wary glances at Sabina over their shoulders.

The Gypsy girl stood a few feet away, running her good hand over the silvery mane of a snow-white horse.

"You rode a horse?" I asked.

Cartwright crooked a brow. "People do it all the time."

"In the nineteenth century."

"A simpler, better age."

Considering the price of gas, he was probably right.

I contemplated Sabina and the horse, which nuzzled her, despite the cobra. "Don't horses hate snakes?"

This one didn't seem to care that a cobra was within striking distance. He didn't even seem to notice.

"I trained Benjamin myself. He works the show, and he can't be afraid of the animals who work it, too."

"You're some horse trainer."

"Yes," he agreed, "I am."

"And so modest."

"Truth is truth. No one is better with horses than I am."

"Why is that?"

He hesitated for so long I didn't think he was going to answer. Finally he looked away, staring at the distant mountains. "I've had a lot of practice. First I trained the draft horses, our Percherons. Then I moved on to the show horses, which requires both patience and time."

"You train horses, and Sabina charms the snake." I glanced her way again. "That one doesn't seem to need a whole lot of charming."

"She's very good with them."

"Them?" My voice squeaked.

"You don't think one snake would make an act, do you now?"

I hadn't thought about the number at all. In my opinion, one cobra should be more than sufficient.

"How many?"

"Hard to say. She picks up snakes wherever we go. A rattler in Texas, another from New Mexico. Then there was the pet python, which grew too large for the owner's house in Mississippi."

"All dangerous reptiles."

"What good is charming those not in need of it?" he murmured, moving closer, crowding into my space just as Balthazar had.

Unlike Balthazar, I didn't want to give Cartwright a swift knee where it counted.

He smelled like water beneath the summer sun, like rain-soaked earth and moon-drenched night. The sudden desire to move even nearer made me take a quick step back. I glanced around, but no one seemed to notice my sudden weakness for a stranger; everyone was going about his or her business with a bustle that said, *Festival coming, festival coming.*

I needed to as well. I opened my mouth to say good-bye and what came out instead was, "Why doesn't she talk?"

Cartwright's gaze flicked to Sabina, who still cuddled the horse. "That's her tale to tell."

Frustration made me speak more loudly than I

should have. "How can she tell anything if she can't speak?"

Sabina glanced in my direction, and I winced. She could obviously *hear* and now knew I was talking behind her back. She might be dumb, but she wasn't stupid.

"Sorry," I muttered, and she gave me a slight smile before turning to the horse.

"She could speak once," Cartwright said softly. "Then she stopped."

Some sort of trauma, I guessed, and felt a sudden kinship.

"After her hand was injured?"

"No injury. Sabina was born with the sign of Satan."

"The sign of what?"

My voice was too loud again. Sabina flinched and buried her face in the horse's mane. The animal whinnied, stomped his foot, and glared at me as if he knew I'd upset her.

"Her parents wanted to drown her," Cartwright continued, "but I wouldn't let them."

"What century are you from?"

"Just because it's a modern age doesn't mean there aren't barbarians everywhere."

I stared into his face. He didn't appear all that much older than Sabina.

I'd heard tales of Gypsy kings, although that was probably as much hooey as the Gypsies-steal-children axiom. Still, Malachi Cartwright behaved as if he'd inherited the mantle at birth.

"Have you taken her to a doctor?" I asked.

"She'll speak again when she's ready. Nothing but time can fix Sabina."

I knew what that was like.

"I meant for her hand."

Cartwright didn't answer, instead moving toward his horse.

"I'm sure there's a specialist somewhere who might be able to help."

He stopped, but he didn't turn around. "We have no insurance, Mayor. No means of payin' a doctor, either. Our life isn't like yours, and it never will be."

He motioned for Sabina to get on the horse, then swung up behind her in a movement so smooth and sure, I paused just to watch.

"Thank you for your kindness," he said, and they galloped away.

7

I SPENT THE rest of my day in the office (a lot of signatures), meeting with constituents (a lot of placating), taking and making phone calls (a lot of headaches).

Joyce was in and out so often, I lost track of whether she was in or out. I wondered where she went when she went, but never got a chance to ask her.

I never got a chance to break for lunch, either. So when Grace showed up around suppertime, I welcomed her with a sigh of relief—until she spoke.

"I hear you and Malachi, call me Mal, Cartwright were chatting it up on Center Street this morning."

I dropped my pen. "Who've you been talking to?"

She lifted a brow. "Who do you think?"

"Balthazar." I hadn't noticed him hanging around earlier, but the newspaper office had a lovely view of the entire main drag.

Grace took a seat. "He's a bastard, no doubt about it. Heard you had a conversation with both of them outside your house last night, too."

"Sheesh, is nothing private around here?"

Grace laughed. "You're kidding, right?"

I hadn't been, but I knew what she meant. Small towns thrived on gossip—a blessing because it was hard for people to get away with anything, a curse if you were the one trying to.

"Did you come over to give me a hard time?" I asked. "Because you'll need to get in line."

"Rough day?"

"No more than any other." I shoved a loose pin into my hair, hissing as it scratched my skull.

"I've been meaning to ask you, why did you take the job anyway?"

"Seemed like the thing to do at the time."

"Not the best reason for a life-changing decision."

"I know."

"You don't have to stay," she said.

She was right, but where would I go? Back to Atlanta? I suppressed a shudder. Never.

"Balthazar would be happy to take over for you," Grace continued.

"Not in this lifetime."

The jerk had aroused my competitive nature. I hadn't wanted the job when I'd taken it, had been trying to avoid becoming the mayor all of my life. But now I suddenly didn't want him to have it, even if it meant I was stuck here. Somehow being stuck here didn't seem so bad anymore.

"That's what I like to hear in a mayor." Grace slapped her palms against the knees of her tan slacks and stood. "Now, we need to take a ride to the lake."

"What did they do now?" I asked, even as my heart lurched in completely inappropriate anticipation.

"I didn't say we were going to talk to the Gypsies. You just jumped to that hopeful conclusion."

"Then what are we going there for? And why do I have to tag along?"

"A tourist was hiking the lake trail at dusk last night and ran into a wolf."

"That's impossible," I said, even as I heard again the long, low howl streaming toward the moon.

"I know that, and you know that, but tell the guy from Topeka. He doesn't believe me. Can't say I blame him, considering the mess that was made of his throat."

I pushed back from my desk so fast my rolling chair kept rolling and slammed into the wall. "He was attacked?"

"Wolf." She held up one finger. "Tourist." She held up another, then smacked them together. "Not a good combo."

"Where is he?"

"In the hospital. Where do you think? He's been stitched and bandaged and given antibiotics, but we're going to have to find that wolf or he'll need rabies shots, too."

"How are we going to find a wolf in the Blue Ridge Mountains? They aren't exactly contained."

The range began as a narrow strip in Pennsylvania and extended all the way through Maryland, Virginia, and the Carolinas to Georgia. Though only a few miles across in their northern region, once the Blue Ridge hit our state they widened to sixty miles in certain areas.

"The tourist wasn't a complete moron. He had a gun. Said he shot the thing. I should be able to track it without too much trouble."

I had no doubt she would. Grace had learned that skill before she entered kindergarten; she'd only gotten better since then.

"I still don't understand why you need me." Not that I'd let her go without me, but I was curious.

"We neglected to read past the first page of our contract with the Gypsies. The second page gives them temporary ownership of the lake while they're here."

My eyes narrowed. "Joyce!" I bellowed.

"Save your breath. She left."

The woman was never around when I needed her. I was going to have to find out why.

"What the hell does temporary ownership mean?"

"They have the rights of owners during the duration of their performances. In other words, we'd be trespassing if we went searching for the wolf. I don't have the time or the inclination to screw with a warrant. And they made a particular point that they wanted outsiders nowhere near 'their land' "—she made quotation marks in the air with her forefingers—"until opening night."

"Fishy," I observed.

"Damn straight."

"Still don't understand why you need me."

"Cartwright seems to have a thing for you."

"You want me to ask him for permission to search?"

She shrugged. "That or distract him while I do it anyway."

I stared at her for several seconds. "It's good to have a plan."

I HEARD SOMETHING funny last night," I admitted as Grace drove an unmarked squad car toward the lake.

"Funny ha-ha or funny weird?"

"Definitely not ha-ha," I muttered. "A howl. And it wasn't a coyote, at least not the first one. Later there were coyotes."

"Is any of this supposed to make sense?"

Quickly I told her what had happened the previous night; I didn't leave anything out except the sudden and overwhelming attraction I'd felt for Cartwright. It wasn't relevant.

"Could have been a dog," she murmured. "Hell, our wolf attack is most likely a dog."

"Because?"

"Putting aside that there hasn't been a wolf in these mountains forever, there isn't a documented case of a wolf attacking a human unless the animal was starving, rabid, or a wolf-dog hybrid."

"Have you been reading the Trivial Pursuit cards again?"

"Why bother when you're not here to beat?"

"I'm here now."

"You won't stay."

I frowned. "Why do you keep saying that?"

"You weren't meant to live in Lake Bluff, Claire. You were meant to live on Fifth Avenue."

I glanced out the window, where the sun was falling down behind the mountains, shooting tendrils of red, orange, and pink across the Great Blue Hills of God.

"I never liked Fifth Avenue," I said.

"Never?"

"Well, maybe the first time. I did find some really great shoes."

"Shoes," Grace snorted. "You're such a girl."

"You say that like it's a bad thing."

"Can be," she said slowly, staring at me with a combination of sympathy and understanding that made me wonder if she'd learned mind reading from her great-grandmother.

I turned away, mentally rolling my eyes at the

thought. Mind reading was as impossible as fortune-telling and happy endings.

Seconds later we slid to a stop near the caravans and got out of the car. The wagons seemed as empty as the land surrounding them. The bonfires were banked, indicating an eventual return. But right now there didn't appear to be a living soul anywhere in the vicinity.

"Stay here in case someone comes back," Grace said, already moving toward the trees.

"What if they do?"

"Stall them. I won't be long."

Before I could argue, she stepped between two pine trees and disappeared into the steadily descending dusk.

I wasn't there two minutes when I began to get squirrelly. Where had all the people gone? When would they return? What would they think if they found me here? What would they do?

To distract myself I began to walk around the camp, studying the wagons. Mostly tableaux of the moon, the stars, and fire, they were works of art in both carving and painting.

I reached the last wagon in the circle. Beyond that the animal cages faced away from the living quarters, perhaps so their occupants could enjoy the view of a forest they would never be allowed to roam.

While I'd strolled, the sun had gone down, spreading spidery tendrils of shadow across the land. However, enough light remained on the western horizon so that the clearing wasn't completely dark, but it would be soon.

I headed toward the nearest animal wagon, both excited to discover what lay inside and a bit scared for the same reason.

"Lions and tigers and bears, oh my." They wouldn't really be transporting any of those, would they?

Tingling in anticipation, I rounded the corner.

The wagon was empty.

8

SO WAS THE one next to it. What the hell?

A gap yawned between the second cage and another, which looked just as empty. I took a single step toward it, then spun when I heard something splash in the lake.

Now a lot of things can splash in the water. Fish jump. Turtles flop. In certain areas, alligators wind their way through the deep. But not here. In the winter these mountains saw snow. Not a lot, but enough to keep the alligators away.

Sadly, the volume of that splash had sounded more alligator than fish or turtle. I glanced again at the empty cages. Were the Gypsies out chasing escaped wild animals? Would Grace run into more than a wolf?

I suddenly wished I'd asked for a radio and, while I was at it, a gun.

Drawn toward the water, I moved past the living quarters until I stood at the top of the sandy incline that led to the lake.

The moon hadn't risen, or if it had, the silvery

glow wasn't visible past the towering trees. The surface of the lake resembled an unbroken sheet of black glass.

Then a ripple began near the center; tiny circles spread wider and wider as it rolled toward the shore.

Panic gripped my throat. I fought the urge to run back to the car and drive away.

"Stop it," I muttered. There was nothing in a lake that could hurt me.

Unless we had a lake monster.

The thought should have made me laugh. Most reports of such things were merely sightings of muskellunge or bass large enough to have been birthed in radioactive waste.

However, standing out here, alone in the night where I didn't belong, I understood how people could believe in monsters.

Whatever had caused the swell broke the surface. At least six feet long, it streamed toward the sand in a smooth flowing motion, like a dolphin wiggling and wagging its seemingly spineless body beneath a late-summer sky.

The monster reached the shallows and rose, emerging inch by inch, until it became a man. Water flowed over broad shoulders, trailed down a smooth chest, twirling past a ridged belly, then trickling lower.

Malachi Cartwright lifted his hands and slicked his hair out of his eyes, the movement causing his biceps to flex, his abs to harden.

I couldn't speak, couldn't move, could only stare. It had been a long time since I'd seen a naked man, and I'd never seen one like this.

He tilted his face upward, breathing in deeply as if trying to draw the very essence of the night within.

I perched at the top of the incline; with no moon, no stars, no streetlights, I remained shrouded in shadow. Frozen, fascinated, I hovered.

The moon burst over the trees, cascading across the water like the sun. When it hit him he sighed like he'd found an oasis in the middle of the desert.

The silvery glow sparkled on the droplets of moisture still running down his skin, making them resemble the melting wax of a pure white candle.

I don't know how long we stood there, him bathing in the light, me watching him do it, but eventually he lowered his head, then began to slog through the knee-deep water toward the shore, and he saw me. Now that the moon was up, the entire clearing was awash with silver.

I could do nothing but stare into his dark, endless eyes as he crossed the sand, climbed the incline, and kissed me.

I shouldn't have been surprised. What did I expect when he'd caught me peeping at him while he was . . . bathing? Swimming? Performing some pagan ritual beneath the moon?

Whatever he'd been doing, I shouldn't have been watching, but once I'd seen him I hadn't been able to stop.

His lips were cool. Moist and sweet, they captured mine. Droplets of water fell from his body, pattering around us, as if we kissed beneath a springtime rain.

He plucked the pins from my hair and filled his hands with the length, his fingers tightening on my scalp as he tilted my head so he could delve more deeply within. My heart skittered a bit at being held captive, but there was also arousal, a sensation so barren in my life, I couldn't pull away, seduced by the possibilities it presented.

His tongue met mine with a force and a boldness that increased both the arousal and the fear. I tamped down on the latter, focused on the former, learning the contours of his mouth with my own.

He nipped my lip, both pleasure and pain, and I gasped, the sound stark against the gentle lap of the waves. His hands moved from my head to my shoulders, before sliding down my back as he crushed me against him.

Water dampened my top, the chill causing my nipples to peak. The lake was fed by an underground spring that ran down the mountain. Even at the height of summer the water was just above icy, which meant most tourists liked to look at the place but not touch. Cartwright obviously had no problem with the temperature of the water, if the erection pressing against me was any indication.

His mouth trailed down my jaw, my collarbone; then his teeth tugged at the neck of my top. One hand slid over my waist, then upward, cupping my breast, a thumb scraping over the nipple before he did some fancy twist, baring me to the night and his tongue.

I panicked, shoving at his chest, kicking at his shins. I couldn't seem to get the word "no" past the alarm closing my throat. Not that "no" had done me any good in the past.

He released me instantly, and I fell, sitting down hard in the sand. Scraped by his beard, my chin burned. My eyes teared, both embarrassment and dread combined. The night brushed my skin, turning the moisture left by his mouth to ice. I glanced down; my breast still hung out, the moonlight causing my pale skin to glow almost translucent.

I yanked my top back in place, then hugged myself tightly and prayed I wouldn't cry.

"I—I'm sorry," I managed, even though my therapist had stressed I had nothing to apologize for in a situation like this.

Cartwright stared toward the lake, and the moon glistened off his body, turning the bronze skin silver. He seemed carved in alabaster, a beautiful pagan god abandoned by the shore. Although I doubted any statue would be carved with an erection of that size.

He didn't make any move to cover himself, but I hadn't seen any clothes nearby, not even a towel. I suppose he'd thought himself alone, protected from trespassers by a contract clause and common decency.

"Why did you come here if not for this?"

I winced at the harsh, angry tone. "I didn't. I—"

"What?" He whirled toward me, and I cringed, hating myself for it but unable to stop.

He froze at my movement, then lowered the hand he'd raised in agitation. "I wouldn't hurt you, Claire."

It was the first time he'd said my name. Too bad I couldn't enjoy the way the word rolled off his tongue. Couldn't sit here and dream about the way his tongue had rolled over mine, because the fear I'd fought for so long was back, and I didn't know how to make it go away.

I got to my feet. I had to get out of here.

"Wait." He took a step forward.

I couldn't help it. I ran blindly, mindlessly, for the cover of the trees. Before I even got close, he caught me, grabbing my arm and spinning me around.

My momentum made me stumble, my palms coming to rest against his chest, so soft, so smooth, so hot. I jerked them back as if scalded.

His fingers tightened, his gaze lowering to my

mouth. My breath caught, afraid he'd kiss me again, afraid that he wouldn't.

"Don't," I said.

"Don't what?" he murmured. "Don't kiss you? Or don't even dare to touch you? I suppose you're too high-class to consort with the likes of me. The mayor and the Gypsy horse trainer. Your family would be none too happy about that."

"I don't have any family," I whispered, then wished I hadn't. He could rape me, kill me, then toss me in the lake. There'd be no one to care.

"Get your hands off her, Cartwright."

Except for Grace.

"Hold them up where I can see them. Do it slow."

He complied, lifting his arms until his palms were level with his shoulders. His gaze left mine and shifted past my shoulder. "Shall I reach for the sky, Sheriff?"

"Move, Claire."

I sidestepped, then turned. Grace stood at the edge of the forest, weapon drawn and pointed at Cartwright.

Her eyes remained steady on him yet her mouth pinched with annoyance. "Out of his reach. Now."

The sharp snap of her voice made me take several quick steps in her direction.

"I thought you had more sense," she said.

I had, too. For future reference, when a naked guy climbs out of the lake, I should run, not let him kiss me. Especially when anything beyond a kiss made me dissolve into a quivering, sniveling mess. However, Cartwright couldn't have known that.

"It's not his fault," I blurted.

"What isn't?" Grace asked, keeping her gun right where it was.

"He kissed me and I—"

My eyes met his. He lifted a brow.

"I let him."

"Oh no. Horrors. Then you said, 'Stop,' and he didn't." She lowered her gun. His erection shriveled. "That's unacceptable."

"No."

Her gaze flicked to me, then away. "It's acceptable?"

"No."

"Claire . . ." Grace's voice took on a distinct tenor of irritation.

"I mean, I didn't say no. Not exactly. I was—"

Entranced. Seduced. Then terrified.

The latter was common enough, the former something new. I wanted to explore those feelings, but after this fiasco, I doubted I'd get the chance, and that was probably for the best.

As Cartwright had so strangely put it: The mayor and the Gypsy horse trainer—what could ever come of that?

"May I lower my hands?" Cartwright asked.

Grace glanced at me; I nodded. She shrugged and holstered her weapon. "How did you come to lose your clothes, Cartwright?"

"I'd think you'd be callin' me Malachi now that we're so well acquainted." He headed down the incline toward the lake, where he snatched a towel from behind a rock and secured it around his hips with a sharp tug.

Grace didn't comment, waiting for him to answer the original question.

"I came to be without clothes because I was bathing. I didn't expect visitors."

"And the rest of your party?"

He pointed. We followed the long line of his bare arm.

The lake was a puddle of melted black wax—murky, still. On the opposite side, tiny flickers of flame danced with human-shaped shadows. They hadn't been there before.

"What are they doing?" I asked.

"Communing with nature."

"When you say communing . . ." Grace looked him up and down. "You mean naked?"

He shrugged. "What other way is there?"

"You've got a caravan of naked Gypsies dancing around the communal fire?"

"Is that a problem?"

"Well . . ." Grace paused. "There are laws about that sort of thing."

"We have little use for laws."

"Oh, really? And why is that?"

Cartwright lifted his face to the sky, staring at the stars that had just begun to twinkle against the cover of night. "In the year 1530, England passed a law that made it illegal to be a Gypsy. The law wasn't repealed until 1784, making our very existence a crime for over two hundred and fifty years."

"You can't not be what you are," I said. "That's like making it illegal for someone to have dark hair."

"The English weren't the only ones," he murmured. "The Nazis declared Gypsies nonhuman and tried to exterminate us along with the Jews. We lost over four hundred thousand in their camps."

I hadn't studied WW II more than marginally, and I didn't remember this tidbit. But I did know that Hitler had ordered more than Jews into the camps. Nuns, priests, those with mental problems, as well as anyone who disagreed with him too strenuously, were rounded up, shoved on a train, and shipped to various outposts in Hell.

"You can see, Sheriff," Cartwright continued, "why we don't trouble ourselves overmuch with laws."

Grace contemplated him with a lot less suspicion and a lot more compassion than before. "You do this dance every night?"

"No. Tomorrow night we'll perform. Tonight we ask the gods for protection and success."

"What gods?" Grace inched closer. She'd always been fascinated with the old ways, and not just those of the Cherokee.

Cartwright's gaze flicked from Grace to me and back again, assessing. "We're Catholics in truth. Every one of us baptized as such."

"I bet the Church just loves it when you worship naked in the night," Grace murmured.

His lips tilted. "I dinna think they know."

I bet not. At least the days when such practices would be punished by a bonfire—of people—were past, although I had no doubt excommunication was still alive and kicking people when they were down.

"This is a ritual of our ancestors, nothing more," he explained. "Some people put flowers on graves, eat turkey at Thanksgiving, or cut down trees like these"—he swept his arm out to indicate the towering spruce—"and drag them into their homes for decoration. We dance beneath Alako—god of the moon, defender of all Gypsies, the one who takes our souls at death."

"And the fire?" I stared at the images of the moon, the stars, and the flames on their wagons. I guessed they were more than just decorations.

"Fire purifies, heals, protects." He glanced across the water. "Fire punishes evil."

Punishing the evil with fire sounded like the Inquisition. Another really fun group on history's hit parade. I liked to imagine them dancing barefoot in Hell along with the Nazis.

Grace fingered her gun again. "You been punishing any evil ones with fire, pal?"

"The Rom are not animals. We leave that to our tormentors. Will you become one of them, Sheriff?"

"No." Grace paused. "I have no problem with nudity, but you can't be running around like this all over the mountain. People will freak."

"There's a reason we asked for the contract we did."

I recalled the bizarre clause that was supposed to keep locals away from the lake until opening night. I'd wondered what the Gypsies were hiding; I hadn't figured it was a pagan moon and fire ritual.

"After tonight, we'll perform," he repeated. "When the full moon comes—" He broke off, frowning for several seconds before he finished. "We will leave."

I had a feeling he'd been about to say something else, but what? *We'll sacrifice a chicken. A goat.*

A child.

I choked and Cartwright's gaze came to rest on me consideringly. I had to look away.

When I did, my eyes caught on the cages, and I remembered what I'd been doing right before he'd emerged from the water. "Did you take your animals across the lake, too?"

"No. Why?"

"The cages are empty."

He muttered something in Romani, then strode away.

"What do they have in those cages?" Grace whispered.

I shrugged. I hadn't seen anything.

Cartwright disappeared around the edge of the nearest wagon just as the call of something big, with teeth, echoed through the night.

9

I STUMBLED OVER my own feet as I hurried to join Malachi in front of a cage that I could have sworn had been as empty as my life. It wasn't empty any longer.

"Mary likes to rest at the back of the enclosure," Cartwright said. "I'm sure you just overlooked her."

A long, sleek, muscular mountain lion slid along the bars. She didn't seem like a Mary to me.

"You have a cougar?" Grace snapped. "Are you fucking nuts?"

"Not lately," Cartwright murmured, seemingly uninsulted by Grace's question or her language.

The animal enclosures were built differently from any I'd seen before—with two sets of bars set far enough apart so that no one could stick a hand inside and lose it, yet visitors could see the animal, hear it, smell it.

Though I might not have seen Mary the mountain lion, there were other wagons that had been empty, too. I skirted Cartwright and headed for the next enclosure.

A grizzly bear waddled forward, flat, dark eyes fixed on my face. He stretched his neck, tilted his head, and roared. Grace appeared at my side, gun drawn.

She stared at the bear for several seconds before turning to Cartwright. "You have got to be kidding me."

"We perform with animals, Sheriff." He spread his hands and his towel dipped lower. I waited for it to fall off altogether, but it didn't. "That means we need animals."

"A monkey, a goat, maybe an elephant. But a cougar and a bear? That's dangerous."

"We raised them from birth." His gaze rested on the still-roaring grizzly. "They are our family."

"Well, your uncle appears a bit teed off. Can you get him to shut up?"

"The gun, Sheriff." Cartwright flicked one long finger at the weapon. "He doesn't like them."

Grace stared at her hand as if she'd forgotten she held the thing, then holstered it with an impatient shove. However, she didn't secure the strap of leather over the butt.

"I hear you don't keep a wolf in your menagerie." She headed for the next enclosure.

Cartwright scowled in my direction before following.

"Was that a secret?" I asked.

He ignored me. "As I told the mayor, wolves are troublesome."

Grace stood in front of the third cage, which *was* empty. I was glad I'd seen at least one thing right tonight.

Logically I knew the cougar and the bear couldn't have been running around the woods with the Gypsies, then miraculously appeared back in the wagons just before we came to see them. But I was also pretty sure I couldn't have overlooked an animal the size of a grizzly when I'd glanced in that second cage. The conflict of what had to be true and what couldn't be made me a little bit dizzy.

"Explain how wolves are troublesome." Grace continued to stare into the empty space.

"They spook the horses," I volunteered.

"And a cougar doesn't?"

"We keep the predatory animals away from them," Malachi said.

"Neat trick." Grace tilted her head. "But they have to run into each other sometime."

"There can be incidents. But my horses are very well trained."

"If they're well trained enough to tolerate the scent of a wild cat and a grizzly, why would a wolf be any different?"

"Wolves are pack animals. They don't do well alone, unless they're rogues, and then they're dangerous."

"More dangerous than a cougar?" Grace asked.

"Depends on the wolf."

She cursed beneath her breath, kicked at the dirt, then stalked down the line of cage wagons, peering into each and every one.

Cartwright watched her go. "What did I say?"

I wasn't sure if I was supposed to mention the hiker who'd been mauled by the wolf. I suspected not, since we'd come out here to secretly search for it. Thankfully Cartwright hadn't asked yet what we were doing on his temporary property.

"Grace is prickly," I said, then headed after her, checking out the occupants of the wagons as she had.

Brass plates identified them with monikers you might find in any phone book. What happened to naming animals after their animal-like attributes—Fluffy, Blackie, and Spot for instance? I guess Teeth, Claws, and Horrific Bloody Death aren't exactly good for business.

"Three monkeys, two zebras, a camel," Grace tallied as I joined her.

"Five crows, an owl, an eagle, and a hawk," I added. "You must really go through the birdseed."

Grace spun toward Cartwright. "What was in the empty cage?"

Confusion spread over his face. "Nothing. That is what makes it empty."

Grace smacked herself in the forehead with the flat of her hand. "I meant," she said between her teeth, "what was in there *before* it became empty?"

"Nothing," he repeated. "We need to have at least one empty cage for an animal to be put into while their enclosure is cleaned."

Why was I disappointed that his explanation made sense? What could he possibly be up to?

I had no idea about the latter; unfortunately, I had a very good idea on the former. I wanted Cartwright to be untrustworthy so I had good reason to avoid him and the attraction I felt.

I *had* wanted him, and I hadn't wanted anyone since . . .

"We should go," I blurted.

Grace glanced at me. "Sure. Cartwright." She nodded and disappeared into the darkness.

I flipped my hand like a three-year-old waving bye-bye and followed.

I was both surprised and disheartened when he let

me go. I couldn't say I blamed him. He probably thought I was crazy. However, *I* didn't keep wild animals within yards of where I slept.

To be fair, he didn't kiss someone as if he wanted to give her everything, then panic and run away. But I doubted Malachi Cartwright had been betrayed by someone he trusted.

D ID YOU FIND anything?" I asked as soon as we pulled onto the highway that led back to town.

"I found you with your tongue down the guy's throat."

"Did not," I returned. When she gave me a bland look, I muttered, "You came too late to see that."

"Who says I wasn't watching for a while before I intervened?"

I narrowed my eyes and she laughed. "Relax, Claire, I wasn't, but it doesn't take a detective to figure out what you'd been up to."

I guess Cartwright's erection gave us away. Or maybe it had been my swollen lips, my tousled hair, even my crumpled top.

"You told me to stall him."

Grace snorted. "I meant talk to him about his work."

"He wasn't inclined to chat."

"I bet." Grace slid a glance at me, then returned it to the dark highway. "I found something."

"Tracks?"

"None that I could see."

Which meant there weren't any.

"If not tracks, then what?"

"I'll show you inside."

I hadn't even noticed she'd used side roads to skirt downtown and approach my house from the opposite direction. I needed to be more aware of my surroundings. That had been the principal rule of the self-defense class I'd taken . . . after.

I hadn't finished the class—receiving the call about my father before I was through. If I had, then maybe I'd have known what to do when Cartwright manhandled me. Anything but freezing like a rabbit in the sights of a wolf would have been good.

Grace followed me to the front porch and waited patiently while I dug out my keys, then opened the door. I flicked every switch as I moved through the house, lighting the place up like Christmas.

The *brrr* a cat makes when surprised sounded from the staircase; then Oprah rocketed down faster than I'd seen her move in years. She twined around Grace's ankles and began to purr.

"Hey, you still alive?" Grace murmured, bending to pick up Oprah.

The two of them had always been pals. Whenever Grace had stayed over, Oprah had slept curled on her chest. I would have been jealous, except I had loved Grace, too.

Her father had refused to let her have a pet of any kind. He didn't like animals. Sometimes I'd wondered if he much liked Grace, which was why she'd spent a lot of time over here.

As each one of the McDaniel brothers had left Lake Bluff and never come back, Sheriff McDaniel, the former, had gotten crankier and crankier. By the time he'd died, everyone in town had been on their best behavior for fear they'd have to deal with him.

I tossed my keys on the hall table. The clatter made Oprah start. Two sets of green eyes—one more yellow, the other more blue—turned toward me.

"You wanna quit smooching my cat and show me what you found?" I asked.

Grace rubbed her cheek across Oprah's dappled head, then set her on the floor. The cat continued to twine between Grace's ankles as if she were in a maze.

"Don't I get a drink first?" Grace asked.

"A drink?"

"Wine. Beer. Whiskey. I don't care. I'm officially off duty." She glanced at her watch. "About an hour ago."

I shrugged and headed for the kitchen. As soon as I filled Oprah's bowl, she abandoned Grace for the food.

I opened my refrigerator. "Merlot. Sauvignon blanc. Bud."

"Whatever you're having." Grace leaned against the counter, her gaze flicking over the cabinets and the windows. She was always on the lookout for something, had been even as a child. Her oddly light eyes and overly inquisitive manner had made people nervous. Except for me.

I grabbed the bottle of merlot and two glasses. "You wanna sit on the deck?"

"Sure." Grace opened the patio door and let me precede her onto the wide expanse of white wood surrounded by the forest.

I lit the wicks on several citronella torches, which served the dual purpose of providing light and keeping the mosquitoes away, theoretically, then poured us each a glass of bloodred wine—why was everything bloodred lately?—and handed one to Grace.

She took a sip. "Ah. Much better than what we drank in high school."

I made a face. "Mad Dog 20/20 and Boone's Farm Strawberry Hill."

"We thought we were so cool." She lifted her glass in a toast. "To improved palates."

"Hear, hear." I mirrored the gesture and took a sip. The smooth berry taste made my tongue curl in pleasure, while the slight scent of earth and oak wafted across my face.

Grace set down her glass and pulled something out of her pocket. I squinted at what appeared to be a piece of bark. "So?"

Grace took a flashlight off her belt and hit the *on* button. When she washed the light over her hand I reared back, curling my lip as if I'd detected a foul odor.

A bright red swastika marred the surface of the wood.

"Hell," I muttered.

"Pretty much."

"You think that's blood?" I asked.

"Hope not."

"Where did you find it?"

"Under the apple tree where our hiking tourist says he was attacked."

"Just lying there?"

"Yeah." She bit her lip. "I didn't see any blood."

"So the guy didn't manage to shoot the wolf like he thought."

"Guess not." She continued to frown, deep in thought.

"What else?" I pressed.

"The tracks were weird. I found his and a few half prints that could have been a dog's. Although it would have had to have been one big dog. But there was also a second set of people feet all over the place."

"Odd."

"Yeah, especially since the only tracks that led anywhere were human."

"I don't get it."

"Me, either. The tourist hobbled away, the mystery guest, too, but the canine? Not so much."

"Where did it go?"

She lifted her hands, then lowered them. "The only other direction is up."

10

"CAN WOLVES CLIMB trees?"

"None that I've ever heard about," Grace said.

"You think our tourist was lying about the wolf?"

"Could be, but then how do you explain the severe throat trauma?"

"I don't. You going to talk to the guy again?"

"First thing tomorrow."

"And this?" I pointed at the tiny piece of wood.

"I'll be asking him about that, too."

"You going to tell him to leave town?"

Her eyebrows shot up. "Why would I do that?"

"If he's some neo-Nazi nut job, maybe he's here *because* of the Gypsies." He had been hiking awfully close to their camp.

"Shit," Grace muttered.

"Yeah."

We both lifted our glasses and drained them. I poured another round.

"All I need are Nazis. I have enough trouble with the Klan."

"Since when do you have trouble with the Klan?"

"This is Georgia, Claire. There's always trouble with the Klan."

"What kind of trouble are we talking about?"

"The usual horseshit—flaming crosses on the lawns, egged windows, nasty notes."

"Here?"

She put her fingers to her forehead and rubbed. "Yes, here. This kind of stuff has been going on for decades."

"Not when my dad was in charge."

"Yes, when your dad was in charge, and mine, too. We had enough crosses on our grass that sometimes we barely had any grass."

"I never knew that."

"My dad was good at camouflaging things. Why do you think he was constantly planting flowering bushes in the center of the yard?"

"I thought it was a Cherokee thing."

"It was." Her eyes met mine. "Partly. The Klan didn't much care for a Native American sheriff, or maybe it was the African-American part they objected to. Nor did they appreciate the lily-white daughter of the mayor and the not-so-white daughter of the head cop being best friends."

I took another gulp of wine. How had I not known this? What else had been going on around here that I'd been oblivious to?

"And now?" I asked. People had to be more enlightened these days. They just had to be.

"Haven't had a good cross burning in quite a while."

"Always a plus."

"Things have been better. Which is why this"—she turned the swastika-marred wood over in her fingers—"is so bothersome. The Klan doesn't care much for Jewish people, either."

"Do they like anyone?"

"White people. Protestants. Who only play with other white Protestants."

"Booooring," I said. "Considering their outfits, I always figured they were short on imagination."

"And style."

"As well as brains." I flicked one finger at the chip. "That looks like a talisman or an amulet, maybe a charm. I'll do some checking."

Before I'd landed the producer's job, I'd spent some time as a researcher. I hadn't been half-bad at it.

"What kind of wood is that?" I asked.

"Seems like it came from the apple tree. If it hadn't been for the symbol, I'd have thought a chunk had just fallen off on its own. The tree must have been struck by lightning—there's a big black scorch mark on the trunk—but managed to survive. Sometimes nature is amazing."

Grace shoved the wood into a pocket and picked up her glass again. "This is nice," she said.

"Yeah. I missed you."

Her face, which had been open and relaxed, tightened. "You had a weird way of showing it."

"What's that supposed to mean?"

"Friends don't leave town without a good-bye. Best friends don't stop calling; they write more often than a card at Christmas."

"I know. I'm sorry. This place, my dad, the people—" I took a deep breath, remembering how stifled I'd felt here. "I wanted to start a new life."

"And I was part of the old one." I nodded. "So what changed?"

"Me."

The word fell between us, a bridge to a secret I didn't want to share.

"What happened in Atlanta, Claire? What made you run back here to hide?"

"I hardly think being the mayor is a good way to hide."

"You know what I mean."

I did. Only Grace would know that something had changed in me. Only Grace would have the guts to ask, and only with Grace would I feel compelled to tell her everything.

"I trusted someone and he hurt me."

"Join the club," she muttered.

I hadn't realized how much my leaving and not coming back had bothered her. I should have. Grace was difficult to say the least, a pain in the ass to be truthful. I doubted people were beating down her door applying for the position of best friend. Around here, I doubted she got many dates, either.

Sleeping with the head cop might have perks, but in macho-man land, which we were smack-dab in the center of, it was probably more embarrassing than anything. That Lake Bluff had a female mayor and a female sheriff was downright progressive, but that didn't mean the guys in town wanted to be seen with us.

Which was probably another reason I'd come home. I wouldn't have to worry about being pursued. Or at least I hadn't been worried until Malachi Cartwright showed up.

"I checked the police reports," Grace said quietly.

My gaze flicked to hers. At first I thought she meant in Atlanta, and my heart thundered, though I wasn't sure why. She wouldn't find anything. Then I realized she was talking about Cartwright and his merry band of Gypsies.

"What did you find?"

"Nothing unusual for towns where a festival is being

held and a lot of out-of-towners have shown up." She took a sip of wine. "Fights. Assault. Reports of strange things going bump in the night."

"Like wolves?"

"Some. Plus huge bats, wild cats, zombies, ghosts, and, in one case, a dragon."

"You don't consider that unusual?"

"Not with all the drinking and revelry."

"Hmm."

"While I was at it, I checked the police reports in Atlanta."

My heart, which had just begun to slow, sped up again. "The Gypsies were in Atlanta?"

"No," she said, "you were."

"You think I was arrested?"

"I was hoping you filed a report on what happened to you."

I shook my head. I couldn't.

"When you say someone you trusted hurt you, you don't mean your feelings."

"Why not?" My voice shook. Damn. I didn't want to talk about this.

"I know you," she said. "You were going to take Atlanta, then the world, by storm. Now you turn up here, and you don't leave."

"Maybe I like it here."

Grace gave me a skeptical look over the rim of her wineglass and waited.

Sitting on the porch with my childhood home behind me, the forest in front of me, and my best friend next to me, I did the one thing I'd been told I needed to do to heal but had been unable to. I talked about it.

"I was dating a nice man who worked in the governor's office," I began.

"Nice ones are always trouble. They're either boring

or not really very nice at all." She tilted her head. "Which was he?"

"Not very nice at all."

"That's what I thought."

"We'd gone out a few months. Three, maybe four. Dinner. Movie. Political soirees."

Grace let her eyes close and her head fall back. "Snore."

My own laughter surprised me. Usually when I thought about that night, I was paralyzed by both fear and disgust. I certainly wasn't laughing.

"I invited him back to my apartment for a drink."

We'd walked in; I'd shut the door, opened my mouth to ask what he'd like, and discovered that what he liked was me.

My chest hurt; I wasn't breathing. I took in a deep, full lungful of air, which caught in the middle.

"Take your time," Grace said in a soothing voice she had no doubt perfected for use with trauma victims.

"There isn't all that much to tell," I managed. "He thought I asked him in for more than a drink."

"But you hadn't."

"No," I said slowly, trying to recall what I'd been thinking, feeling.

Maybe I *had* meant to have sex with him. Maybe he'd sensed that and just jumped the gun. I couldn't remember anymore what I'd felt for Josh Logan before that night in my apartment.

"Go on, Claire," Grace murmured. "You can trust me."

My eyes met hers, and I knew that she was right. Grace might have been annoyed that I'd left, might still be a little annoyed, but she loved me. She'd do anything for me. I'd never had another friend like her and I never would. Old friends truly were the best friends. They knew you when—and they liked you anyway.

"He . . . ," I began, and choked as if something had blocked my throat.

Grace shoved my wine into my hand. "Drink." She pounded on my back a few times for good measure.

When I'd stopped coughing, taken a sip of wine, then several breaths, I tried again. "We had sex and then he left."

"That's not what happened."

"Were you there?"

"You wouldn't be shaking, choking, and stuttering if all that had happened was sex."

"Extremely bad sex," I muttered.

"He raped you."

I jerked, sloshing wine over the side of the glass. Dark red drops cascaded down my hand and dripped onto the deck. I watched them roll over my skin and thought of Snow White's mother pricking her finger while sewing and letting the droplets fall upon the white linen. The strangest images came to mind when I was trying to deny the truth.

"He was my . . . boyfriend." Or near enough. "I invited him in."

"For alcohol, not sex. You told him no?"

"I—I think so. Everything's fuzzy."

"You struggled?"

"A bit." I'd had to wear long-sleeved blouses in the midst of a scorching Atlanta summer until the bruises on my arms went away. "Obviously not enough."

"It wasn't your fault," Grace said.

Deep down, I knew that was true. But higher up, near my head, I couldn't get past the sense that I'd brought what had happened on myself, that I'd led

Josh on, given him false signals. I'd liked him, been attracted to him. I would have had sex with him eventually. So what was the big deal?

God, I sounded like every other date rape victim on the planet. I hated myself.

"Why didn't you file a report?"

"I couldn't."

"Of course you could. You want him out there doing that to someone else?"

My gaze lifted. "He isn't like that."

"Sounds to me as if he's exactly like that."

"He was moving up in the governor's office. There was talk he might even *be* the next governor." I took a deep breath. "I didn't think anyone would believe me. I figured they'd chalk my story up as one more scum ex-girlfriend scamming for her few minutes of fame."

"You don't think this will come back to bite you on the ass later?"

"How? I never told anyone but you and a therapist. I doubt she'll say anything. You plan on going to the tabloids with this, Grace?"

"You didn't see a doctor?"

"Why? A couple of bruises. I lived."

"Diseases. Pregnancy. You moron."

"Thanks. That helps."

"You need to see a doctor."

"He used a condom."

"In other words, he planned it."

"Men carry condoms in their wallets. It's what they do."

Of course Josh's condom hadn't been in his wallet; it had been on his cock. Talk about being prepared.

"It's behind me now," I said. "I want to forget."

"Which is why you ran home."

"I didn't run anywhere. My father died. Lake Bluff needed a mayor. I accepted."

"You are so full of shit I'm surprised you don't smell."

"And once again . . . thank you. That helps so much."

"You haven't forgotten, Claire. I saw you tonight with Cartwright. You were scared half to death." Her face darkened, and she stroked the butt of her gun. "Did he try to do more than kiss you?"

"No. Not really."

He'd grabbed me, made me feel trapped. That's what had started the flashback. Until then, I'd been enjoying myself. A lot.

"Cartwright's out of your league."

I stiffened, insulted, but she continued.

"Guys like him pick a woman in every town. They have their fun, then leave at the end of the week."

Sounded good to me. No commitments. No need to tell the whole truth and nothing but the truth. Just a little horizontal mambo and away they went, never to be seen or heard from again. I wondered if I could find that kind of deal more than once a year.

Grace watched me closely. "You wanna talk about Atlanta some more?"

I shook my head. I'd talked and talked about it with a therapist—or at least I'd talked as much as I was going to. Talking hadn't done much good.

Grace stood, picking up her glass and the bottle. "I should go."

"Sure." She was disappointed in me. I couldn't blame her. I was disappointed in myself.

Grace would not only have arrested Josh; she would also have carved him a new hole—right where his uncontrollable penis used to be.

Standing abruptly, I grabbed my glass and led the way inside.

We set everything on the counter. Grace touched my arm. "If you want to talk again, I'm here. Any time. Day or night. If you want to file a complaint, I can help you."

"It's a little late for that."

She went to the front door and glanced at me over her shoulder. "It's never too late."

"I just want to forget, Grace."

"Looks like that's really working out well for you," she said, and closed the door behind her.

She was right. I hadn't moved past that night. My life had become divided into before and after. If I'd truly forgotten, I'd have . . . well, forgotten.

What had happened with Josh would forever be a part of who I'd become. It had been a life-altering experience, because here I was, right back where I'd started, and I didn't even mind.

I returned to the kitchen, planning to load the dishwasher and recork the wine. I'd just lifted both goblets when a tiny tap made me glance up.

A man peered through the sliding glass doors.

11

I DROPPED THE glasses. They shattered at my feet.

Oprah, who must have been snoozing in the hall, squalled, then thundered up the stairs. The man opened the glass door and stepped inside.

"Are you all right?" Malachi Cartwright knelt and began to pick up the larger pieces.

"What the *hell* are you doing here?" I demanded.

He tilted his head, and his hair swung back from his shoulders; his earring glinted sharply in the overhead light. With him kneeling at my feet I felt like Cinderella. Too bad I'd learned the hard way that life was not a fairy tale.

Slowly he rose, just as he'd risen out of the water only hours earlier. Except this time he had on all his clothes. Too bad.

The thought was so out of character for me—the new me, the "after" me—I almost laughed. What was it about this man that made me want him? Could it be that he wasn't going to stay?

My therapist had recommended I have sex with

someone I trusted. I didn't trust Cartwright. I didn't even know him. But that also meant he didn't know me. That anonymity, the promise that there'd be nothing more than sex between us, was unbelievably appealing.

"I came to see if you were all right," he said. "You seemed upset."

He didn't know the half of it. I liked that in a man.

He stood so close the heat of his body warmed me; I caught the scent of chill lake water and sunshine. The contrast was so enticing I swayed, my body yearning for the promise of his.

Cartwright stepped back, then glanced around helplessly. "Garbage can?" He lifted hands full of shards.

"Oh! Sorry. Under the sink." I opened the cabinet, pulled out the basket. "The cat gets into it otherwise."

The jangle of broken glass sent me to the closet for a broom. Then I gathered the remaining mess and bent to sweep everything into the dustpan.

Black-clad legs appeared in my line of vision. I glanced up to find Cartwright staring down. I was possessed by the sudden urge to press my cheek against his thigh, turn my face, and mouth him through the thin cotton layer of his pants.

I stood so abruptly the glass rattled in the pan; then I marched across the floor and dumped the refuse in with the rest.

When I turned he was right there, and I jumped back, banging my tailbone against the counter. He took the broom, the dustpan, out of my hands, setting them aside.

"Claire," he murmured. "Don't be afraid."

"I—I'm not."

He leaned forward, nuzzling my neck, his breath

brushing my collarbone, making me shiver. His mouth slid upward, caressing my jaw, hovering near my ear. "You are," he whispered.

He touched me nowhere, but he was so close everywhere. I found myself straining forward—wanting, needing, desiring him.

His erection brushed my stomach, just a hint, so minute I wasn't even certain he had in truth touched me. He grazed my jugular with his teeth, and I gasped, the sound pure arousal. I wanted to grab his head, pull it to my breast, let him suckle me as he lifted me onto the countertop and plunged into me again and again until we both came screaming.

Whoa! Where had that come from? Even "before," I'd never been one to get naked anywhere but the bedroom. And screaming? Sex wasn't all that.

"I want you more than I've wanted any woman in . . . aeons." The word whispered across my skin. "But we'll take it as slow as you wish."

I stilled. "What?"

"Some men are animals. I am not."

I shoved at his chest, and he moved away. Stalking to the floor-length windows, I glanced outside where the citronella tapers still blazed merrily, their light not strong enough to penetrate the thick forest surrounding the deck. "You were in the woods."

"Yes," he said simply.

I spun around. "You were listening?"

He spread his long-fingered hands. "I dinna mean to."

"A gentleman would not eavesdrop."

"There are no gentlemen anymore."

He had that right.

"Get out," I said.

Cartwright started toward me, and my eyes widened.

At first I thought he meant to grab me, shake me. It had happened before. But then I realized he meant to leave, just as I'd asked, but I was standing in his way.

I sidestepped, tripping over my own feet, and he steadied me with gentle hands. "I would never have—" He stopped, took a breath, tried again. "I would never have been so forceful with you earlier if I'd known."

"I'm not made of glass," I muttered.

"But you are. Spun fine in fire. Hard enough to keep out the rain and the wind." His knuckle rapped against the pane. "Fragile enough to shatter if handled poorly."

He reached for the handle, and suddenly I didn't want him to go. When I touched his wrist, his gaze met mine. Desire leaped between us, so strong, so strange.

"Fire is sacred to the Rom," he murmured, and his eyes trailed over my red hair.

"I thought it punished evil."

His lips tilted. "That, too. My ancestors worshipped the fire." He lifted his hand slowly and trailed it down my cheek. "As well as the moon."

I couldn't stop staring into his dark, dark eyes. There were secrets there. But I was so tired of being alone, so tired of being scared, so tired of never wanting anyone, and now I wanted him. I couldn't help it. I pressed my mouth to his.

Warm. Sweet. Soft. He let me take the lead, hanging back, making me follow, allowing me to be the aggressor, and I liked it.

I nibbled at his lips, trailed their seam with my tongue, and he opened to me. I tensed just a little, expecting the usual invasion, but none came.

Patiently he waited, letting me kiss him, barely kissing me until it wasn't enough and I just had to taste.

Behind my closed eyelids, images burst free. Cool

spring water running beneath a blazing summer sun. Snowflakes drifting through a silvery sky to land atop a field of purple wildflowers.

I wasn't a woman prone to pretty words or beautiful daydreams, yet kissing this man brought to mind all sorts of odd things.

Fire beneath the moon. A rainstorm hitting the pavement after a scorching August day. Steam rising up, drifting past my face.

I pulled away, staring at him wide-eyed, trembling. For the first time in months I wasn't afraid. The arousal had pushed away every shred of fear.

"I will never touch you unless you ask it of me." I saw his lips moving, but his voice was like the wind swirling through my head. "Perhaps you must even beg."

The thought of telling him what I wanted, of never having to fear his pushing me further than I could handle, was seductive. But—

"You can trust me, Claire."

How did he continue to take the words right out of my mouth? Or maybe out of my head? I made a derisive sound.

"You don't think I'm trustworthy?"

I met his eyes. "I don't know you."

"You could tie me up." He leaned forward and I tensed, but all he did was rub his mouth along my forehead, his lips caressing the sensitive skin at my hairline. "Then I couldn't touch you, unless you set me free."

I shuddered at the image, which was far too appealing. "Maybe later," I managed, and he laughed.

"I must go," Cartwright said, but he didn't. He stood with his back to the sliding glass door as I stood so close his chest nearly touched mine every time he filled his lungs with air.

"You'll only be here a week," I said.

"After your festival, we must head for another. In Pennsylvania." His head tilted. "Why?"

"I may not be able to—" I took a breath, let it out. "In a week."

"You think all I care about is sex?"

My eyebrows lifted. *Well, yeah.* He certainly couldn't care about me. We'd just met.

"You think I have a woman in every town?"

I winced at the echo of Grace's words. Well, eavesdroppers rarely heard good about themselves.

"You think I share my body with them, and then I go away?" I inched back a few steps. "You don't know much about the Rom. We aren't supposed to consort with *gadje* except for business."

"What's *gadje*?"

"Those who are not Rom."

"Sounds like a custom from the fifteenth century."

"An ancient custom, to be sure. But one we try to uphold. The outside world has never been kind to us."

I recalled Mrs. Charlesdown accusing Sabina of stealing when the girl had done nothing at all.

"In the old days, people would leave unwanted children near our camp," he continued. "Then, when we took one, adopted him, made him one of us, we were accused of kidnapping."

"So that's how the Gypsies-steal-children rumor got started."

"Yes," he said. "I do not have a woman in every town. I am not supposed to have a woman at all. Or at least not one who is *gadje*. I would be declared *marime*. An outcast."

"But you're the leader."

"That doesn't matter." He stared straight into my

eyes, then very deliberately lifted his palm to my cheek. "To touch you is forbidden."

"Then why are you here?"

He looked out the window, toward the wood. "I couldn't stay away."

The idea of him being forbidden to touch me, that touching me could get him exiled, or as exiled as one could get in the twenty-first century, was strangely intriguing.

"Kiss me," I murmured, and his gaze returned to mine.

"You accept my offer then?"

I hesitated. Once I did, I'd be committing to more than a kiss. I knew that, despite what he'd promised. But I wanted to heal, to get past what had happened, to move on, and this was the perfect opportunity.

What if I tried to have sex with someone from Lake Bluff and I . . . couldn't? I wouldn't be able to stay here, either.

But Cartwright was leaving. And best of all, he couldn't tell anyone that he'd touched me or risk being ostracized himself.

I reached past him and yanked the cord on the drapes so that they slid across the window, obscuring us from the rest of the world.

"Kiss me," I repeated. "Then touch me"—I pointed to the curve of my neck—"right here."

He smiled and did exactly that.

12

I DON'T KNOW how much time passed as we kissed and then kissed some more. He touched me nowhere but my neck, my mouth, yet my entire body hummed at the nearness of his.

My breasts ached; my legs wobbled. I was damp, desperate. "Bedroom," I managed against his mouth.

He stepped back and I nearly fell. "Not yet."

"What?"

"Too soon." He brushed my hair out of my face. "You aren't ready."

I felt more ready than I'd ever been.

"I thought I was the one calling the shots."

"To a point. I am not going to do anything foolish."

The double entendre of his words made me flush. His turning me down when my body screamed for a release I hadn't had in . . . I forget, made me angry.

"Fucking the forbidden is already foolish," I snapped.

"I haven't fucked you." He opened the sliding glass door and slipped through, pulling it closed behind him.

Right before the latch clicked, I heard him murmur, "Yet."

I reached for the handle, yanked the door open, got tangled in the curtains, and impatiently shoved them aside; then I stood staring at the empty deck, the deserted yard, the silent wood.

To disappear that quickly Cartwright would have had to vault over the edge and sprint into the trees. Even then, he'd have to be very, very fast. Guess he couldn't wait to get away.

I went inside, checked all the windows and doors. By the time I reached my room and completed my nightly tossing-Oprah-off-the-pillow ritual, I was calmer.

Malachi had been right to say no. I wasn't ready. Although—

As I stepped out of my clothes and pulled on a nightgown, I let my hands drift over my breasts, let my fingers trail between my legs.

I felt ready.

But the body was different from the mind. I might want him more than I'd ever wanted anyone, physically, but mentally . . . I wasn't sure.

I had a difficult time waking up the next morning. My head heavy, my eyelids stuck together; I felt dopey yet strangely on edge.

When the shower spray hit my body, I yelped as if the droplets were electrical charges. The water pressure had never bothered me before—except for a lack of it—now the pounding set my teeth on edge.

I didn't want liquid cascading over my skin; I wanted his hands sliding down my arms, up my rib cage, cupping my breasts, thumbs tracing the nipples.

My head fell back; the water beat on my throat; my own hands followed the path my mind made. It had been a long time since I'd done this, too.

As my skin hummed again as it had hummed last night, I slipped my fingers between my legs and began to finish what a mere kiss had started.

The combination of the memories, the pounding spray, and the rhythmic press of my own hand made me come gasping in less than half a minute.

To my amazement, the self-inflicted orgasm did little to diminish the frustration I'd awoken to, a feeling that hung around me like Pigpen's cloud of dust throughout the day, making me jumpy and far too short with everyone I met.

The Full Moon Festival officially opened with a short ceremony in the town square at 9:00 A.M. I was set to give a welcome speech; the high school band would play "Georgia on My Mind," and we'd be off and running with a sidewalk sale by all the local merchants, as well as the first show by the Gypsies that evening.

Instead of a suit or slacks, I donned a mint green dress that complemented my figure, the waist nipped in, the skirt full and fabulous, the hemline hitting just below the knees. When this dress was accented with my grandmother's pearls and pumps in the same shade, I resembled June Cleaver with a French twist.

I'd just finished my speech and stepped back from the podium to light applause from the fifty people who'd bothered to show up when a stray breeze caught the skirt and made it billow nearly to my waist.

The warm air on my bare legs, the brush against the still-damp crotch of my panties, made me cry out in both arousal and alarm. I slapped my hands against the fluttering material and glanced up to check how many people had noticed.

Luckily, the band had started to play the Ray Charles classic as soon as I'd finished, and no one heard my outcry. A few people smiled at my discomfiture, but not maliciously. Everyone had an embarrassing moment or two in their past.

Then I noticed a man dressed in black and white walking away from the crowd. Even without the long dark hair and lithe, almost-catlike gait, I'd have recognized Malachi Cartwright. He stood out like a crow among peacocks.

Had he been listening to my speech? I'd passed my gaze over the crowd before, during, and after the welcome, but I hadn't noticed him.

The last notes of the song faded and what was left of the crowd, mostly the parents of the band members, clapped.

I hung around to make sure everything was being broken down and put away before I headed for the office.

"Lovely performance," Joyce said as I entered.

"The band's really coming along."

"I meant your Marilyn Monroe imitation." She waved at my skirt.

My face heated. "I was going for June Cleaver."

"Unless you were auditioning for *Leave It to My Beaver,* you missed by a mile."

"Leave it to *what*?"

"Porn," she said simply, and tapped a few keys on her computer. "Actually has a plot. June and Ward enjoy a rare weekend without the kids and—"

"Stop." I slapped my hands over both sides of my head. "My ears. Are they bleeding?"

"Just because I'm old doesn't mean I'm dead."

I wasn't sure how old Joyce was, and I'd never had the guts to ask. I always figured she was near my dad's age, give or take.

"You aren't that old," I said.

She lifted her hands, palms out. "The pickings around here are mighty slim at any age."

True. And for someone nearing Social Security, probably even more so. Joyce was out of luck unless she wanted to date See, Hear, or Speak No Evil. I wrinkled my nose. Forget about Have No Fun.

"How come you never married, Joyce?"

Her head came up; her eyes widened. "Me?"

"Yes, you. You obviously liked kids or you wouldn't have been a teacher."

Joyce snorted. "Honey, in my day, you were a nurse or you were a teacher. I preferred a career choice that didn't involve blood." She pursed her lips. "Though I have to say, being a phys ed teacher, I saw my share of it."

"You didn't like kids?"

"I liked you." Joyce smiled.

I smiled back. "Thanks."

I don't know what I'd have done as a teen without Joyce. There'd been things I couldn't ask my dad. Things Grace hadn't known. But Joyce had always been available. And while she'd often mothered me when I didn't want her to, she'd also been a friend when I needed her to be, and that was something I'd always be grateful for. I wanted her to be happy.

"Wasn't there ever anyone you considered marrying?" I pressed.

Joyce stared at her desk and I knew.

"Dad."

She shrugged. "He never saw anyone but your mom. Even after she was gone."

"I'm sorry—"

"No." She held up a hand. "I could have pushed it. Could have talked him into marrying me on the loneliness factor alone, but I didn't want to be second all my

life. Here"—she waved a hand at the desk, the office—
"I was first. He depended on me. He needed *me,* and no
one else."

"I feel the same way. I couldn't do this without you,
Joyce."

"Thanks, girl. That means a lot."

"Where do you go when you . . . go?" I asked.

"The ladies' room."

"Not that kind of go. Sheesh. I mean when you disappear sometimes."

She faced her desk. "I don't know what you mean.
Now, did you want to borrow that video? Because from
where I'm sitting, you could use a little excitement in
your life."

My mind went immediately to the excitement I'd
had in my life last night, and I had to turn away so she
wouldn't see me smile. "I'll be fine."

For the first time in a long time, I actually thought I
might be.

With the festival begun I was both busier and less
busy than usual. Citizens didn't stop in for a chat or
even make an appointment. They had too much to do.
However, tourists wandered through, as if the town
hall were part of a guided tour.

Many of them wanted to meet the mayor and thank
me for the lovely event, then ask questions about Lake
Bluff, the mountains, and the history of both.

After the fifth family had traipsed through my office, I called for Joyce. "Next year we hire someone to
do tours and speechify about historical . . ." I waved
my hand. "Stuff."

"Got it," she said, and made a note on her ever-
present notepad. "Think you'll be here next year?"

"Huh?" I glanced up from the mountain of crap on
my desk, which appeared to have grown since yesterday.

"Balthazar is determined, and it isn't like you wanted to be the mayor."

"Who said I didn't?"

"Your dad."

Guilt and sorrow flooded me. I missed him. I should have stayed and taken over the job as he'd wanted me to. If I had, I never would have met Josh and—

Straightening my spine, I lifted my chin. "I don't plan on leaving anytime soon."

"Even if Balthazar wins?"

"I don't plan on letting Balthazar win."

Joyce grinned. "He'd be so proud."

I let myself bask in the notion of my dad at last being proud of me.

He'd always hoped I would take over for him, been very disappointed that I would rather eat dirt, and while I'd been too caught up in my own plans to worry about his feelings at the time, now that he was gone, I wished I'd been a better daughter. I'd try to make amends by keeping the town he'd adored safe from idiots like Balthazar Monahan.

"I hear you made the council vote last night," Joyce said.

"So?"

"I don't think they've actually voted in years."

"Is that bad?"

"No. Your dad was a good guy, but sometimes he slacked off on things."

"He did?"

I'd never heard that before.

"Everyone does if they can get away with it. Jeremiah was good with people. He listened to them. They liked him and trusted him."

"Unlike me."

"Where'd you get that?" Joyce asked. "Everyone likes you fine."

"They don't trust me. No one talks to me like they talked to him."

"They will. The people know you can do this job, or they wouldn't have asked you to take over."

"How can they know?"

"The apple doesn't fall far from the tree, Claire. No matter how hard you might have wanted it to."

I suddenly felt lighter, happier, than I had in months, maybe years. In Atlanta I'd always been seen as less than I could be; here I was seen as more than I was.

I glanced at the clock. Not quite noon. No one had come through the door for fifteen whole minutes. "I'm going to try and get a little work done," I said.

"Hold your calls?"

"Unless it's an emergency, yes."

I headed directly for the Internet. I could rationalize all that I wanted to, but deep down I knew that the discovery of a swastika-bearing chunk of wood could not be good. I needed to find out what it meant. I had to protect this town and its people at all costs. They'd put their trust in me, and I wouldn't let them down.

I found out all sorts of things I really didn't want to know about the Nazis. Was there anything good to know about them?

However, under "Origin of the Swastika" I discovered something else. The sign dated from prehistoric times and was an Icelandic symbol of both protection and rebirth.

My search for totems, charms, and amulets made of wood caused thousands of sites to spill onto my screen. The first ones referenced Native American tribes—Inuit and Ojibwe specifically, but nothing on the Cherokee.

The second set referenced Wicca. Spells, natural cures, good luck, bad luck, and anything in between.

I rubbed my forehead. This wasn't going anywhere.

My phone rang, the shrill *brring* slicing through the lovely quiet of my office. I shot a glare at Joyce through the glass.

She motioned furiously for me to answer, and I remembered that I'd told her to interrupt only in the case of an emergency. I snatched up the phone. "Claire Kennedy."

"Get your butt to the hospital."

"Grace?" I asked, but she'd already hung up.

13

I WASN'T SURE what I expected to find at the Lake Bluff Community Hospital. Certainly not Grace sitting quietly in an empty room, staring at her hands.

"Where's the fire?" I asked.

She glanced up. "He's gone."

"He, who?"

"Ryan Freestone." At my blank expression she elaborated. "The tourist who was attacked by the wolf."

"So?"

"Gone as in disappeared and can't find a trace of him anywhere."

I sat, too. "You'd better start from the beginning."

Grace spread her hands. In one she held the swastika-marred slice of wood. "I came here to ask him about this. He was gone. No one's seen him since last night."

"He got sick of the place and left. I know I would."

"He didn't return to his hotel. His car's still in the lot."

"He's enjoying the festival."

"Maybe. I have my people keeping an eye out. But so far no one's seen him."

"He'll show up."

"Maybe," she repeated, turning the wood over and over in her hand like a worry stone.

"What's the matter with you?"

"I watched the security tape."

A prickle of unease washed over me. "And?"

She picked up the controller for the VCR and pointed it at the television mounted on the wall opposite the bed. A low thunk and flickering images appeared.

A dimly lit hall. The tiny clock in the corner of the tape read 3:23 A.M. A door opened and a man stepped out.

A completely naked man.

"That him?"

"Mmm."

"Guess he didn't care for the hospital gown."

Grace didn't bother to comment.

He crept toward the front entrance, cringing back when the image of a nurse moved to and fro behind the desk. He turned toward the camera, and I got a good glimpse of his face—awfully hairy, with wild, burning eyes that brought to mind a zealot or a crazy person. Because the film was black-and-white, I couldn't distinguish the color of his hair beyond lighter than black, nor the color of his eyes beyond lighter than dark.

"Not the most attractive guy in the world," I murmured.

"He had a fever, a bad one according to the nurses. He was saying all sorts of weird things."

On the tape, Freestone caught sight of an open window. He sprinted toward it with an odd, loping shuffle, then sprang onto the sill and went through.

"We're on the second floor," I said.

"No moss on you."

"What did you find under that window?"

"Footprints leading into the woods."

"Usually a fever makes you weak."

"Usually." Grace hit the *off* button, then pressed *rewind,* waiting several seconds before choosing *pause.*

"Take a look." She lifted a pile of white tape from the bed and held it out to me.

I made a face. "Do I have to?"

She quirked a brow, and I took the offering gingerly. The tape and gauze were wrinkled and torn, but there was no blood—or anything else I didn't want to see.

"I don't understand." I handed them back to her.

"Freestone had extreme throat trauma. Defensive wounds on the hands and arms, but watch this." She hit *play.*

I observed again Freestone creeping out of this room, seeing the nurse, turning back; then Grace froze the image.

He'd lifted his hands to smooth his hair out of his face. There wasn't a mark on them.

I stood and moved in closer, staring at his smooth, unmarred throat. "You're sure this is the same guy?"

"Yep."

"What did the doctor say?"

"He didn't have a clue. Since I couldn't find the wolf, they were going to start rabies shots today."

"Those are painful, right?"

"Better than they used to be, but I doubt treatment for rabies is anything you want to do if you don't have to."

"You think that's why Freestone pulled a Houdini?"

"Maybe." Grace ejected the tape. "Hell, I don't know what to think anymore."

Neither did I.

"I so don't need this right now," she muttered.

With the festival in full swing, Grace and her minions had their hands full. Even with the rent-a-cops she'd hired—retired officers from Lake Bluff and surrounding areas—they had to be swamped.

"I've got to find him," she said.

"What happens if he's got rabies and he doesn't receive the shots?"

"You don't want to know."

"I don't want to, but I think I have to."

She tilted her head, studied me, then nodded. "Pretty much what you've seen in the movies—extreme thirst, foaming at the mouth, inclination to bite everyone you meet, spread the wealth."

I cringed at the idea of the guy loping down Center Street at the height of the festival. That would kill the fun for everyone.

"The incubation period in humans is one to three months," Grace continued.

"Oh." A trickle of relief flowed through me. "That's good."

"As long as he doesn't leave town or disappear into the mountains. Freestone was a hiker and, according to his family, a good one. Been known to stay in the wilderness for weeks on his own. He knows the out-of-doors."

"Crap." The guy could survive indefinitely.

"There's also the chance that the virus has mutated."

"Which would mean?"

"A much faster incubation period."

"Like one to three days instead of one to three months?"

She shrugged. "Viruses are wonky that way."

"I have to call the CDC."

"Already done."

"And?"

"They'll get back to us."

I rolled my eyes, and Grace's lips tightened. "I can't wait around for them. Once the disease starts to exhibit symptoms, the vaccine is useless."

"We do not need a death associated with this town, or the festival."

"We don't need a rabies outbreak ever."

"Right. Do rabies victims usually take off like this?" I asked.

"I've never dealt with a rabies victim."

"Never?"

"According to the doctor, human infection is rare. I don't think he's seen it before, either."

"Swell."

"In my experience, normal people want to be cured. ASAP."

"So what's wrong with Freestone?"

"Normal people don't heal traumatic throat wounds in less than twenty-four hours."

I contemplated Grace's worried face. "What are you trying to say?"

"He might seem normal, but he isn't."

"What is he?"

"That's what we have to find out. But I'm not going to have time to trace down similar instances of miraculous healing. I'm assigning that task to you."

"Me?"

"You're research girl, right?" Grace didn't wait for me to answer. "And while you're boning up on miraculous healing, find out if there have been a lot of wolves appearing in places where there aren't supposed to be any."

"Okay."

"Anything turn up on this?" She wiggled the talisman.

I filled her in on the origin of the swastika.

"Protection and rebirth," she murmured. "Interesting."

I hadn't found it that interesting, but whatever. "Did it belong to our missing hiker?"

Grace shook her head. "I had to call his family to tell them he was gone. His wife said she'd never known him to carry a charm, amulet, or talisman, and she doubted he'd carry anything with a swastika on it."

"Because?"

"His mother's maiden name was Wasserstein."

"Oh."

"Yeah."

"I don't like this one bit."

"What 'this' are you talking about?" Grace asked. "The part where we have reports of a wolf where there hasn't been a wolf for a century? Or the part where the wolf that shouldn't be here mauls a tourist? Or maybe the part where the tourist miraculously heals, then disappears before he can be treated for a potential epidemic-producing disease?"

"I was talking about the part where we find a swastika where a person with a Jewish background was attacked in a part of the forest where Gypsies are camped."

"Ah, hell." Grace kicked the bed. "I hadn't thought of that."

"What now?"

"I'm going to get a search party together to find this guy."

"I'll help."

Grace laughed. "Have you ever been in the mountains?"

"I live in the mountains, Grace, same as you."

"*Not* same as me. I went into these hills with my father when I was four. He left me out there and made me find my way home."

I frowned. "You never told me that."

"It was . . . private."

"It was child abuse."

"What?" Grace appeared genuinely shocked by my comment.

"If someone called you and said a four-year-old girl had been left in the woods alone, on purpose, what would you do, Sheriff McDaniel?"

"Find the kid."

"And then? Would you give that kid back to the people who'd abandoned her at an age when she should be watching Big Bird instead of dodging his relatives as they swoop down and try to eat her eyes for breakfast?"

"You've been watching too much Hitchcock. Birds don't usually do that."

"I might not be 'heap big hunter' like you, but I know what vultures do, and scavengers of any type prey on the weak." Boy did I know *that*. "You could have died out there, Grace. I would have been really pissed off."

She smiled. "Thanks."

"So what else did your dad do in the name of tradition?"

She shot me a look that had me tightening my lips over any further questions. I guess we'd shared all we were going to for one day.

"I'll let you know what I find out there," she said. "Meanwhile you can search for that info."

"I'll need the talisman."

She reached into her pocket and slapped the icon into my palm. "Don't lose it."

"Have I ever lost anything?"

"Your mind," she muttered as she walked out of the room.

14

I MEANT TO go straight to the office, but I became sidetracked.

As mayor I needed to make an appearance at the sidewalk sale, so I walked up and down each street, peering at every table, speaking with the merchants, being complimentary while managing to refrain from buying a single item lest I show favoritism to anyone.

Politics.

Returning to Center Street, I discovered a line trailed out of the café, blocking the sidewalk so that people had to divert into the street to pass. This caused a backup of traffic that had *ruckus* written all over it. I hurried over and suggested another place to eat to those at the end of the line, then wound up getting yelled at by Bobby Turnbaugh.

Talk about a ruckus.

I was only able to mollify him by promising to hold the next four town council meetings at the café.

A trio of kids had set up a lemonade stand at the corner of Center and Bailiwick. They were cute as puppies, so eager to please they became downright wiggly when I gave them a dollar instead of a quarter for a glass. I took a sip and sprayed it onto the pavement.

The three stared at me with wide blue eyes. "We just made the lemonade the way our granny does."

"What's your name?"

"McGinty."

Great. Their granny ran the biggest moonshine operation in the county. No wonder my teeth felt like the enamel had been eaten off.

"How much of this have you sold?" I eyed the industrial-sized cooler from which they'd dispatched my share.

"Only one jug." The kid pulled out an equally mammoth cooler from beneath the table.

"You're going to have to pack this in," I said.

"What?" they shouted. "Why?"

I didn't want to explain that their granny was a moonshiner and their lemonade about 150 proof, but I couldn't let them keep selling the stuff.

"Did you sell more than one glass to a single person?"

Solemnly they shook their heads. Well, that was good news. I doubted anyone would get sick from one glass. The way it tasted, I doubted anyone but a local would be able to finish the stuff. And locals were used to the effects.

"It's getting too crowded out here for you to take up the corner," I improvised.

"Aw, what're you givin' them a rough time for?" said a man with a thick Boston accent. "They're cute."

"Yeah, that's local color," added a woman whose hands were full of shopping bags with logos from nearly every store in town.

The kids beamed. "Want a glass, mister?" one asked.

"No!" I exclaimed. "I—uh—I'm buying the whole jug. I mean cooler. I need it for . . . the police."

Three little faces went white.

"They're thirsty," I continued. "Been out in the sun all day directing traffic."

"Good idea," the man said. "Gotta keep our men and women on the force hydrated."

The tourists moved on—thank God—and I pulled a twenty out of my pocket. The kids snatched the cash and began to pack their stuff. I took the cooler and poured it down a storm drain in a nearby alley. The scent that wafted up could have peeled paint from a barn.

When I returned, they were gone. I should tell Grace what had happened, but I figured by the time she got out to the McGinty place, Granny would have moved her still. *Again.*

This might be the twenty-first century, but in the Blue Ridge Mountains, the southernmost section of Appalachia, old habits died hard.

The Scotch-Irish were double immigrants who'd traveled from their native Scotland in the 1600s to settle Ulster in Northern Ireland. When things began to suck there, long before the potato famine, they'd traveled across the sea. At the time of the Revolution 10 to 15 percent of the population of the Colonies had been Scotch-Irish, which had contributed in no small amount to the uprising against the English.

"Mayor Kennedy." Balthazar's cool, slick voice made me tense. I was tempted to just keep walking and pretend I hadn't heard him in the noise of the crowd. Unfortunately, he'd just follow me back to the office and then I'd never get rid of him.

I plastered on a smile, turned, and nearly got a faceful of camera. I reared back as he clicked the shutter.

Asshole.

"That'll make a lovely shot for our front page." He smirked.

I could imagine how lovely I'd look this close. "Knock it off."

"Sorry," he said, not sounding sorry at all. "A public figure like yourself is fair game."

He hit the button again, and the camera fired like a machine gun. I was tempted to hold my hand in front of my face or shove my fist into his nose. Instead, I spun on my heel and headed for town hall.

"What do you think of this caption?" he called. " 'Mayor Kennedy allows moonshine lemonade to be sold on Center Street.' "

I stopped, turned, and stared him down. "I don't plan to give up, Balthazar. I *will* fight for this job."

He covered the few feet separating us, crowding too close as usual. "Why? You didn't want it in the first place. You should quit."

My hands curled into fists. "I'm done quitting."

"Then you'll be fired. Or at least voted out of office."

"Don't count on it."

"If the festival doesn't produce, or those filthy Gypsies cause trouble, you're finished."

He lifted the camera and took another picture. " 'Mayor Kennedy giving her concession speech.' " Another. " 'Mayor Kennedy cleaning out her desk.' " Another. " 'Mayor Kennedy,' make that just plain 'Claire Kennedy,' 'what will she do now?' "

"Stop taking my picture."

He lowered the camera, fiddled with something, then hit the button again. The flash went off right in my face.

Luckily, I'd figured he was up to something and closed my eyes. I opened them just as Malachi Cartwright snatched the camera out of Balthazar's hands.

"You, sir, are a prick."

"What's your point?" Balthazar sneered.

Cartwright opened his fingers, and the camera tumbled toward the pavement. Balthazar surged forward, but he was too big and slow to catch it. I doubted anyone could have. It smashed into the cement with a sickening crunch.

"What a shame," Cartwright murmured.

A crowd had gathered. Everyone stared. No one moved. For an instant I don't think anyone breathed.

"That was my only camera," Balthazar roared.

"You should take better care of it."

"Me?" Balthazar's face reddened. "Me?"

He was so furious, I wondered if we'd need to call the rescue squad. He might just pop a blood vessel. One appeared to be pulsing quite close to the surface of his forehead.

The big man lunged at Cartwright, who sidestepped easily. Balthazar swung at the other man's head. Cartwright ducked.

People began to choose sides, shout encouragement. At the edge of the crowd, Sabina, sans snake, stared at Balthazar and Malachi with a tense, almost frightened expression. Poor kid.

"Don't do this," I said, but the men were past hearing me.

Balthazar had four or five inches and about a hundred

pounds on Cartwright, but he wasn't quick enough. He couldn't catch the man. Sadly, that only seemed to make Balthazar madder and more determined. Sooner or later he'd land a punch, and from the size of him, one would be all it would take to do some serious damage.

I stepped forward, planning to put myself between them, and someone yanked me back.

"They'll kill you," Grace snapped.

As she finished speaking, Balthazar swiped at Cartwright, who narrowly missed getting his nose broken as he jerked his face out of the way of the flailing, ham-sized fist.

"We have to stop this."

"You think?" Grace muttered. "Where's a fire hose when you need one?"

She strode forward, putting herself between them, just as I'd planned to do. Cartwright backed off immediately. Balthazar came forward with a roar. She drew her gun and pointed it at his chest. "Stop."

He did, first staring at the gun, then lifting his gaze to her face. "Are you crazy?" he snarled.

"Are you?"

"I'll have your job for this."

"Oh no. I shake. I shudder." Grace gave an exaggerated wriggle of fear. "Now pick up your toy and go home."

"What about him?" Balthazar jerked his head toward Cartwright.

"What *about* him?"

"Aren't you going to make an arrest?"

"For what?"

"Assault."

"*You* took a swing at *him*."

"He broke my camera."

"Then I guess you're even."

Balthazar cursed, kicked the camera, and stalked away.

Grace holstered her weapon. "Nothing to see here, folks. Y'all move along now."

Leaning over, she scooped the ruined camera into her hands and tossed it into the trash, then turned to Cartwright. "You probably want to stay out of his way while you're here."

"Perhaps he should stay out of mine."

"I doubt that'll happen. He seems the kind of guy to hold a grudge."

Cartwright shrugged. "Wouldn't be the first."

"Well, watch your back." Grace's gaze met mine. "I'm off."

Time for her to head into the woods and look for our missing tourist. I only hoped she found him—alive and well and eager to begin treatment for rabies.

Sabina inched closer, in her hands a sheaf of papers. A quick glance revealed the Gypsies' showtimes for the week.

"You're putting those up?" She nodded. "Left your snake at home, I see. Good idea. Less trouble that way."

"It didn't seem like less trouble to me," Malachi murmured, his gaze on Balthazar as the other man skirted the offices of the *Gazette*, heading for the large warehouse at the back.

"You didn't have to get involved," I said.

"He needed a lesson in manners."

"I doubt he'll learn any from your breaking his camera."

"And I'm betting he will."

"He could have killed you."

"Me?" Cartwright's smile was far from friendly. "I dinna think I would have been the one who wound up dead."

15

B Y EVENING, DOZENS of discarded flyers tumbled down the sidewalk and dozens more blew up against the buildings. On my way home I snatched one and read:

Come one, come all, to the greatest performance
in the world. Live animal acts! Different show
every night! Come twice, come thrice!
Bring your friends.

Tonight's show began at 9:00 P.M. After running home to change and eat dinner, I drove the familiar route to the lake.

Rows of cars spread across a medium-sized grassy area. Not a huge turnout, but not a bad one, either. If the performance was all the Gypsies had promised, the crowd would increase with each subsequent night. Everyone would make more money, and good word of mouth on the Lake Bluff Full Moon Festival would increase traffic for this year as well as the next.

A ring had been set up, surrounded by portable grandstands. The menagerie wagons curled in a semi-circle, bars facing the seats so the audience could view the animals during the show. The conveyances used for living quarters had been moved halfway around the lake; I could barely see their roofs from where I stood. Twinkle lights graced the nearest trees, and spotlights illuminated both the ring and the area surrounding it.

A ticket booth stood in the center of the path that led to the performance. An elderly man sat within, while two younger men flanked either side, scowling at everyone, daring them to try to slip by without a ticket.

One was big, bulky, with thick dark hair and a fierce expression. The second had lighter hair, nearly brown as if bleached by the sun, and he was so thin and tall he hunched over as if trying to disguise his height, or perhaps his prominent Adam's apple.

A tall young woman with a white streak through her black hair galloped past carrying a bushel of apples. She handed them to a squat middle-aged man with large, curious eyes and a beaked nose who began to dip each one into a vat of caramel. Balloons bounced in the hands of children. The scent of popcorn and cotton candy filled the night.

I handed my ticket to the burly bouncer type, and he growled what might have been a thank-you, but I doubted it. Beyond him, tables had been set up for the sale of trinkets. I trailed past, glancing at the items on sale. A sign caught my eye.

AMULETS. TALISMANS. CHARMS.

Interesting.

I'd left the swastika-marred wood at home, figuring the Gypsies might be understandably testy about a

Nazi symbol. Even though the war had been over for sixty-plus years, that didn't mean they should forget. No one should.

I examined everything on the table but didn't find a single item that resembled the one Grace had found nearby.

"Do you have anything in wood?" I asked.

The ancient Gypsy's face was so wrinkled and brown it resembled a dried-apple doll. Her hair was covered with a brightly colored, coin-fringed scarf, and huge hoops swung from her ears. Every finger sported a ring, and ten bangles dangled on each of her arms. Whenever she moved, a cacophony sounded.

She stared at me for so long, I wondered if she spoke English. I'd started to turn away when she reached under the table and pulled out a box. I took the offering, nearly dropping it when something moved inside.

"Uh, no thanks." I tried to give it back; she wouldn't take it. Instead encouraging me with nods and motions to open the lid.

I did, but the container was too shallow and the night too dark for me to discern what was inside. I up-ended the box, and a shriveled paw fell into my hand.

I didn't shriek. Instead I said something like, "Glurg. Blah," and threw the thing away.

The old woman snatched it nimbly out of the air, cackling, and tossed it back inside.

"What was that?" I demanded.

I didn't expect her to respond. I truly didn't think she spoke English.

"A joke, dearie. Didn't you ever hear the tale of the monkey's paw? Ancient curse? Three wishes?"

I forced myself to take a deep breath, then another. My heart, which had been pounding far too fast and too loud, slowly settled. "Sounds familiar."

"We like to give the people what they want."

"I didn't ask for a monkey's paw!"

"What monkey's paw?"

"The one in the box!"

"This box?" She picked up the container and up-ended it. Nothing came out.

A spattering of laughter, then applause erupted behind me. We'd drawn a small crowd.

"If any of you are interested in having your fortunes told," the old woman said, "I'll be doing readings after the show."

I'd been set up for an advertisement. I didn't think I liked it, but since we both needed the festival to do well, I couldn't complain.

I hurried to the performance ring. Joyce waved at me from the middle of the crowd and I waved back. Most of the seats were taken, but I managed to squeeze onto the last one in the first row just as the lights dimmed and a drum began to beat a rhythm that sounded as if it had come out of Africa.

The mountain lion snarled; the grizzly growled and somewhere out in the forest, the same something that had howled the other night answered.

I glanced around, but everyone was focused, fascinated, on the center ring.

Suddenly one of the lights flared, illuminating Sabina. She seemed to have materialized out of nowhere. One minute the ring had been shadowed, empty. The next, there were lights and a girl wearing a snake.

Theoretically, I knew she'd slipped through the shadows while the music and the animals had distracted the crowd, but with the night settling gently around us, I could swear I felt the magic; I almost believed in it, too.

Sabina appeared different in the spotlight. Her inability to speak didn't matter there. Her shyness gone, she danced as if she'd been born to; she no doubt had.

Her eyes appeared lighter than I remembered, more gold than green, not in the least bit brown, most likely just a reflection. Her hair was loose, swirling around her face and shoulders in time to the music, which had changed, becoming faster, more Oriental than African, although that drum still pulsed beneath the surface.

Her skirt swayed; brightly colored, it caught the light, playing hide-and-seek with the golden toe rings adorning her bare feet. From the waist down she was completely covered, but from the waist up she wore more snake than cloth. Her bare arms glowed beneath the lights, writhing up and down, back and forth, mimicking the cobra's movements.

The snake danced, yellow eyes glowing, seemingly as hypnotized by Sabina as the rest of us.

Someone gasped and I tensed, afraid the cobra had become aggressive; then I saw what made the crowd shift and mutter uneasily.

Close to a half a dozen snakes slithered into the ring, moving pretty quickly for snakes. If they wanted to, they could continue right across the circle, over the raised wooden edge, and into the crowd. Since I saw at least one rattler, that could be a problem.

However, the reptiles headed for Sabina, and once they reached her, they paused. She smiled, welcoming them, and when the music slowed, deepening toward the blues, she knelt, leaning backward until her head nearly touched the ground as she bowed her body like a gymnast.

The crowed went "ooooh." Then, when the snakes began to slither onto her as if she were a bridge, the crowd went "ahhh," although my personal response was "ew!"

Sabina lifted her body until she rested on her knees, then rose to her feet. Her entire torso was covered with writhing snakes, the cobra wrapped around her neck, two rattlers twined around her arms like bracelets, and she appeared to be wearing a python as a belt. She sashayed out of the ring to thunderous applause.

It wasn't until Sabina was gone and the lights had dimmed again that I thought to wonder about her hand. I hadn't noticed during her amazing performance any deformity at all.

Ta-da!

The band blasted a traditional "Wasn't she wonderful?" sally, followed by a single thud of the drums.

Bam. The lights went back on, revealing an empty ring.

The crowd held its breath. At first the staccato beat seemed to come from the band, but as the sound became louder, I distinguished the rhythm of a horse's hooves.

A ghostly shadow wavered, and then a white horse leaped out of the darkness, landing at the center of the spotlight. Atop the animal's back stood Malachi Cartwright. How had he stayed on the horse?

Cartwright was dressed in his usual black pants, his feet bare, the better to cling to the animal. His shirt red, the sleeves billowy, only a few buttons had been fastened, so that his chest played peekaboo with the fabric, blowing open and closed in the breeze kicked up as he put the horse and himself through their paces.

I'd never seen anything quite like it, and from the silence of the crowd, neither had they. Cartwright and the horse appeared to be one being. I never saw the man direct the animal. I never saw the animal await instructions. Whether Cartwright stood, knelt, or lay flat on the horse's back, he never lost his balance, never faltered.

The music rose to a crescendo, signaling the big finish. Cartwright jumped off and perched on the edge of the ring. The horse circled, faster and faster, around and around.

I figured Malachi would do some fancy jump and land on top of the animal; instead he raced in the opposite direction, until he stood in front of the audience. He bowed low and everyone cheered. Then he turned to me and held out his hand.

I stared, uncertain of what he expected. The crowd went silent, waiting.

"Would ye be wantin' a ride then?" he asked, playing up his brogue shamelessly to the audience.

My gaze switched to the horse, which still galloped in a circle. "No thanks."

"I'll be with you the entire time."

I shook my head, but the crowd began to shout encouragement. "Go on, Mayor."

"Come on, honey."

"Try it; you'll like it."

Maybe I would. Curious, I put my hand in Cartwright's.

He snapped his fingers, and the horse stopped dead. Since there was no saddle and therefore no stirrup, Malachi boosted me up, then climbed on behind. I held my body rigidly upright, trying not to lean against him. His arms came around me, and the horse rose, pawing at the air.

My gasp sounded more like a shriek. I was thrown against Malachi, my back to his chest; my rear nestled into the curve of his thighs. He tightened his legs, and while I should have felt trapped, even threatened, all I felt was anticipation. What might happen next?

Benjamin's front hooves met the earth, and he began to run. Instead of skipping over the barrier with ease—it was only a foot high—the animal bunched his muscles and he leaped, as in the dancing-on-air performances of the Lippizaner stallions, clearing the ring with several feet to spare.

The three of us seemed to fly, and that sense of magic returned for just an instant before Benjamin returned to the ground, then carried us into the night amid the thunderous roar of an appreciative crowd.

16

WE DIDN'T GET far before Cartwright stopped the horse with a soft cluck of his tongue. He'd probably been doing that the entire night, so what had seemed to be silent communication was anything but. Regardless, the show had been beyond impressive. What was a guy like him doing in a place like this?

I shifted, the movement bringing me more firmly against Cartwright. Either the performance had excited him or I did.

I tried to inch away, but his arms tightened. "Don't."

The band began to play softly, a waltz, smooth and sweet. I glanced toward the ring, but our mad dash had taken us several yards into the forest and I could see only trees.

"The show," I began.

"Nothing but a bird act. They fly to and fro. You aren't missing a great deal."

"Considering what I saw already, I'd have to say that I am."

"Did you like it, then?"

"Very much. Why do you stay?"

His body tightened against mine. "What do you mean?"

"You could perform in New York. Las Vegas. Even on television. Or you could train animals and give up performing."

"No," he said quietly. "I could not."

I waited for him to explain, but he didn't.

"You enjoy wandering the country in a wagon?"

Cartwright shrugged, the movement rubbing his chest against my back. I resisted the urge to curve against him like a cat rolling in sun-warmed grass. "Wandering is what we do. The Rom are not welcome in this world."

"Sometimes you talk like you're stuck in the seventeenth century."

"Sometimes I feel as though I am."

"Your horse is beautiful."

"He is. Did you know that the Rom believe a white horse is touched by magic?"

"You think he's magic?"

He chuckled. "When Benjamin flies through the air with such ease, I wonder if the angels carry us."

I couldn't help but snort. I'd never been one to believe in such things.

"In truth," he continued, "animals with white coats are best for performances like mine because the chalk I use on my feet, which helps me keep my balance, doesn't show. If you ever go to a circus, you'll notice the ring stock is usually white, perhaps gray."

His hands, which had rested lightly at my waist, holding me safely astride, slipped around to rest on my stomach. I forgot all about white horses and magic.

When he leaned forward, his breath brushed my

ear. I shivered, and not from the slight mist that had begun to swirl in off the lake.

His lips pressed against the curve of my neck, taking a bit of me between his teeth, gently nibbling, sucking. The sensation was glorious, both sharp and tender, causing my body to tremble against his.

Benjamin shifted and I jumped, but Cartwright soothed me with soft murmurs and gentle touches until I quieted along with the horse.

My head fell back against his shoulder, and I stared at the slice of sky visible through the tall canopy of trees—navy blue punctured by glistening sparkles of white and the silver sheen of a rising moon covered with mist.

His fingers traced my rib cage, my collarbone; my blouse gaped open. How had he gotten the buttons undone so fast?

I didn't care, enjoying the drift of the night along my heated skin. His palms cupped my breasts through the bra, and my nipples tightened as he rubbed the center of his hand against them in slow, firm circles.

"This is crazy," I whispered. "Anyone could see."

"Everyone is watching the show."

For an instant I thought the show was us, then I heard the distant music, a smattering of applause, and I understood what he meant. We were alone in the forest. Just him and me.

And Benjamin.

"Tell me what you want."

His thumbs and forefingers rolled my nipples through the fabric and I moaned. I would have been mortified if I hadn't been so aroused that I had no room to feel anything else.

His breath warmed my ear; his tongue flicked the

lobe. "Where shall I touch you? How hard?" His thumbnail flicked the tip of one breast. "Or how soft?" His forefinger ran gently across the swell of the other. "Anything you want of me, Claire, you've only to ask."

I wanted to see him. To touch the chest he'd displayed beneath the harsh fluorescent lights. But I couldn't find the words, so I shifted until we were face-to-face.

He steadied me, settling my knees over his thighs, unbuttoning the last few buttons of his shirt when I tugged at them, murmuring nonsense words to the horse when the animal shuffled nervously.

I couldn't tear my gaze from the angles and planes of his chest. The moonlight sprinkled through the trees, sparkling like fairy dust across his earring. Shadows scampered along his skin. I wanted to trace them with my tongue.

His flesh was cool from the fog that crept around us yet warm with the blood pulsing beneath. I scored his collarbone with my teeth, flicked his nipple with my tongue, caught the scent of the lake either on his skin or in the air, and licked him, just to see.

He tasted of both summer and winter; I wanted to rub my face against him and remember his flavor, his scent, forever.

He leaned back, his neck bowed, face open to the night, and let me do whatever I wanted.

Most men would have been unable to keep themselves from touching me, from grabbing my head, showing me what *they* wanted, forcing my mouth down, down, down until—

I sat up. Hell. I needed to keep my mind on *this* man, *this* moment, no other.

His skin glistened with the moisture left by both my mouth and the mist. His black pants were tight, tighter still at the juncture of his thighs.

"Do you want to touch me?"

My gaze lifted. His eyes were so dark, with just a tiny speck of silver, a reflection of the moon, at their center.

"Not"—I swallowed—"yet."

"May I touch you?"

I hesitated. How far was I going to let this go? How far *could* it go in the forest, on the back of a horse? I didn't think very far, so I nodded.

He reached out, running one finger down my cheek, across my lips, his fingernail scraping the lower one before tracing my chin, my neck, the swell of my breast above my bra, then beneath it.

Suddenly my clothes were too tight. I wanted to be naked in the night, feel the air caress my body, right before he did.

There was something incredibly erotic about the mist on my face, the wind in my hair, the distant drift of the music, and the murmur of the crowd. We were alone yet not alone. I didn't feel trapped as I had in the past, and I wasn't sure if that was because of him or me or the great outdoors. I only knew that I didn't want this to end. Not yet.

His eyes held mine as his finger rolled in a slow circle around my nipple. "May I keep touching you?" he whispered.

In answer, I let my head fall back, offering him more of me. His hands pressed against my shoulders, lifting me to him like an offering beneath the moon. My legs slid open farther; his erection pressed against me right where I needed it to, and I crossed my ankles at the small of his back. If I fell, then so did he.

I waited for his fingers to fumble at the catch of my bra; instead his dark hair sifted across my chest as he mouthed me through the fabric.

Pressing him closer, I tangled my fingers in the soft, curling strands. His tongue swept beneath the edge, and heat shot from my breast to my groin. I tightened my legs, pulling myself more firmly against him. His fingers moved to my bra strap; in just an instant, he'd free me to the night, to him, take me in his mouth, and suckle me as I came writhing in his arms.

He inched back, and I nearly shrieked in disappointment, thinking it was over, and I hadn't even started.

"Shh," he murmured, the sound but a breeze across my damp skin.

Then I heard it, a rustle, a footfall. Someone was coming.

Cartwright cursed; I wanted to. Quickly we rearranged our clothing, or at least I did. His shirt had flown onto a nearby bush and lay there like a flag.

"Ruvanush?" a man called.

"What's that mean?" I whispered.

"My title. Leader, elder."

"Elder?"

"The translation is vague. It means I give the orders and they obey."

"Feudal much?"

He frowned, but before he could answer what hadn't really been a question, the call came again, closer this time.

"Ruvanush?"

"What is it?" Malachi asked.

Whoever was out there knew better than to show himself. He murmured something in their language, and Cartwright muttered several words in that language himself. From his tone, they weren't endearments.

"I must go." He jumped from the horse, then lifted his arms for me.

"Now?"

The question was as stupid as I was. I flushed, happy for the trees, the night, the mist; he couldn't see.

My body screamed for release; my mind spun at the combination of lust and embarrassment.

I scooted off the horse. It was a long way down, and I slammed into Cartwright awkwardly rather than sliding gracefully.

He caught me, holding on when I tried to duck under his arm and run away.

"I'm sorry, but they need me. I'm—" He took a deep breath, then let it out on a sigh. "The leader. You know how that is."

I did. If someone had called, if someone had needed me, I would have had to go, regardless of what I'd been doing. Or whom.

"I should get back," I said. I had to call Grace, find out what had happened on her little jaunt into the woods. I was surprised I hadn't heard from her already.

"Yes," he said, obviously distracted. "I will see you later."

I turned toward the lights and the music, figuring Cartwright would follow me to my car, maybe kiss me good night. I was trying to figure out how to avoid that—all I needed was for the townsfolk to catch a glimpse of me swapping spit with a stranger—when the sound of hoofbeats had me spinning in the other direction.

Just in time to see Malachi Cartwright and his horse disappear.

17

THE SHOW HAD ended by the time I slipped into the circle of lights. No one seemed to notice I'd been gone.

Where had Cartwright been headed? What could possibly require his attention in the depths of a forest that wasn't his own?

Good questions, neither of which I'd probably ever get an answer to.

The fortune-teller was mobbed. Not that I wanted my fortune told, but I had wanted to ask her again about the talisman. However, without it, I doubted I'd have gotten any further than before. I'd probably end up with another monkey's paw, and that I could do without. I'd return tomorrow night and bring along the chunk of wood.

A serpentine line led away from the menagerie wagons. A large crowd clustered in front of the cougar; another equally large one peered into what I assumed was the grizzly's cage. Plenty of Gypsies milled about, keeping an eye on things.

I tried to find Joyce but had no luck. She must have left right after the show. I couldn't blame her. The woman was in the office long before I was every morning.

I headed for my car, but as I pulled away I caught a glimpse of Sabina at the edge of the trees. I lifted my hand in greeting, but she didn't respond.

I felt sorry for her. She seemed lost, lonely. I wondered if the Gypsies treated her poorly because of her infirmities or watched over her as if she were an injured puppy.

I slowed my car, intent on trying to communicate with her, but when I glanced a second time where she'd been, she was gone.

The road to Lake Bluff was deserted. Without streetlights, it was downright cavelike with the canopy of trees rimmed by the mountains on either side.

I drove slower than the speed limit, alert to any movement at the edge of the woods. A deer darting into my path could cause quite an accident. At the very least, my air bag would engage. I hated when that happened.

For several minutes my headlights revealed nothing but asphalt; then suddenly a dark shape raced toward me. I swerved, slamming on the brakes. My tire caught in the gravel at the edge of the road, and I skidded sideways, coming to a stop with the nose of the vehicle in the ditch.

Taking a shaky breath, I turned my head and came nose to nose with a wolf.

Luckily, the window was shut. Nevertheless, I reared back, squeezing my eyes closed, expecting the glass to shatter inward and rain against my face.

Nothing happened.

I opened one eye, then the other. All I saw was trees. "Hell."

Had I seen a wolf, or hadn't I? I didn't plan on getting out to check if there were tracks, even if I'd been capable of distinguishing the print of a dog from a coyote or even an albatross. That was a job for Grace.

I shoved my car into reverse and floored it, bouncing out of the ditch and onto the road with a squeal. Then I held on to the steering wheel with a grip so tight my fingers ached as I sped much more quickly back in the direction I'd come.

There'd been something strange about that wolf. Something I couldn't put my finger on since it had been there and then gone so fast I was left wondering if I'd even witnessed it in the first place.

The fur had been tawny brown, gold, gray all mixed together, and the eyes had been strange, though I couldn't determine why I thought so. I'd never seen a wolf except in a book or perhaps on television.

I passed the turn for the lake and kept going. Grace's house was about a mile farther down, on a hill with a view of the mountains on one side and the lake on the other. It had been in her family for centuries, a miracle considering the government's penchant for taking anything worth having from the Indians.

But one of Grace's ancestors had possessed the wherewithal to cede their property to a white friend. That friend had kept it for him when the Cherokee were herded onto the Trail of Tears. For years the Aniyvwiya, or the principal people, as they called themselves, had remained in the desolate corner of Oklahoma where they'd been exiled. But they'd missed their mountains.

A few had come back, hiding in the hills with others who'd slipped away and never left. When the time came for the Aniyvwiya to reclaim some of what was theirs, the McDaniels had taken back their land forever.

I turned onto the narrow road that tilted upward at a

sharp angle, winding through spruce trees so thick and overgrown there were times I couldn't see past the brush of their boughs across my windshield. When they parted, the house appeared like a castle before me.

I don't know why I thought the thing resembled a castle, as it was built of wood, not stone. No turrets. No moat. No dragon. In truth, Grace's house resembled something you might find on the front of a Halloween card.

Not that it was broken down. I doubted it was even haunted. But the way it rose up out of the high, narrow ridge, shining white against the ebony night, with a gabled roof and . . . were those bats circling the chimney?

At least she was home. The windows were ablaze with light, her cruiser parked next to the toolshed.

I probably should have called, but after seeing the wolf I hadn't wanted to take my eyes from the road even to dial my cell phone.

As I stepped out of my car the sounds of the night surrounded me—bugs, the wind, a distant rustle. The space between my vehicle and the front porch loomed large. I slammed the door and hurried across it.

A bat swooped low, chasing those bugs, and I stifled a shriek. If I started screaming, I'd scare Grace to death. Although Grace didn't scare as easily as I did.

I reached the porch, thundered up the stairs, and rang the bell, hitting the button so hard the thing rang three times in a row. There'd be hell to pay if I dragged her out of the tub.

She didn't come. I glanced at my watch. Not even 10 P.M. Where the hell was she?

I rang the bell again. Then stood impatiently tapping my foot, straining my ears, trying to catch the sound of her approach.

I started to get nervous. Lights on. Car here. Maybe she'd fallen and she couldn't get up?

I jiggled the doorknob. Locked. Leaning over the porch rail, I peered into one window, then crossed the creaky wooden floor and peeked into the other. New furniture but no Grace.

I should go around back and see if I could get in that way. Glancing at the sky, I flinched as something flew past, making the silvery light of the moon flicker.

Taking a deep breath, I hit the ground running and was pounding up the back steps before I realized I'd gone the whole way with my eyes closed. Luckily, Grace hadn't added any lawn ornaments lately, or I'd be flat on my face in the grass, skewered by a grinning ceramic gnome.

I knocked. No one answered. Tried the door. Locked, again. Checked the windows. Nada.

"Damn."

I pulled out my cell and dialed her number. Inside I heard the echo of the ring that played in my ear, over and over and over until finally her machine picked up.

"I'm not here. Leave a message. If this is an emergency, call—" Grace's voice recited the number for emergency services, though I was certain most locals knew her cell phone number, like I did.

I dialed that next and caught the faint drift of a ring—I turned and stared into the dense cover of the trees—out there. I waited for her to pick up, but she didn't.

Had Grace dropped her phone when she was taking a stroll? Had she dropped her phone after she'd fainted? Or perhaps when the wolf that appeared to be stalking us all had attacked.

I wished, not for the first time, that I carried a gun.

Then again, who knows what or whom I might shoot if I had one?

I crept down the steps, pausing as the phone stopped ringing and went to voice mail. I waited a few seconds, then hit *redial,* and when the ring, which was actually a song, "Stray Cat Strut," began again, I inched toward the edge of the yard.

The moon cast me in shadow, and I stared at my outline with a frown. I was hunched, cringing, and that would not do.

I straightened so fast my spine crackled. I would go into those woods, find Grace, and deal with whatever had to be dealt with. My days of cringing and hiding were gone. I was the mayor; I was in charge, and I'd damn well act like it.

"Grace!"

I stood at the edge of the trees, with Grace's empty house blaring light behind me and the dark shrouded hills before me.

The mist tumbled down. Tendrils of white snaking through the branches, swirling, whirling, coming closer and closer, faster and faster.

"Oh hell," I muttered.

That wasn't mist.

18

I CLOSED MY eyes, then opened them. The wavering white cloud remained, more solid than a fog yet unidentifiable as anything else.

The phone had stopped ringing again. I held my own stupidly against my ear. With stiff movements, I closed it, then shoved it into my pocket, never taking my eyes from the billowing white. Maybe the place was haunted after all.

I wouldn't be surprised. Four thousand Cherokee had died on the Trail of Tears. Why wouldn't some of their ghosts come back here?

I wasn't afraid of spirits. I didn't think. I'd never seen one.

Nevertheless, I held my breath, my entire body tense, quivering as I hovered between flight and fight. How did one fight a specter?

The worry became moot as the wavering mass solidified into a woman, and Grace popped out of the trees wearing nothing but a white cotton robe.

She came to a stop when she saw me in the yard. We stood blinking at each other.

"What are you—?" we said at the same time, then fell silent.

"Problem?" Grace tilted a brow.

I wasn't sure if she meant in town or with her running around the forest wearing not much more than a bath sheet. It didn't take X-ray vision to see that beneath the robe she was naked.

"Claire?" Grace stalked past me toward the house. "Is there a problem in town?"

"No. I mean yes. Well, not in town."

She cast a withering glance over her shoulder, her dark hair swinging loose, appearing even darker against the white of the robe.

"Focus." She turned the knob.

I frowned. The door had been locked. Or maybe I didn't know how to twist it just right. Old houses were tricky that way.

"I tried to call you," I said. "I heard your cell phone ringing—"

Grace reached into a pocket, then held up her phone and waggled it.

"Why didn't you answer?"

"Must have fallen out. Lucky you called or I might never have found it."

"What were you doing out there?"

Grace disappeared inside, leaving the door open, which I took as an invitation, and I followed her.

The place was much as I remembered—an old house, updated bit by bit over the years. The color of the paint had changed. New carpet brightened the hall, as well as the new furniture in the living room. The hardwood floors shone a bit brighter than they had when Grace's father lived here.

Other than that, the kitchen had been remodeled in the eighties and still sported teal appliances and peach and white vinyl floor tile. Yummy.

Water ran in the small half bath off the hall, then the door opened, and Grace appeared fully dressed in cut-offs and a blue tie-dyed T-shirt. "Want a drink?"

She headed for the kitchen. I had no choice but to join her or stand in the hall alone.

Grace straightened away from the refrigerator, then tossed a beer at my head. I bobbled the can but managed a save. When I popped the top, the beer fizzed up so fast I had to slug some down or make a mess.

Taking a long sip of her own brew, she stared out the dark square of window that overlooked her yard. "I heard something," she said slowly.

"And ran out in your robe?" That wasn't like Grace. Come to think of it, neither was the robe.

She shrugged but didn't elaborate.

"What if what you heard was the wolf?" I pressed.

"I think that wolf is long gone."

"Think again."

In the middle of taking another swig of beer, Grace paused, swallowed loudly, and set the can on the countertop with a click. "You saw it?"

"Yeah."

After I told her what had happened, I half-expected her to grab a gun and barrel into the hills, but she didn't.

"I couldn't find a trace of the thing today," she said, "and no one's seen Ryan Freestone, either. I'm going to have to organize a hunting party."

"When?"

"Tomorrow."

I winced. Grace had been in the public life as long as I had; she knew what I was thinking.

"I'll keep it quiet. We'll leave just after dawn and be out of town before any of the locals are awake, let alone the newcomers."

"Thanks."

"I can't put this off."

"I know."

"I really thought the animal would have disappeared into the mountains by now. Why stay so close to people? That's not like a wolf."

"Could be like a rabid wolf."

"You're just full of good tidings, aren't you?"

I took another swig of beer. "That's me. Susie Sunshine."

Grace snorted. "I'll kill it tomorrow."

"I know," I repeated.

Silence settled over us, not companionable but tense, and I wasn't sure why. I had to break it.

"Place looks almost the same."

"I don't have the time or the money to redecorate much."

"Is that a hint for a raise?"

"I'm always hinting for a raise. Get used to it."

"I didn't mean anything by that," I said. "I don't have the time or the energy to mess with my house, either."

"I—" She broke off, took a sip of beer, glanced up at the ceiling, then sighed. "I've done a bit upstairs."

"Oh?"

"I turned Dad's room into an office and I updated mine."

"Got rid of the *NSYNC poster?"

"Had to. It was embarrassing."

"And the Barney sheets?"

"Those, too."

In truth, Grace's room had never had an embarrassing item in it, unlike mine. Those pom-poms, the unicorns, the pink and white lace—let's not even go there. I slept in the guest room now so as not to become nauseous on a nightly basis.

As a youngster, Grace had collected panthers—her walls papered with magazine photos, dresser and nightstand covered with stuffed replicas and figurines, bookshelf filled with both fact and fiction.

This would seem odd unless you were familiar with ancient Cherokee tradition. In this matrilineal society, Cherokee children were born members of the clans of their mother. There were seven, and Grace had been born to the Blue Clan, otherwise known as the Wild Cat Clan, or the Panther.

She took this membership seriously, partly because in this day and age most Cherokee's knowledge of their clan affiliation had been lost. Very few knew for certain where they'd come from.

"Can I see what you've done?" I asked.

Grace shrugged, then led the way upstairs.

Unlike my house, Grace's had three floors: the main-level living quarters; the second floor, where Grace and her brothers had slept; and the third floor, which had been her father's.

Every door on the second level was closed. I wondered momentarily if her brothers had taken their things or just left them behind to gather dust. The question flew right out of my head when we reached Grace's room and she pushed open the door.

Gone was every trace of her collection, in its stead a slick, modern rendition of a jungle.

The walls had been painted mossy green. The carpet was a thick bed of blue. The bedspread brought to mind a hundred thousand blades of grass marching across the mattress. Pillows like lily pads, muted violet and evergreen, had been tossed about haphazardly. The curtains, drawn closed over the glass, blended into the wall.

Water gurgled—not the drip, drip, drip of a faucet but the smooth tones of a brook or a stream. At first I thought a new-age CD was playing; then I discovered a miniature fountain behind a screen that resembled a swamp shrouded in moss and flowers the shade of the sunset after a hard summer rain.

It even smelled different from the rest of the house—like dried grass and the remnants of lightning. I looked around for candles, potpourri, the little electrical-outlet air fresheners, but I didn't see a single one.

"This is amazing," I said.

"I feel at home here."

The room was beyond soothing. With the green curtains over the windows, the babbling water, the soft colors, the thick, cushy carpet and quilt, I could easily imagine burrowing in—spring, summer, winter, or fall—and sleeping like an exhausted baby.

Maybe I needed to do a little redecorating myself. But what kind of room could I fashion that would make me feel at peace when the real lack of peace rested within me?

Blah-blah-blah. Sign me up for the next Dr. Phil show. I was sick and tired of psychoanalysis. Even my own.

Grace glanced pointedly at her watch.

"Oh! Sorry." I moved toward the door. "I know you have to be on the move early tomorrow."

It wasn't until we'd said our good-byes and I sat in the car that I realized Grace hadn't shown me what she'd done with her father's office.

I glanced toward the lone window on the third floor. Instead of shining brightly with cheery yellow electricity as the rest of the house did, that single window glowed softly, as if lit by a dozen wavering candles.

That wasn't safe. What if Grace went to bed and forgot to put them out?

My hand was on the door handle, as I was thinking I'd just ring the bell and remind her, when Grace appeared in the office window. She leaned down to peer outside. Seeing me, she lifted a hand in farewell, then drew the shade over the glass.

I was antsy on the drive home, and not just because I kept scanning the woods for a deer or a lone wolf. Something about my visit with Grace bothered me, and I couldn't figure out what.

Not the secretive way she'd drawn the shade. It was nighttime; I should close my own shades more often. But why draw a third-floor shade at all? Who was going to see anything unless they had a fire ladder or had learned to fly?

What was she doing up there anyway? Why have an office lit by candles? That was the quickest way to ruin your eyes short of poking them with a stick.

I shook my head. Not my business. Grace had always been a little different, which was why I'd liked her.

I drove past the turn to the lake. All the show lights had gone dark; the place seemed deserted. Had Malachi returned? Where had he gone in the first place?

My car trailed down the streets of Lake Bluff. Any other week but this and we'd have rolled up the sidewalks before the sun set. But during the Full Moon Festival, people strolled around until midnight or later.

The ice-cream shop was open, as were the candy store and the café. Couples walked arm in arm eating out of bags of popcorn bought from the brightly lit wagon in the town square. Kids raced across the grass chasing fireflies. A mother pushing a baby stroller window-shopped as she slowly ate an ice-cream cone.

I caught sight of one of Grace's employees and a few rent-a-cops loitering on the street corners. Everything appeared to be under control. I only hoped the noise and the lights and the food—the popcorn and the ice cream as well as the people—didn't attract a wolf.

Since there was nothing I could do about it short of ordering the streets cleared and the doors sealed from the outside, I took comfort from the fact that Grace knew her job, knew what we were up against, and she'd no doubt warned her people.

When I saw two additional guards at the end of Center Street patrolling the small open space between the town and the trees with rifles, I pointed my car toward home. Everything had been done that could be done for now.

Seconds later I turned into my driveway. My house did not look inviting. Since I'd forgotten to turn on a light, it looked downright hostile.

I parked the car in the carport, then sprinted for the door, hoping I'd be able to get it open before my headlights timed out.

I'd just removed my keys from my pocket when the lights went off with a dull thunk. The streetlights didn't penetrate very well up the hill and around the bend; clouds had drifted over the moon. I heard the distant trill of laughter, the slam of a door, but that only served to remind me of how alone I was.

My car's engine made the usual clicking, settling noises that should have been reassuring but weren't. For some reason they sounded like footsteps.

I was being foolish. I knew it, yet my hand still shook

as I tried to shove the key into the lock. I dropped the key ring onto the ground, the loud clash against the pavement making me jump, even though I'd been the one to drop the thing in the first place.

With an annoyed sigh, I bent, retrieved the keys, and thrust one into the lock. My front door swung open on more darkness; in the center two glowing yellow eyes made my breath catch before the vicious hiss made me snap, "Oprah! What's the matter with you?"

The slight scrape of something hard against pavement—a shoe or a claw—had me spinning. In that instant before my eyes caught up to my mind, I knew the wolf was behind me, poised to spring and tear out my throat.

Too bad I was wrong.

19

"CLAIRE."

Josh Logan stepped closer, and the moon chose that moment to reappear, bathing his handsome face in silver. He looked more like a bloodsucker now than he had in my dreams.

"I've been waiting for you."

I glanced into the house, wondering if I could dive inside and slam the door. But that would be childish.

Oh well.

I made it into the foyer, even got the door nearly closed, before he grabbed it. Josh had always moved quicker than spit.

"What's the matter with you?" He followed me in.

I backed up, not wanting to remain in grabbing distance. Calmly he closed and locked the door behind him, then flicked on the lights.

He appeared exactly the same as he had the last time I'd seen him, but then, I doubted he'd lost as much sleep over the incident as I had.

Young, blond, buff, Josh was the darling of Atlanta.

Born in Washington, D.C., which might be the South geographically but was a far cry from Earth technically, his father was a congressman who'd once been a lawyer. Hadn't they all? Josh's mother was a lawyer who'd become a lobbyist. So had his sister.

Josh was the bright light and shining hope of the Logan family. He'd attended the University of Georgia, then gone on to Harvard Law, before returning to work for the governor. An up-and-coming run for that very office would be the next step on Josh's path to the White House.

Ah, hell, I was going to have to turn him in. I saw that now.

"What do you want?" I asked.

"The same thing I've always wanted, Claire. You."

Goose bumps rose all over my body. I'd dreamed of this a hundred times, but I'd never really thought it would happen. Why would Josh return to the scene of the crime, so to speak? Why would he take the chance that seeing him again would make me realize how completely stupid I'd been? Make me understand quite clearly that I had to call the police and make certain he never did to anyone else what he'd done to me?

Maybe he wasn't as smart as he said he was.

Oprah began to growl from the stairs, and Josh's gaze went past me to the cat. The sound of her yowls was replaced by that of claws scrambling on hard wood as she fled up the steps and disappeared into the darkness on the second floor.

Josh's attention returned to me, and I had to resist the urge to turn tail and scuttle upstairs like the cat. If I did that, he'd grab me, and I wanted to avoid grabbing at any cost. What I needed to do was get him out of the house, and me along with him. Outside I might have a chance.

"Why don't we go onto the deck?"

Bracing myself, I turned my back on him. When he didn't knock me to the ground and start tearing at my clothes, I walked into the kitchen, then over to the sliding glass doors.

The sound of the refrigerator opening made me pause. Josh had his head inside. "No champagne?" He reached forward and withdrew a bottle of sauvignon blanc. "This will have to do."

He helped himself to two of my wineglasses, then nodded for me to continue. I should have kept going while he had his head in the fridge; I might have made it to the woods. My wits were not as sharp as they should be. I needed to focus so I could seize the next opportunity and get out of here.

On the deck, Josh set the wine on the table and poured each of us a glass. He held one out to me. "We need to talk."

"Talk?" I took the wine but didn't drink. Maybe I could throw it in his eyes and run.

Josh flashed his campaign smile—courtesy of thousands of dollars in orthodontia—and chuckled. "I want you back, sweetheart. I've missed you so much."

"Missed me?" I couldn't seem to stop repeating whatever he said.

"I know we didn't date long, but you got to me." He smacked himself in the chest with one fist. "Right here."

A hysterical giggle threatened to burst free. Was he serious? Why would he be here otherwise, unless—?

My mind rebelled at the idea of what else he might want. I'd die first. Or he would.

"I'm making my bid for governor soon. We'll have to tie the knot right away."

"I—uh—what?"

"You're perfect. We'll play up the Appalachia thing." He gestured toward the mountains with his wineglass, sloshing a little over the side as he did. "You're from the hills, but you made good. Don't suppose you've got an old granny without her teeth we could parade around?"

"Huh?"

He *tsk*ed as he came closer. "You'll have to come home with me tonight. You've only been here a few weeks, and already you're losing that polish I love so much."

He reached for my hair, ignoring or perhaps not even noticing my flinch, then rubbed a lock between his fingers. "It would be better if you were blond. We'll take care of that tomorrow." He strode across the deck. "Pack your things."

"You—you actually think I want to marry you?"

Slowly he turned. "Why wouldn't you? I'm going to be the next governor of Georgia."

"No," I said quietly. "You aren't."

He gave an impatient sigh. "Claire, I thought you understood what all this was about."

"All what?"

"I took you everywhere. I made certain everyone saw us together. Then my people did a survey— grassroots, you understand, but good enough. I got the results the day we made love."

I couldn't help it. I choked. "That wasn't love."

His face relaxed into an expression of abject relief. "I'm glad you understand. At least I won't have to pretend. You won't care if I keep a girlfriend? You have to admit you're a little cold in the sack."

All I could do was gape. He was insane.

"Americans love an underdog and"—he lowered his voice—"truth be told, I'm not one. But you are. To come from this"—his lip curled as he waved in the general direction of Lake Bluff—"and accomplish what you did, to leave behind your hillbilly past and lose that horrible accent. Why, if I didn't know you were white trash, I'd never suspect. A large percentage of those surveyed trusted you. So if you stand beside me, as my wife, if you tell them they should vote for me . . ." He spread his hands and winked.

"Let me get this straight," I said. "You dated me to see how I played to the public. You took a poll and then—"

"I made you mine."

"Made me." Well, at least he'd gotten one thing right. He had *made* me.

"I staked my claim." He lowered his hands. "It's a guy thing."

"It's a rapist thing."

Shock spread over his face. "What?"

"You raped me."

"Did not."

I wasn't going to play " 'Did not' and 'Did, too,' " with this guy. I was going to call Grace.

I pulled my cell phone out of my pocket and he grabbed me. So much for avoiding it.

"We dated for months," he said.

"My mistake."

"I must have shelled out thousands wining and dining you. You owed me."

"You're right. And the time's come to pay up."

He relaxed a little, though he didn't let me go.

"How about this?" I continued. "You get to go directly to jail, do not pass go, do not become governor of Georgia." Not that he'd actually go to jail—I had no evidence and it was his word against mine—but it sounded so good.

My head rocked back when he slapped me. I tasted blood. My cell phone fell from my suddenly boneless hands, hitting the ground with a clunk.

For a minute I'd actually thought I could stand up to him. Turn him in. Make him pay. Then one slap, and I couldn't think, let alone defend myself and call the police.

I'd never been hit before. Grabbed, shaken, raped, but never hit. No one tells you what a shock it is—not the pain so much as the degradation, the knowledge that someone can do that to you and there's not a damn thing you can do to stop it.

Suddenly Josh was yanked backward. "Strike a woman, will you?" Malachi Cartwright lifted Josh into the air by the neck of his shirt and shook him. "Bastard."

Josh's legs flailed, shoes striking shins, knees pounding against thighs. Cartwright didn't seem to notice.

"Would you like me to kill him?" he asked mildly.

Josh's eyes nearly bugged out of his head.

"Put him down," I said.

"I dinna think I will," Cartwright murmured, his brogue thickening.

"Put him *down*."

Cartwright crooked a brow. "You're certain?"

"Yes."

He tossed Josh over the side of the deck. Josh's shout of protest was cut short with an "oof" when he landed.

"What did you do that for?" I demanded.

"He should not be breathing the same air as you, and well you know it."

A bellow of fury made us turn. Josh barreled up the steps. His suit was torn and muddied. He had scratches on his cheek. He was limping but still moving at quite a fast clip and headed directly for me.

"You bitch. I'll kill you for this."

Cartwright stepped between us. Josh roared with anger again; he didn't sound quite human. He didn't look very human, either, until he pulled the gun.

"Shit," I muttered, scanning the ground for my cell phone. Not that I could get help here faster than a speeding bullet, but at least I could throw the thing at his head.

"You think that scares me?" Cartwright asked.

"It should."

Malachi laughed and punched Josh in the nose.

Blood spurted; the gun tumbled to the plank floor as Josh slapped both hands to his face. "You broke my nose."

"You're lucky I didn't break your neck." Malachi grabbed him by the shirtfront and yanked him close. "Come near her again, and I'll make you wish you were dead."

The threat should have been laughable, words straight out of a John Wayne movie, but something in Cartwright's face must have convinced Josh he wasn't kidding, because his eyes widened and his face went white.

Cartwright let him go with a disgusted shove, and Josh crumpled to the ground, eyelids fluttering. "Call the sheriff," Cartwright ordered.

"Shouldn't I call an ambulance?"

"Ach, nothin' that can be done about a broken nose."

"I think he's unconscious," I said.

"He fainted." Cartwright nudged Josh with his boot. "Nothing that can be done about that, either."

I retrieved my cell phone. One glance at the display

and I cursed. "Broken." Was anything made to last these days? "I'll have to go inside."

Cartwright nodded, bending to pick up Josh's gun.

"He could have shot you."

The moon glanced off Cartwright's black eyes, making them glow silver at the center. "Not with the safety on he wouldn't."

He held out the gun, using his thumb to flick the catch off, then on again.

"He still could have removed the safety and shot you quicker than you could have punched him."

"Perhaps."

"You're either very brave or very stupid."

His face hardened. "Men do not hit women. If they do, they're not men; they're beasts." Cartwright turned his face toward the moon. "This one deserved far more punishment than he got."

Malachi was right. But if I'd let him punish Josh, then Malachi would be the one going to jail. Cops were funny that way.

"May I wash?" Cartwright held out his hands, which were dotted with Josh's blood.

"Of course." I glanced at Josh, but he remained unmoving.

"He'll be all right for a minute," Cartwright assured me. "And it isn't as if you don't know where to find him if he decides to go."

True enough. Together Cartwright and I went into the house.

Grace answered on the sixth ring; she sounded wide-awake. "I'll be there in five."

Cartwright turned away from the sink, drying his hands on the dish towel. "I'm sorry I didn't come sooner. I was . . . delayed."

I remembered what had happened between us earlier

that night and what hadn't because he'd been called away.

"Is everything all right at your camp?"

He began to nod; then his gaze swiveled toward the open doorway. "Hell."

Josh was gone.

20

CARTWRIGHT WAS OUT the door and down the back steps before I could catch up. "Wait!"

"He'll be getting away."

"It isn't as if I don't know where he lives, as you said. Where he works and where he plays, too. He won't get away."

Cartwright paused with his long fingers curled around the wooden handrail, the white moons of his nails stark against the darker shade of his skin. "I'd feel better if I found him now."

I stared at the prehistoric trees, and I remembered what was out there. "There's—uh—a presumably rabid wolf on the loose."

Cartwright turned to look at me. "I thought there were no wolves in these woods."

"Someone neglected to tell that to the wolf."

His lips twitched. "Has anyone seen the beast?"

"I have."

"You?" His lighter expression turned dark. "When?"

"Earlier tonight. I nearly ran it over on the road near your camp."

"I suppose it was hanging about because of the menagerie," he murmured.

"Or your people. You need to be careful. Grace is going to go out with a hunting party tomorrow."

"Is she now?" He seemed amused again.

"She's the best tracker in town."

"She will be hunting in the daylight?"

"It's kind of hard to hunt at night. Illegal, too, I think, though I doubt that would affect Grace."

"As long as they don't muck about near the lake once the sun has set, I give my permission."

Permission? I opened my mouth to ask what in hell he was talking about, then remembered the Gypsies' weird contract with Lake Bluff.

"Why does she have to stay away once the sun's set? You got a few vampires in your caravan?"

"I haven't seen a vampire in years," he said wistfully, then laughed at my expression. "We have shows at night. I don't think it would be safe to have people with guns traipsing around the lake."

That made sense. Or at least more sense than his harboring vampires. "Grace will track the thing down tomorrow. I'm sure of it."

Cartwright grunted, obviously unconvinced.

"Maybe you should wait here," I said. "Grace will want to talk to you."

"I'm sure she will." He straightened his shoulders, as if preparing for a battle. "But she knows where I live, work, and play. She can find me."

"She won't be happy."

"Right now, I'm not happy." He suddenly touched my cheek. Strangely, I didn't flinch, nor was I possessed by the sudden urge to back away; instead I leaned into him, needing his warmth and comfort. "I swear no one will ever hurt you while I'm here."

Before I could make any comment, he disappeared into the night.

I stared after him, wondering where he was going, if he really thought he'd find Josh, who'd no doubt arrived in a BMW and was driving it hard all the way back to Atlanta. Knowing him, he'd have the authorities here by tomorrow with an arrest warrant for Malachi Cartwright.

"Damn," I muttered. If they arrested the Gypsy leader, would the rest of the Gypsies continue to perform? If they didn't, our festival was ruined.

And I couldn't believe I was worrying about that at a time like this, but someone had to. I guess it *was* my job.

A howl burst from the trees, drifting toward the bright silver moon. I stood on the porch and waited for another, but none came.

A few minutes later, my doorbell rang and I went inside, closing and locking the glass door behind me.

Grace stood on the doorstep attired in her uniform, though her blouse was buttoned crooked and her shoes weren't tied. Her hair wasn't braided, either, and it hung past the base of her spine, making her appear younger than I knew her to be. Maybe she had been asleep.

"I've been dying to arrest this guy." She shouldered her way inside. "Where is he?"

"Gone."

"Don't bullshit me, Claire; it's late."

"I wish I *was* bullshitting. We thought he was unconscious, turned our backs, and poof. Malachi went to look for him."

Her eyebrows shot up. "Malachi, is it?"

Oops.

"Seems silly, not to mention ungrateful, to keep using his last name after what he did for me."

"I suppose." Grace reached for her shoulder mike. "I'll get an APB out on Logan."

"No. Don't."

"Claire." Her voice held a warning note. "You *are* going to prosecute this dickhead. We can definitely get him for assault after this."

"I am. I promise. But could we skip the all points bulletin? I really don't think Lake Bluff, or me for that matter, needs the attention we'd get if this hits the wires. Can we keep it quiet, at least until the festival is over?"

Grace contemplated me for several seconds. "All right. I'll call the Atlanta PD in the morning. They can pick him up on the Q.T."

"Thanks. Is everything set for tomorrow?" Grace stared at me blankly. "The wolf hunt?" I reminded her.

"Oh yeah. I got hold of everyone after you left." She glanced at her watch, winced. "We're meeting at Lunar Lake at four A.M."

"I heard something howling right before you got here."

Her head lifted. "Where?"

I pointed in the direction of the mountains.

"You sure?"

"No."

Instead of getting annoyed, which was what I expected, Grace merely nodded. "Howls are weird that way. Can't pinpoint their location unless you're a wolf. And two can sound like a dozen."

"But one just sounds like one, right?"

"Right."

"One is what I heard."

"Good. We don't need a pack out there. I'd have to call the DNR." She made a face. "I'd like to avoid that if possible."

No one cared much for the hunting and fishing police—aka the Department of Natural Resources—and those who hunted cared for them least of all. Probably because sportsmen, and -women, were throwbacks to a time when hunting and fishing kept a person alive, and pioneer spirits like those became seriously annoyed when someone tried to regulate them.

"Is Cartwright coming back?" Grace asked. "You should probably tell him what's going on, let him know we'll be in the area tomorrow."

"I already did."

"And?"

"He said as long as you're gone by dusk, you have his permission."

"I don't think I need his permission."

"The contract," I reminded her.

"Extenuating circumstances outweigh a contract. There's a potentially rabid wolf roaming the forest. Cartwright will just have to lump it."

"You're sure? Maybe I should have Catfish take a look at that contract."

Catfish Waller was the only lawyer left in Lake Bluff. There wasn't much call for legal advice in a town that existed on tourism. Sure there was the occasional personal injury or real estate disagreement. But the big cases were found in the big city, which was where all of our lawyers had gone—except for Catfish.

Seventy if he was a day, Catfish spent his free time, which meant most of his time, smoking a cigar on the front porch of his combination office and living quarters. He'd never been married, probably because no one could stomach the cigar.

"No need to bother Catfish," Grace said. "I know what I'm talking about."

Grace headed for the front door, pausing with her hand on the knob to glance at me. "You gonna be okay?"

"Sure."

Her head tilted, and her blue-black hair swung across her hip. "Seriously. Do you want me to stay? We could make popcorn. Watch movies."

I smiled. "Thanks. But you need to be sharp tomorrow. Or as sharp as you can be on the small amount of sleep you're going to get, thanks to me."

Grace shrugged. "I've made do with less. If you're scared, I'm right here."

And she would be; I knew that, had always known it. Even though she'd been hurt when I left, angry when I came back, if I needed her, she would be there. No matter what.

"Grace," I began, "I should have kept in touch after I left."

"Yes, you should have."

"I'm sorry. It was just . . . I wanted to make a new life."

"And I was part of the old one. We already had this talk. I get it."

I put a hand on her arm. "I was wrong. You were the best friend I ever had. The best friend I'll ever *have*."

"Yes, I am."

I laughed. "So, we're best friends again?"

"No." Grace opened the door and stepped outside as my heart took a dive toward my feet. "We were *always* best friends, Claire. That never changed, even when you did."

I waited until she started the squad car, then backed down the drive and onto the road before I went to bed.

I didn't think I'd sleep. Having my nightmare show up on the doorstep should have been ... well, my worst nightmare. But it had turned out okay. In fact, I felt like I'd faced my demon and survived.

Sure I'd frozen when the going got tough, but with a little help from Malachi I'd managed to keep from retreating into a corner and talking to myself. I'd taken steps to end Josh's days of freedom. I'd make certain he hurt no one else, and I'd prevent him from assuming a position of trust and power in my home state. All in all, a good night's work.

I fell asleep the moment my head hit the pillow, or at least I thought I did. Because, what happened after the mist drifted in my window again felt very real.

I lay on the bed as the fog spilled over the sill, crept across the floor, across me. The cool, gentle trail was a touch upon my naked body, making me writhe and thrash and beg for more. I floated above myself, a voyeur, yet I could feel every stroke.

My nipples pebbled; my breasts swelled; my legs fell open so the mist could swirl across the damp, red curls. I felt the lap of a tongue just once, and I arched off the bed, my body bowing, straining for a release that was so close I heard it humming just out of reach.

The mist retreated as if it were being sucked out the window by a whirlwind.

"No," I said, and the sound of my own voice woke me up.

I'd kicked off all the covers, but I wasn't naked as I'd been in the dream. However, my body was perched on the edge of orgasm, skin tingling, chest heaving, mind whirling as wildly as the mist had.

Something shifted at the foot of the bed. A set of

yellow eyes seemed to hover a few inches above the mattress, and I gasped. Oprah jumped to the floor and stalked away, disgusted with me.

I didn't blame her. These erotic dreams were becoming as bad as the nightmares.

The wind blew in the window, fluttering the curtains. Wait a second. . . .

The window had been open in my dream, but I thought it had been closed when I went to bed.

Slowly I turned my head in that direction.

21

"DINNA BE AFRAID."

I started up, grasping at the covers, yanking them to my chin, even as I recognized the voice, as well as the man thrown into midnight silhouette by the light of the moon through my open window.

"What are you doing here?" My fear had turned to fury. "How did you get in?"

"The window was open."

I frowned, trying to remember. Had it been? Maybe. But—

"This is the second floor."

"Did you think someone could not get in if they were of a mind to?"

I'd thought exactly that. The house was big in the way of old houses, the ceilings high, which put the second story much farther off the ground than most second stories. There was no convenient drainpipe near my window, and only slick, painted wood surrounded it.

"You couldn't have climbed," I murmured. "That's impossible."

"Obviously not, since here I am."

His accent pronounced, his words had gone formal in a way that made me remember English was not his first or his only language.

"Why are you here?" I asked. "Did you find Josh?"

He hesitated, then sighed. "No."

"Not a trace?"

"Blood from his nose led to his car." He spread his hands wide.

"Never mind. Grace will take care of him tomorrow."

"Men like that . . . They have a way of slipping out of trouble."

"Not this time," I said.

He tilted his head, and the moon glanced off the cross tangling in his hair, nearly blinding me. "Why do you wear a crucifix in your ear?" I asked.

His lips curved. "Where should I wear one?"

"Most Catholics wear a crucifix around their neck."

"I said we were *baptized* Catholic."

"But you really aren't?"

"What else would we be?"

"Question with a question," I muttered.

"What's so wrong about answering a question with a question?"

"It makes you look guilty."

"I wasn't aware you suspected me of anything."

"I'm just making conversation." What else was I supposed to do when a man climbed in my window in the middle of the night?

Actually, I knew what I was *supposed* to do, especially with him, but I wasn't sure I was ready to do it.

Malachi seemed to sense my unease, because he stayed near the window, even leaning against the sill, a picture of tranquility, no threat to me at all.

"We've always worn the symbols of the people who inhabit the land around us," he said.

"Why?"

"To avoid persecution."

"People aren't persecuted for their religion anymore."

He smiled at me as a father might smile at a foolish but dear child. "Do you think if your townsfolk knew we were worshipping the moon and the fire, they'd be so quick to flock to our show and give us their hard-earned money?"

Probably not. But—

"They wouldn't *persecute* you."

"You saw what happened in the drugstore with Sabina."

I had.

Silence fell between us. I could feel him staring at me, even as I stared at the shaft of moonlight spilling through the window and spreading across the rumpled quilt on my bed.

"Claire?"

I glanced up and found myself captured by what I saw in his eyes. He wanted me, but he wouldn't make the first move. He wouldn't make any move. That would have to come from me.

There was power in that, control, strength, everything that had been taken from me by Josh Logan. I wanted it back.

Tonight I would take it, by taking Malachi.

In truth, this man should have terrified me. He'd broken Josh's nose, picked him up easily and shaken him like a doll. Malachi's physical strength was superior not only to mine but also to that of anyone I'd ever known. However, he'd used his strength to defend me;

he'd never used it against me, and I didn't believe he would.

I'm not sure why I trusted him, why I felt as if I knew him, as if I'd always known him, why the sight, the scent, the taste of him seemed familiar, but it did.

I crossed the floor. He continued to lean against the windowsill, his fingers gripping the wood. He'd said he wouldn't touch me unless I asked, unless I begged.

I stopped in front of him, my bare feet framed by his black boots. I held out my hand, and when he put his palm against mine, I urged him to stand.

Our bodies were a wisp apart. If I swayed just a little . . .

His breath caught as my dream-hardened nipples brushed his chest. My head tilted back. "Kiss me," I whispered.

Our lips met; he tasted like the mist—a cool, damp rain. I wanted to draw him inside and feast on the flavor. My teeth nipped, then laved the tiny hurt before I sucked on his tongue until he groaned.

I expected him to take me in his arms, but he didn't, touching me nowhere beyond the kiss. His control was nothing short of phenomenal. When the man made a vow, he kept it.

I lifted my mouth only centimeters from his and whispered, "Touch me everywhere."

His lips curved, the movement a ghost against mine. "Do you have rope?"

"Huh?"

"I promised you could tie me up. Then you'd have no need to be afraid."

I inched back. "I'm not afraid."

"No?"

"No," I said firmly.

And I wasn't—a miracle. What did I know about this man beyond what he'd told me? None of it might be true. But he'd had every chance to hurt me, to take me and force me the way Josh had. Instead he'd been patient and kind. He'd protected me.

I wanted to give him something. Like me.

Taking his hand, I led him to my bed.

I had to see his body in the moonlight, the way I'd seen it as he'd come out of the lake. I'd wanted to touch him then, to run my hands and then my mouth over every inch. Now I could.

As I reached for the top button on his shirt, his gaze remained on my face, both gentle and heated at the same time. Slowly I released each one, revealing inch after glorious inch.

The shirt fluttered to the ground, and I learned his shape with my lips, the rise of a nipple, the curve of his waist, the hard sear of ribs beneath the sleek expanse of skin.

The band of his trousers hung loose from wear, so I lowered myself to the floor and dipped my tongue beneath it while he shuddered.

The screech of his zipper rang loudly in a room where the only sound was the steadily increasing pace of our breath. One tug and his pants pooled near his ankles, caught on the tops of his boots.

He kicked them off, and they landed with twin thuds against the wall; his socks followed, as did the discarded slacks.

I gazed all the way up his body, fascinated with the play of light through the window. The shadows of the trees chased the moon's glow across his skin, turning him into a statue both bronze and silver.

His head thrown back, his hair swirled across his

shoulders. His earring swayed, mixing with the strands. His hands clenched and unclenched at his sides while he waited with complete trust for my next move.

I just looked at him, memorizing this moment forever.

On my knees in front of him, the position should have been one of submission, but it wasn't. I was completely clothed; he was completely at my mercy—naked and aroused, the most intimate part of him bared to me. Leaning forward, I closed my mouth over his tip.

He didn't groan, moan, or make any sound at all beyond a soft sigh. He didn't grab my head and show me what to do or mutter instructions about speed, pressure, technique. He did nothing that every other man of my acquaintance had ever done in a situation like this. Malachi Cartwright just let me be.

I took my time, learning everything about him. His taste, his texture, the shape and length of him. How he fitted best, when he didn't, what made him swell and nearly come. I took him to the edge, retreated, then took him to the edge once more. And through it all, he never touched me. Not once.

It was the best sex I never had.

I increased the speed and pressure, but at the last instant he backed away. I reached for him, but he stayed me with a slash of his hand.

His shoulders heaved as he fought free of the tide. I sat on the bed. "You didn't have to stop," I said.

"I did, or there'd be nothing left for you."

"I don't mind."

He lifted a brow. "You're not ready?"

I hesitated. I'd enjoyed being in control. Was I ready for him to be?

"Shall I get the rope then?"

I couldn't help but smile. He was so easy with me, with this. I wished that I could be.

"Lie back, Claire; I want to do something for you."

For me, not *to* me. I did as he asked.

His shadow blotted out the light, and for an instant I became almost overwhelmed with bad memories. But he murmured to me as he might murmur to his horse, soft words in the language of the Rom, with perhaps a little Gaelic thrown in, and soon all I knew was him.

He went down on his knees, nudged my legs apart, leaning over to lift the hem of my top and press his mouth to my stomach. The muscles fluttered to life.

Tracing his palms over my hips, down my flanks, he then ran his thumbs up my quivering thighs, sliding them outward across the sensitive line where pelvis and leg became one.

I opened to him, and his mouth came down hot and hard upon me, just like the dream, except he wasn't made of mist and I still wore all my clothes. The thin cotton of my pajama bottoms didn't provide much of a barrier, which was just fine with me. He continued to put pressure right where I needed it the most until he had me begging, just as he'd promised. I was the one who pushed off the pants, kicking at them frantically until they hung from one ankle.

Then his mouth and his tongue were doing innovative things as I tangled my fingers in his hair and held on. His earring tickled the inside of my thigh, and my breath caught between a laugh and a moan. I shifted just enough so that at the next stroke of his tongue I was no longer able to laugh or moan, only come.

He didn't stop, pushing harder, stroking longer, drawing out the orgasm until I didn't know if there had been one or perhaps two, and I didn't really care.

When the tremors died, he pressed a kiss to my stomach, just below my belly button, before inching back. My hands slid limply to the mattress, and I opened my eyes.

Mist swirled through the room, so thick I could no longer see anything.

Not even him.

22

I SHOT INTO a sitting position, heart racing. Was I dreaming again?

"Malachi?" My voice sounded breathy—scared or satiated? I wasn't sure.

A shape moved in the fog. "I'm here."

I exhaled in a whoosh. "What is this?"

The bed dipped. He drew me into his arms, his skin hot and damp. "Mist."

I'd seen the fog creep over the hills, watched it curl through the trees and settle over the lake. But I'd never seen it creep in a window—except in my sleep. I'd never seen it so thick I could distinguish little beyond the swirl. As I stared at it now, the fog seemed almost otherworldly. I didn't like it.

"From the mountains." Malachi's palm smoothed over my hair. "There's nothing to fear in the mist."

He was right, of course, but that didn't make my heart stop pounding far too fast.

"Hush," he whispered. "We'll rest awhile."

He lifted the quilt, tucked me in, then lay down on top.

I felt slighted. "What's the matter?"

He turned to face me, his eyes endless pools of black in the dim, gray, mist-shrouded room. "If I lie next to you, skin to skin, there'll be no rest for us."

"That's okay."

He put his hand against my cheek. "For now, this is enough. Close your eyes, *a ghrá*."

My eyelids were suddenly so heavy I couldn't keep them open. "What's *a ghrá* mean?"

He hesitated, as if he couldn't quite remember, then whispered, "*Pixie*. You look like one with your red hair all wild and your mouth so sweet."

Smiling at the image, I let the night slip away.

I awoke just before dawn and lay staring at the ceiling, wondering what had disturbed me. Then I realized it was so many things.

I could see the ceiling. The mist was gone.

I was alone in my bed. The window was closed.

And somewhere, out in the forest, something was howling.

I jumped up, then froze, frowning at my bare legs. I guess Malachi hadn't been a dream after all. Although I had been known to throw off all my clothes in my sleep.

I went to the window, yanked it up, and stuck my head and shoulders through the opening. Out here I could hear the howling so much better.

"More than one," I murmured.

That couldn't be good.

The eastern horizon glowed pink. Very soon the sun would burst over, slanting orange, red, and yellow fire across the mountains and the trees.

I waited, watching, listening, enjoying the cool morning air, sans mist for a change.

Daylight exploded across the sky, and at that very same instant the howling stopped as if the rays of the sun had silenced it.

The sudden quiet after the burst of sound was eerie. My skin prickled, and I pulled my head back into the room.

Grace would be out there now with her handful of hunters. She'd find the wolf, or wolves, and she'd end at least one of our problems.

I glanced around. Not a trace of what happened last night remained. Not his shirt or a sock, not even a note.

I scowled into the vanity mirror. Malachi wasn't the type of man to leave a note; I wasn't the type of woman who needed one.

Last night had been about sexual freedom. I'd taken back my life. I'd done what I wanted to do with the man I'd wanted to do it with, and it had felt . . .

"Fantastic," I announced, my mood lightening at the memories.

If they'd even happened.

"Don't be ridiculous," I told the brand-new woman in the mirror. "You aren't insane."

Isn't that what all insane people said? Especially when they talked to themselves in the mirror?

AN HOUR LATER I walked down Center Street, nodding to the people I met and wondering why everyone kept whispering.

I found out soon enough.

I hadn't been at the office five minutes when Joyce barreled in. She saw me at my desk and tossed the *Gazette* in front of me with such force I had to slap my palms on top of the newspaper to keep it from tumbling off the other side.

"What are you thinking?"

"Not . . . much," I said slowly. "I haven't had my coffee."

"You've had just about everything else."

"Are you okay?"

"No." She stabbed a finger at the paper.

I glanced down and choked. In the center of the front page was a photo of my house, with Malachi climbing out the window. In a smaller photo below, the photographer had zoomed in and caught the Gypsy leader's disheveled appearance: His shirt hung loose, framing his beautifully sculpted chest; his pants were zipped but not buttoned, and his hair looked as if someone had run her fingers through it in a fit of passion. I guess I hadn't dreamed last night after all.

"I'm going to kill him," I muttered.

"Doesn't seem like you want him dead, seems like you want him naked."

"I didn't mean Mal." Joyce's eyebrows went up at the familiar term of address. "I meant Balthazar. This is his idea, if not his direct handiwork."

"Goes without saying," Joyce agreed. "But what in Sam Hill were you doing letting that guy in your bedroom?"

I hadn't *let* him in, but that was neither here nor there. "Did you take a look at him?"

"Pretty is as pretty does."

"That's the truth."

"You slept with him?"

"What do you think we did, Joyce, play Monopoly?"

"Ah, hell." She put her fingers in her hair and tugged. "How am I going to spin this so you don't lose your job and ruin everything your father worked for?"

"My private life is private."

Joyce snorted. She was right. I was a politician, or near enough. My private life would never be private.

"If you hadn't slept with him," she continued, "I might be able to make something up."

"I can't think what."

Joyce glanced at the picture again. "You're right. No fixing this." Her eyes lit with an idea. "Gypsies'll be gone in a week. Maybe it'll blow over. As long as you stay away from him from now on."

I went silent.

"Claire?"

"Hmm?"

"You'll stay away from him?"

I took a minute to ponder. "No."

"He's that good?"

I didn't need a minute to answer that. "Yes."

"Hell."

"This picture is going to seem like less than nothing soon enough."

Joyce stilled. "What else did you do?"

I told her about Josh, past and present, as well as the wolf, the missing tourist, and Grace's hunting party. By the time I was done, Joyce's hair was a mess and I was worried she'd make a bald spot somewhere if she kept yanking at it.

"You should have put that bastard away on day one," she said.

"I know."

"I can't wait to see him in cuffs."

I couldn't, either.

"You should have come home right away after that happened, Claire. Come home to the people who love you."

"I didn't want anyone to know."

"By 'anyone' you mean your dad."

"Especially him." The one bright light to his being gone was that he'd never know about Josh.

"He'd have broken out the family shotgun, that's for sure," Joyce said. "I'd have chipped in for the shells."

I smiled. "Thanks, Joyce."

She shrugged. "People in this town stick together. Always have, always will. I'd do anything for you."

"Same goes," I said, amazed to realize I'd do whatever I could not only for her but for anyone in Lake Bluff. Except maybe Balthazar.

"What are you going to do about this?" Joyce lifted the paper.

"Not much I can do, except hold my head up and give Balthazar another piece of my mind." At the rate I was going, soon I wouldn't have any mind left.

I wasn't able to get over to the offices of the *Gazette* until nearly noon. Joyce wasn't the only one who'd seen the paper. The way my phone rang and my office filled up, I started to think there wasn't anyone in three counties who hadn't seen it.

"Not the image we want to project, Mayor," said the high school principal.

"I realize that."

"Be a little more discreet next time." Then he winked. I nearly fell out of my chair.

Catfish wandered in, chewing on his cigar along with his mustache, and asked, "You wanna sue 'im? I'm game."

I wanted to, but I didn't think I'd win. I also figured a lawsuit would only call more attention to the situation. I said as much to Catfish.

"Most likely, but that don't mean it wouldn't be fun."

The tenor of the visits remained the same. Citizens expressed mild disapproval, then shrugged the whole incident off and went on to ask my advice or suggest an improvement or complain about the same thing they'd been complaining about since my dad was in office.

I guess after the Lewinsky scandal, a photo of the mayor's lover wasn't enough to make people tar and feather me. I couldn't wait to rub *that* in Balthazar's face.

Except he wasn't in.

"Rushed out right after the fella in the paper came in and shoved him around," said one of Balthazar's underlings, a slimy little man I'd noticed following me on several occasions.

"What fella in the paper?"

"You know what one." He leered. I hadn't seen anyone leer in so long that at first I thought he might be having a stroke. "The Gypsy king." He held up the paper and tapped Malachi's face. "This guy."

"He was here?"

The man squinted at me. "You know, you don't seem all that bright for a mayor."

I ground my teeth together and counted to ten. "What happened?"

"The Gypsy came in and told Balthazar he'd better mend his ways or else. Then Balthazar got in his face."

Uh-oh.

"Gyp shoved him so hard I swear Balthazar flew into the wall. Then he left."

"Balthazar?"

He rolled his eyes. "The *Gypsy.*"

"And where's your boss now?"

"Not sure. He heard the sheriff was huntin' wolves—"

Who'd blabbed that info?

"So he ran over to the station. Called and said he was going to head out and see what he could see."

If Balthazar screwed up Grace's hunt, I wouldn't have to worry about him bothering me anymore. We'd be finding parts of him all over the place.

"Tell Balthazar I want to see him."

"He was within his rights to print that picture." The man's pencil-thin lips curved into something that might have been a smile—on someone with lips. "Besides, everyone's seen it. Not a thing that can be done anyhow."

"Whatever," I muttered.

Back at town hall, I skirted the side of the building until I reached the sheriff's department. Grace not only should be back with news about the wolf, or wolves, but she should also have called Atlanta about Josh.

I was right. She sat in her office, talking on the phone. Whispers and snickers rose as I wound through the desks of the others in the department.

"Save it for high school," I said.

"Doesn't look like you saved it," someone called.

Everyone laughed. Oh yeah, this was great.

Grace saw me through the glass and waved me in, motioning to a chair.

"Uh-huh," she said. "I see."

She lifted the paper, pointed to the photo, wiggled her eyebrows, then shook her finger.

I gave an exaggerated shrug—code for "What can you do?"—then pointed at the phone with a quizzical expression.

She signaled for one more minute and tossed the *Gazette* into the trash where it belonged.

"Thank you for your help, Detective. I'll be in touch." She put the receiver back on the cradle.

"Are they going to pick up Josh?"

"I don't think so."

"What?" I straightened so fast I banged my tailbone against the back of the chair. "They have to."

"They would, except they can't find him."

"Explain 'can't find.' "

Grace, who'd been staring at the top of her desk, tapping her nails, and working on putting a permanent frown line between her finely arched brows, lifted her head.

"Josh Logan has disappeared."

23

"BY THE TIME I called the Atlanta PD," Grace continued, "they'd already heard from his people. Logan never made it home last night." Grace pulled out a notepad. "I need to ask you a few questions."

I'd been staring out the window trying to process what she'd just said. I jerked my gaze back to her face. "I already told you everything."

"Now you'll make a statement."

"You think I lied? You think I . . ." I paused. "What *do* you think?"

"Personally, I think Logan knew you were going to press charges and ran."

"Why would he do that? It makes him look guilty."

"He *is* guilty, Claire."

"He doesn't think he is. He actually believes I owed him sex."

"They all do," Grace said drily. "But most of them don't force the issue."

"I still don't think he'd run. Not yet."

Grace shrugged. "Doesn't really matter. When we

find him, we'll prosecute. But right now I need to know exactly what happened at your house from the minute he showed up until the minute he left your sight."

I told her, not stopping until I reached the part where I walked into her office and she showed me the newspaper.

"Cartwright said Logan got into his car and drove away?"

"That's what he said."

"You didn't see it yourself."

"No."

"Mmm."

"What's 'mmm'?"

"Cartwright could have done something with him."

"Why?"

"He hurt you. *I'd* like to kill the guy."

My eyes widened. "You just skipped from missing to murdered."

"I'm funny that way."

"Grace, you can't actually think Malachi killed Josh."

"I think all sorts of things until I'm proven wrong."

"He wouldn't—"

"You barely know him, Claire." Grace shuffled her papers impatiently. "You have no idea what he's capable of."

She was right, so I changed the subject. "What happened this morning?"

"Nothing."

"You went hunting?"

"Yes."

"I love it when you give one-word answers. Gets me all tingly."

She scowled and slapped my statement into a file. "There isn't anything to tell. We went into the woods, traipsed around for hours, and found absolutely nothing. No wolf, no tracks, no missing tourist, no signs of a camp."

"Weird."

"Not really. The mountains go on for miles." She spread her hands. "If someone, or something, really wants to hide, and knows how . . ."

Her voice trailed off, but I heard what she wasn't saying. We could look for years and never find the man or the beast. Except—

"This morning, just before the sun came up, I heard wolves."

"Plural?" Grace asked.

"Yeah."

"Fuck."

"Mmm."

"Could you tell where they were?"

I shook my head. "When the sun broke over the mountains, they went silent—*bam*—mid-howl. It was . . . kind of spooky."

"I like this less and less every day."

We remained quiet for several minutes, thinking about what might happen with more wolves than one. None of it was good.

"Did you see Balthazar in the woods?" I asked.

Grace frowned. "No. Why?"

"Weasel-faced guy at the *Gazette* said he went after you to get a story."

"Never saw him. Maybe he got eaten by the wildlife."

"Grace!"

"It could happen."

The rest of the day passed quickly, and when dusk arrived I found myself once again driving toward Lunar Lake.

Only one bouncer—the dark burly man—stood next

to the ticket booth tonight. Since the crowd appeared even larger than the one on the previous evening, I wondered why the powers that be—Mal—had decided less was more.

I dug money out of my pocket and along with it came the wooden chip with the swastika. I set the talisman on the shelf and shoved the money through the small hole beneath the barred window.

"Where did you get that?"

I glanced up to find the ticket taker's gaze had fallen on the amulet. He spoke English with an Irish accent that wasn't half as charming as Mal's—probably because of the permanent scowl marring his face.

"It was found near here."

"That's powerful Rom magic." His skeletal fingers tried to reach beneath the bars and snatch it, but I got there first. "A *gadje* should never touch that!"

The bouncer turned toward me and emitted a low rumble that had me backing up fast.

"W-why?" I managed.

"You're *marime*," the old guy said. "Give it to me."

"Uh, no." Grace would have my head. This was evidence. Maybe.

"Hogarth," he said, and the big man moved forward. I turned to run and smacked into Malachi.

"What's going on?" he demanded.

Hogarth subsided with a *grrr*. The old man came out of the booth. "She's got a rune."

Malachi jerked his head at the ticket seller, who scuttled behind the iron bars before he turned to Hogarth. "Don't you have a show to do?"

The bouncer lumbered away, but not before glaring in my direction. I didn't like his eyes. They were small, dark, and a little wild.

"May I see it?" Mal asked.

I handed him the chip. He stared at it for a few seconds, lips tightening.

"Is it yours?" I blurted.

His eyebrows shot up. "Mine? No."

"Your man said it was powerful Rom magic."

"This is an Icelandic rune."

Icelandic, which made sense considering the origin of the swastika. But— "Why would an Icelandic rune be used in Rom magic?"

"Not magic. Not in the way you think. My people consider good luck a type of magic."

"You're saying this is a good-luck charm?"

"Yes. Roms have taken for their own many of the traditions of the countries they wandered through. This is one of them."

"How are they made?"

"Simply enough. Fruit trees are seen as giving life; they bear fruit. A bit of their trunk, a little red paint—"

"Not blood?"

Mal gave a short, sharp laugh. "No."

"The swastika seems an odd choice."

"It's an ancient symbol."

"Protection and rebirth." At his questioning expression, I shrugged. "Internet. Still, considering what you told me about the Nazis . . ."

"My people don't look at things the way others do. Whoever made this was only thinking about its original intent, which is where the power would come from. Using the symbol as it was meant to be used removes some of the stain of the past."

I doubted the stain on the swastika would ever go away, but one could always hope.

"This was found in the forest where a man was attacked by a wolf," I said. "The man who's still missing and in dire need of rabies shots."

"I don't see what one has to do with the other." Malachi tilted his head, smiled a little. "I doubt a wolf was carrying a rune."

I doubted it, too.

"Well, it didn't belong to the man who was attacked, or so his family said." I paused, considering, then plunged ahead. "Your ticket seller said I shouldn't touch the rune, that I was *marime*. I thought that meant outcast."

Malachi's smile faded; he suddenly appeared much older. "*Marime* is both the act of being outcast for unclean behavior and the state of being unclean itself."

"I'm unclean?" I whispered furiously.

Malachi's lips compressed. "Of course not, but—"

"You're not supposed to touch me."

His eyes heated. "What I'm supposed to do and what I *will* do are two different things."

"What would happen to you if your people found out that you and I—" I broke off. He knew very well what he and I had done.

"I'm their leader. They can do nothing to me."

I had my doubts about that.

"Is that why you came to town and threatened Balthazar this morning?"

His head went up. "You know about that?"

"It's a small town, of which *I'm* the leader. What do you think?"

He let out his breath in a rush. "I saw that photo, and I wanted to—" His fingers clenched.

"Me, too." I put my hand over his. "I'm sorry you got caught in our little war."

"War?" His face crinkled in confusion.

"Balthazar wants my job. He thinks he can get it if he discredits me."

"So he'll continue to harass us?"

"Most likely. If we continue to see each other."

I waited for him to say last night had been a one-time thing. Considering the taboo that hung over us, how could it be anything else?

Malachi's hand turned beneath mine, relaxing the fist and linking our fingers together, even as he tugged them to the side, behind his leg so no one could see.

"I want to be with you again," he said softly. "Tonight. But perhaps I should come in the back door and leave the same way."

"Not perhaps." I smiled. "Definitely."

"Until later then." Malachi released my hand as the band began to play, signaling the beginning of the show.

"Do you have to perform?"

"No. Tonight is for Hogarth and Mary."

Hogarth didn't look like a performer; he looked like a hit man.

"What does Hogarth do?"

"Wrestles the grizzly."

"Isn't that a little dangerous?"

"What would be interesting about the show if it wasn't dangerous? You think it's safe for Sabina to dance with snakes?"

"I guess not." I only hoped Hogarth didn't end up Swiss cheese while performing in my town.

"And Mary—" I tilted my head. "I thought Mary was a cougar."

"She is."

"You let the cougar do her own show?"

"Ah, no. I meant tonight is *Jared's* night. He's Mary's . . ." He paused as if searching for the word. "Trainer."

"The animals aren't loose, are they, free to dart into the crowd and wreak havoc?"

"We take every precaution."

I didn't like the sound of that. "What kind of precautions?"

"We charm the circle. The animals won't go past it."

I stared at him for several seconds. "Tell me you're kidding."

"Yes and no. We do charm the circle. It's our way. But we also have guards with guns. You don't have to worry about your people or your guests. We've never had an incident. Never."

I relaxed somewhat, though I still wanted to shake Joyce for booking such a strange and potentially dangerous show. If I didn't know how much she loved me, I might think she was trying to sabotage me—either in cahoots with Balthazar or maybe to take the mayorship for herself.

But I did know Joyce. She was family—or as close to family as I had these days, except for Grace.

Besides, if Joyce hadn't hired the Gypsies, I wouldn't have met Mal. He'd brought me out of the prison my fear had built; he was leading me back to myself, and I couldn't regret that for an instant.

"I have to go and . . ." Malachi waved his hand in the direction of the performance.

"Of course."

He hesitated, his gaze dropping to my mouth. I took a breath; my tongue swept my suddenly dry lower lip, and he turned sharply and walked away.

Just his eyes on me had made me want him. If he'd stayed here another second, *I* would have kissed *him,* which was probably why he'd taken off in such a hurry. Would his people stone him if they found out about us?

This was the twenty-first century. Malachi could sleep with whomever he wished, just as I could.

Maybe we needed to keep it quiet, but that only added to the thrill. Of course, I didn't know how quiet we could keep it, considering the photo in the paper.

The band went from soft introductory music to a rousing polka, and I glanced at the ring as Hogarth ran in leading an amazingly docile grizzly. Hogarth wore a bright red one-piece Lycra wrestler's suit. Considering his size, his breadth, his huge gut, that was nothing I ever wanted to see again. Lord only knew what might be revealed in the midst of wrestling fever.

My gaze searched for and found several rifle-bearing men, who lurked on the outskirts of the performance ring. From their sober expressions and the professional manner in which they held the guns, they appeared to know what they were doing.

I turned away, planning to wander over to the cotton candy wagon. Not to eat any—the very thought made my teeth ache—just to take a whiff and enjoy the kaleidoscope of colors.

All the usual pastels—pink and blue, as well as the less popular green and yellow—were available, but in the intervening years since I'd been near a cotton candy machine, they'd discovered neon orange, blue, green, purple, as well as silver and black. Times certainly had changed.

As tempting as it was, I never made it to the cotton candy. On the way, I had to pass the fortune-teller's tent.

Five dollars. No waiting.

What the hell? I thought, and slipped inside.

24

BENEATH THE CANVAS I found a prime candidate for the cliché of the month award.

Two chairs flanked a table covered with a purple cloth, which reached to the floor. On top lay a deck of cards and a lump covered by black silk. The lump had the distinct outline of a crystal ball.

"What is it you wish?"

The fortune-teller had appeared in front of a set of multicolored draperies that separated the front of the tent from the back; I hadn't even heard them swish.

She'd removed the scarf with the coins—revealing dark brown hair with only a few threads of gray. She'd removed her bracelets as well, but her fingers still sparkled with rings, and the hoops in her ears flashed despite the dim light.

I pulled five dollars from my pocket and set it on the table.

She glanced behind me. "Tie the flap."

I did as she asked. When I turned, the money had disappeared and she sat behind the table. "I am Edana." She waved impatiently. "Sit."

I settled in a rickety card table chair, and she laid her palm faceup atop the purple cloth. I stared at it, unsure of what she wanted. "Give me your hand."

Hers was thin, sinewy, dark, very similar to the dreaded monkey's paw. I didn't want to touch her any more than I'd wanted to touch that.

"Why?" I stalled.

She made an impatient sound. "I am *filidh,* a seer. I read the palms, the tarot; then we will look into the ball."

She yanked the black cloth from the lump in the center of the table. The light that hung above us—an oil lantern, talk about a fire hazard—reflected off the surface, and the rainbow colors of the draperies swirled at its center.

"Why do you need all three?" I'd planned to be here five minutes, but this appeared to be a major undertaking.

"Everyone is different. I may see something in your hand, the cards or the ball—perhaps a bit in each. I do what I must to give those who visit me what they pay for."

She flexed her fingers, asking without words for my hand. I clenched my teeth and gave it to her.

Her skin was hot, dry, or maybe it just felt that way because mine had gone cool and damp. She stroked a long, sharp nail down the center of my palm and I jumped.

"Hold still," she snapped.

She was awfully cranky for someone whose livelihood depended on the whim of strangers. But I guess she didn't have to worry about repeat customers, since the caravan moved to a new town every week. I wondered if this meant she actually told people what she saw rather than what they wanted to hear.

I did a mental rolling of the eyes. I didn't believe she was going to see anything. I'd come in for fun. A curiosity.

She traced the line that ran from just above my thumb and curved around the pad toward my wrist. "A long life," she murmured. "With the possibility of death, here." She pointed to a place where the line faded, right next to the base of my thumb.

"What does that mean?"

"You may die or you may not."

I refrained from pointing out the wishy-washiness of this statement.

Her dark eyes lifted to mine. "Soon."

A chill went over me. "Soon" wasn't wishy-washy at all.

"When?"

She shrugged and returned her gaze to my hand, rubbing her nail over a tiny couplet of curved lines beneath my ring and middle fingers. "The girdle of Venus is strong. You like sex."

I jerked back, but she didn't let go.

"Although"—she pointed to a break in the lines—"you did not until recently. Trauma," she murmured. "But that is over now."

My eyes narrowed. How did she know? Could Malachi have . . . ?

No. He wouldn't.

Would he?

I'd read about fortune-tellers having accomplices who went into whatever town they were near to learn all that they could about the people. Then the supposed clairvoyants used the information to appear psychic when they were merely masters at planning ahead.

I was torn between wanting to run and wanting to hear more so I could figure out where she'd gotten her information. Curiosity won out.

"What else?"

Edana bent closer, squinting, then shrugged and let go. "There is nothing."

"I many die soon and I like sex. That's it?"

"We are not done." She picked up the cards, mixed the deck a few times, then handed them to me. "You shuffle."

"How much?"

"Until you feel you are done."

While I did that, she spread a piece of navy blue velvet in front of her, smoothing the fabric until it was straight and flat and reminded me of the endless night sky above the mountains.

"I'm done." I attempted to hand her the cards, but she shook her head.

"Cut them into three piles; use your left hand only." I did. "Now stack them into one pile." I did that, too.

Finally she picked up the cards and laid them, faceup, in a pattern—three in a row for three rows, making nine cards altogether.

"This is the past," she said, pointing to the top three. "The wheel of fortune." She went silent, pursing her lips.

"Do I need to buy a vowel?"

Edana didn't laugh. Maybe she'd never seen the show. Maybe she didn't like Vanna. Maybe I wasn't as funny as I thought I was.

"The wheel brings change. You were at a cross-road."

I had been, but so were a lot of people.

"This card"—she pointed to the center of three—"is the six of cups. You returned to your childhood home."

No kidding. Anyone would hear that if they meandered into Lake Bluff for more than a minute.

Edana flicked her gaze to my face, frowned as if she'd heard my thoughts, then returned to studying the cards.

"This is the knight of cups. You were longing for love."

I coughed. *Not.* I'd been longing for—

I wasn't sure. Safety? A home? Certainly not love. I needed love like I needed Balthazar on my back.

I'd never really considered a home or a family because I'd been running so fast toward my goal. Sure, I no longer wanted to be Barbara Walters Jr., but I still hadn't given any thought to the home or the family most women craved because I'd been stuck in my past, focused on what *had* happened instead of dreaming of what might.

In truth, I'd been deliberately avoiding the thought of settling down, remembering the tales of my mother's unhappiness, her need to be forever somewhere else.

I'd felt the same wanderlust in Atlanta and feared I was more like her than I wanted to be, that I'd never be happy anywhere, doing anything.

But now that I'd come home and begun to feel that this *was* home, I saw that what I'd really wanted was to be out of Atlanta. Despite my belief that the big city was the place for me, it never had been and never could be.

A home and family sounded nice. I was sick of being alone.

"We move on to the present." Edana's hand slid to the three cards that lay in the center. "The fool."

"Terrific," I muttered, wondering if she was going to give me a lecture on the mistake I'd made by trusting Mal, by letting him touch me—if not for my own sake, then his.

"This is a good card," Edana continued. "New beginnings. Hope. Throw caution to the winds and enjoy your journey."

That didn't sound like me.

"Eight of wands," she continued. "Everything is about to change. Surprises, good and bad, await you around every corner. Expect the unexpected."

I'd never been very good at that. I liked my life orderly; I did better with a plan. Which might be why I was so on edge lately. Every plan I'd ever had was gone.

"The moon," Edana continued.

I glanced at the card, which showed the moon in various stages—full, crescent, gibbous, and one I couldn't figure out. The moon was round and flame red, as if something had exploded on impact.

"What's that?" I pointed.

"Hidden moon," she said, "a very special time."

I wanted to ask what the hidden moon was, but she didn't give me the chance. "The moon changes nightly. It is full of mystery and power. When you look at it, you long for what you can never have."

"Me personally or just a general 'you'?" I couldn't remember looking at the moon very much at all. Even during the festival there'd always been so many other things to do.

"This card indicates . . ." She closed her eyes, then allowed her palm to hover above the surface of the card, not touching it at all. "Dishonesty, infamy." Her eyes opened and for an instant the lantern reflected in their depths, a fiery dot of flame. "Madness," she whispered.

"Great."

Edana shook herself as if coming out of the water. "The future," she continued, moving her finger to the third row. "Death."

"Again?"

"Not necessarily literal death." She tilted her head as if listening. "Though it can be. The death card indicates an end, cutting ties, moving on. Something familiar will go out of your life."

"Like my *life*?"

"One never knows when the end may come. And the end as we know it is not the end. Nothing dies without being reborn. Death is a doorway."

I suppose that was meant to be comforting, but it wasn't.

"Page of swords." Edana pointed to the final card with a frown. "Someone is watching you."

Balthazar and his minions most likely. They never went away.

She muttered something in Romani that sounded suspiciously curselike, and I glanced up. She stared, transfixed, at her crystal ball. Within the glass, smoke swirled, gray, like fog or mist.

"Here we go again," I muttered. What was it lately with mist?

"Beware the devil"—Edana's eyes and her voice had gone flat, as if she was in a trance—"who is a shape-shifter."

A shape-shifter?

I lowered my gaze, just as the mist parted inside the crystal ball. At the edges, shadows of different shapes and various sizes milled, none distinct enough to be classified as man or beast.

Until the lean, black wolf appeared in the center of the crystal ball, paw lifted as if it had heard the scuttle of something small and tasty. As the animal tilted back its magnificent head, its eyes met mine.

They were human.

25

W HAT THE HELL is that?"

My voice was so loud I brought Edana out of her trance.

"What?" She shook her head as if to clear it.

"In there." I pointed.

The crystal was empty.

She peered at me curiously. "You saw something?"

"Didn't you?"

"I . . ." She paused and rubbed her eyes. "Don't remember."

" 'Beware the devil who is a shape-shifter,' " I recited.

Her hands fell down; her eyebrows flew up. "I said that?"

She glanced uneasily behind me. I did, too. Nothing was there.

"You did. There were shadows, everywhere; then a wolf appeared in the damn ball." I yanked up the tablecloth, peering beneath the table. "How did you do that?"

There was nothing under the table but Edana's skirt-shrouded legs.

I stared at the ceiling, searching for a camera or a projector; then I stalked to the drapes and yanked them aside. All that lay behind them was a beach-type lounge chair, which had seen better days, and a cooler full of water and Gatorade.

Gatorade?

I returned to the front of the tent. "What's going on?"

"My magic is seeing the future and the past. I cannot make things appear that don't exist."

I had my doubts about that. I also had my doubts about her sight. Before, I hadn't thought she had any; now I wasn't so sure. Which meant that all she'd told me might be true.

"What do you know about the wolf in the mountains?"

She lifted her hands, lowered them again. "I know only what the cards, the palms, the ball, tell me."

"Yet you don't recall what appeared in the crystal or what you said?"

"I'm an old woman; sometimes I don't recall my name."

I narrowed my eyes. She was lying, but why? Did she truly know nothing? Or was she afraid? Either way, I doubted I'd get any more info from her.

Questioning Gypsies was like trying to catch a floating feather. You kept snatching and snatching at the air, and the thing floated higher, remaining just out of your reach.

"Edana?" The tent flap rattled. "I have your supper."

I untied the entrance, and a young woman entered carrying a tray. I hadn't seen her before. Her hair was an interesting combination of blond and light brown, a shade that should be dishwater yet glowed tawny in the light of the oil lamp. Her eyes were light, more green than blue, and tilted up at the corners. The more I saw of these Gypsies, the more I thought they'd fraternized early and often with their Irish neighbors, despite any taboos to the contrary.

The girl gave me a quick, somewhat harried nod and crossed the tent to set the plates in front of Edana. "I'm sorry to be late."

The old woman waved away her apology. "Understandable, child."

I slipped outside; the show was over. People streamed away from the bleachers toward their cars. A few stopped at the trinket tables, a few more bought popcorn and cotton candy, while several formed a line in front of Edana's place.

Mal was on the other side of the camp astride Benjamin. His head lifted; our eyes met, and he turned the horse toward me.

Mal was only a few feet away when the girl ducked out of Edana's tent. Her sudden appearance must have startled the animal, because he threw up his head, nostrils flaring.

Malachi's forearms bulged as he attempted to control the horse, but the horse's eyes rolled wildly and he began to buck. Everyone in the immediate vicinity scattered. Then Benjamin reared, and when his hooves met the ground again, he galloped for the trees.

The girl stood rooted to the spot, face white. I ran after Mal, though I had no hope of catching him.

Just before the two would have disappeared into the forest, the horse suddenly stopped, planted his front feet, lifted his hindquarters, and sent Malachi sailing over his head to smack against the nearest tree trunk with a bone-crunching thud before sliding to the ground. Then Benjamin lowered his head and nudged his master's still form.

I reached Mal first. He was already sitting up, patting the horse's nose, and murmuring in both Rom and Gaelic.

I fell to my knees, my hands fluttering over Mal, though what I expected to do I wasn't certain. I wouldn't know what a broken bone felt like if I touched one.

"Are you okay?" I asked, my voice unsteady.

He contemplated me with a confused expression. "Why wouldn't I be?"

"You went flying into the—" I waved my hand vaguely.

His eyes softened. "I can't count the number of times I've been thrown from a horse. I know how to fall. I assure you, that looked much worse than it was."

It looked like he'd broken his neck, yet he climbed to his feet easily, then held out his hand to me.

I laid my palm against his; just the touch of skin on skin made me want to go into his arms and remain there while he murmured soothing words in another language until my heart stopped racing.

However, when I reached my feet, he let me go and stepped back. I frowned at his withdrawal, then noticed we'd drawn a crowd.

Someone is watching you, Edana had warned.

Make that a whole lot of someones.

When everyone realized that Malachi was fine and the horse, too, they drifted away.

"What got into him?" I asked.

Mal's gaze went past me and I turned. The young woman who'd brought Edana her supper still stood outside the tent.

"He's never liked Molly," Mal murmured. "I'm not sure why."

MALACHI WAS CALLED back to whatever he'd been doing; Molly disappeared into the crowd, head hanging.

Poor kid.

I returned to my car, which by now was one of the last left, and started the engine. Sabina appeared in the glare of my headlights.

I got out. "Hi."

She lifted her good hand.

"Did you want to tell me something?" I wasn't sure how she might do that.

She shook her head. Her eyes, intent on mine, caused an odd tingle of recognition.

"Sabina!"

The girl, who'd been coming toward me with a quick, determined gait, stopped. I turned and, at the sight of Edana, understood why I'd had that weird tingle. They had the same eyes.

"You're her—"

"Grandmother," Edana interrupted. "And all she has since her parents . . . died."

I frowned at the hesitation on the word. Had they died or hadn't they?

I recalled Mal saying they'd wanted to drown their daughter and he'd stopped them. But *how* had he stopped them?

"Come along, child," Edana ordered.

Sabina shuffled toward her grandmother. Her long, dark hair shrouded her face so that when she moved past me, she bumped into me.

I reached out to steady her, shocked at how cold her arms were despite the heat of the summer night.

"She's lonely," Edana said when Sabina had passed out of earshot. "She knows she isn't supposed to consort with the *gadje,* but there's no one here her age."

Sabina *was* the youngest Gypsy I'd seen, and she had to be in her late teens or early twenties.

People lived, loved, married, and procreated. It was what people did. So what had happened to the children?

Before I could ask Edana, she walked away. All of the tourists and locals had gone; the Gypsies bustled about cleaning up. I went home. What else was there to do?

As soon as I got there, I checked the windows and doors. Josh was still on the loose, though I doubted, after last night, he'd come back here. However, one never could tell.

Then I wandered around the house unable to settle down, waiting, watching, wondering. Would he come or wouldn't he?

Midnight had arrived when a sharp rap drew me into the kitchen. Malachi stood framed in the clear pane of the sliding glass doors.

He must have taken another dip in the lake, or maybe just a shower, because his hair was slicked against his head, making the spike of his cheekbones more pronounced and his eyes blacker than polished ebony.

He wore black, too, though he'd only buttoned two buttons near the bottom of his shirt and a long, supple slice of his chest glistened beneath the light of the moon.

I crossed the room and opened the door.

26

A BREEZE BLEW in that smelled of rain. In the distance, thunder rumbled. Malachi was a dark silhouette against a darker, turbulent sky.

I waited for him to come in; instead he captured my hand and drew me out. "Something's coming."

I cast him a quick glance. *Something?* What an odd way to describe a storm.

We stood at the wooden railing and watched the clouds billow over the mountains, then skate across the tops of the trees. Soon the only illumination came from heat lightning.

I'd always been fascinated by it. The way the sky seemed to flash outward, the fissure opening in the black velvet curtain, allowing the electric sizzle to escape.

"When I was a child," I murmured, "I thought that Heaven was spilling out."

"Perhaps it is."

He laid his hand over mine where it rested on the

railing. Our hips and shoulders brushed. The chill of the storm front stirred our hair.

We watched in companionable silence; I couldn't remember feeling this in tune with anyone except Grace. I'd never been this comfortable with a man, ever. What was it about him that made me trust?

The wind picked up; the lightning broke right overhead. "We should go in," I said.

He turned toward me and touched my cheek. I couldn't see his expression, only the slight glint of his eyes. "I don't have to stay."

I smiled, reaching up to brush his partially dried hair back from his brow. He kissed the inside of my wrist. My breath caught. "I want you to."

"Stay?"

"And all that staying implies."

I linked our fingers and led him into the house. Sanity still lingered, and I paused to shut the sliding glass door, then stick the iron bar between the two panels for good measure.

Malachi watched me with somber eyes. "He willna hurt you again. I swear."

"You can't be with me every minute. And you'll be leaving soon."

Something flashed across his face, there and then gone the next instant. I thought it might be regret.

"I don't want him breathing the same air as you."

He'd said that before; the old-fashioned phrase made something warm and solid shift just below my heart.

"And that other one, the big man, with the hairy hands and the big nose he sticks into business he should not."

"Balthazar."

"He will not come near you again, either."

I sighed. Wouldn't that be nice?

"Balthazar lives and works here," I said. "I have to deal with him."

"I wouldn't want your job, Claire."

I remembered how he'd flown over the head of the horse to smack into the trunk of a tree. "I wouldn't want yours, either."

For an instant I thought how different we were, how odd that our lives had crossed, and what a gift that we'd have these few days together.

"Let's not waste any more time," I said.

"I don't want to frighten you."

I stared into the endless darkness of his eyes and told him the truth. "You don't."

"You're too trusting, Claire."

"You plan to hurt me?"

He looked away. "How could you think that?"

"Exactly. So why shouldn't I trust you?"

"Sometimes people are not what they seem."

I knew that better than anyone. Josh had been nothing like what he'd seemed.

But the time had come to move beyond the past. I couldn't let the bastards win. By running back here, I'd done just that, and it hadn't helped. Josh had just followed me.

But I'd stood up to him, and now I needed to stand up to what was left of my fear. I wanted to do that with Malachi.

"I believe you're exactly what you seem," I said. "A man who works hard. Who takes care of his people. Who's honest about what he wants." I stepped closer, leaning up to brush my mouth across his. "And I'm glad what you want is me. I want you, too."

I'd never said that to a man. Not that there'd been

all that many, even before Josh. I'd been too busy getting through school, working, trying to make a name for myself. All of which seemed foolish now.

"Come with me."

I led him through the house, shutting off lights as we went so that darkness spread behind us as we continued to walk into the light.

We reached my room, and I flicked off the last switch. Night fell; I could barely see the outline of his face.

Suddenly he jerked his head toward the hall where Oprah's eyes glowed eerily disembodied. The sudden movement caused her to hiss.

I shut the door. "She doesn't care for storms."

"Poor beast," he murmured.

I started toward the bed; anticipation made my heart flutter, then pound. When Malachi hit the light switch and the harsh electric glare flooded the room again, I jumped like Oprah after a loud noise and spun around.

"I want to see you," he said.

That I wasn't ready for. My body wasn't bad, but it wasn't good, either. It certainly wasn't on the caliber of his.

"Please," he continued. "I've been waiting to see the pale moon of your skin and the fire of your hair when I'm inside you."

My moon-pale cheeks blushed fiery red. "I—I can't."

The thought of having sex with the lights brightly shining was too much for me. I couldn't do it. I'd panic at the worst possible moment, and once I did, I doubted I'd ever be able to go through with something like this again.

"You're so beautiful," he murmured. "I just want to gaze at every inch of you."

He started toward me, and I held up my hand in a staying gesture. "I *don't* want them on!"

I was making a big deal out of something small, but then, Malachi knew why, or at least the root of it. Still, I expected him to turn around and leave. I was too much work. Especially for a man who could have anyone he wanted in any town, anywhere. But Malachi surprised me again.

"That's all right, *a stor*." The lightning flashed, making the windowpanes glow white. "I swore to you I'd never make you do anything you didn't want to do." He flicked the switch. "I meant that. Would you like me to go?"

Silence descended, broken only by Oprah's muttering on the other side of the door and the distant rumble of thunder. The storm was moving away.

I opened my mouth; I wasn't sure what I meant to say, and a large *crack,* followed by a bolt of lightning so bright I had to close my eyes, yet still I saw it etched on my eyelids, froze the words in my throat.

Oprah squalled and the *scritch-scratch* of her claws tearing at the wood floor as she ran to her safe place downstairs seemed almost as loud as the rasp of the startled breath I drew into my lungs.

When I opened my eyes, Malachi stood right in front of me. He smelled like summer rain, new grass, the night, and I knew I didn't want him to go—not now, maybe not ever. I inched closer, resting my cheek against his chest, and his arms came around me so gently I wanted to weep.

Since that would kill the mood even quicker than any panic on my part, I kissed him as passionately as I knew how.

Lip-to-lip, tongue-to-tongue, I tangled my fingers in his still-damp hair, and the curls tumbled over my wrists. The cross that swung from his ear tickled the sensitive V of skin between my thumb and forefinger, and I moaned into his mouth, licked his teeth, backed us up until my thighs hit the bed, then tugged him onto the mattress with me.

We bounced once before he pulled away. "Claire, it doesn't have to be like this."

"Like what?"

"So fast, so—" He broke off.

"Desperate?"

"I know you're not desperate," he said softly. "Neither am I."

No, I was certain *he'd* had good sex in the last year.

"We'll go slowly." He sat up, bringing my knuckles to his lips and kissing them.

"If I wait too long, I might not go at all."

He dropped my hand and turned away. "Then we shouldn't."

"We should." I touched his shoulder. "I need this. I need you. Mal, please."

His skin twitched beneath my hand, almost a flinch but more likely pain caused by crashing into a tree. The guy probably had bruises everywhere. Maybe I needed to be gentle with him.

The notion intrigued me. What if I treated Mal as if he were the broken one?

Slowly I eased myself into a sitting position, then laid my cheek against his shoulder, pressed my breasts to his back. "Make me forget," I whispered. "Everything but you."

He turned in my arms. Lightning flashed, weaker, hardly a flicker, and in it he appeared anguished. "There's so much about me you don't know."

"I don't want to know. It's just you and me. No one else, nothing else, matters."

He hesitated, seemingly torn, and for an instant I wondered what he might confess. A hundred thousand lovers? Thievery? Murder? STDs?

Crap.

"Do you have a condom?"

"Of course."

Of course. What man wouldn't? Especially a man like him.

And why did that bother me? I certainly didn't have any handy, and I knew better than to sleep with him without one. Desperate passion is one thing, desperate stupidity another.

"Don't leave," I murmured, and I wasn't sure if I meant tonight or next week.

He put his forehead against mine and sighed. "I can't."

He kissed as if he'd been doing it for centuries and getting better with every one. He made love to my lips with varying degrees of pressure, tiny scrapes of his teeth, but no tongue. Not yet.

He touched me nowhere but my face, his long, hard fingers tracing the line of my jaw, his calloused thumbs stroking my cheeks and then my forehead. Who knew being touched on the forehead could be so erotic? Pretty much everything this man did was.

"Touch me," I gasped.

"I *am* touching you." He kissed my closed eyelids.

I grabbed his hands, pressed them to my quivering stomach. "Everywhere."

He lifted one palm to my chest and pushed me backward until I lay flat against the mattress, then stood and took off his clothes.

The storm had passed leaving only clouds behind. The room was so dark I could only tell what he was doing by the sound of it. For an instant I regretted the necessity of that darkness; I wouldn't mind seeing *him*. Then the bed dipped, and I sat up.

"Where are you going?" He reached for me; even in the complete darkness he managed to catch hold of my arm.

"I want to feel your skin against mine."

"You will, *a ghrá*. I promise." He pushed me back again. "But let me." His fingers brushed the waistband of my pants, curving beneath; then he ran the smooth surface of his nails along my belly, running his thumb down my zipper and flicking over me just once.

I arched, gasped, and he quickly divested me of every stitch of clothing below the waist.

He went onto his knees to take off my socks. My legs hung over the end of the bed. He kissed his way back, running his tongue up my inner thigh before skipping right over the good part and pressing his mouth to my stomach.

His weight lay over one leg, his skin hot against mine. I draped my ankle over his back, rubbed my heel at the base of his spine, and he scored my skin with his teeth, then swept his tongue into my belly button. I never would have imagined that such a thing could almost make me come.

My shirt went the way of my underwear, and he buried his face between my breasts, filling his hands with their weight, gathering them together so he could flick his tongue back and forth over their tips so languidly I had to bite my lip to keep from ordering him to both hurry up and never stop.

"Your body, so soft and round, I dream of it in the night," he murmured. "I want to see every curve."

I tensed, thinking he meant to turn on the lights again. Despite being aroused so deeply I might have agreed to anything, I still wasn't ready for that.

"Shh." He ran his hands over my arms. "I'll learn all there is to know like this."

He explored every inch of my skin with the tips of his fingers, tracing each curve with the tip of his tongue. He cupped my feet, pressing his thumbs against the arches until I moaned as the tension flowed free. His palms skated across my calves, my thighs, sliding over the hollow at my waist before teasing my breasts until they throbbed.

He nibbled my earlobe. "Turn over, Claire."

I was both relaxed and on edge. Since I didn't want him to stop, I turned over.

Then he started again at my feet and worked his way upward, mouth first this time. I never knew how good it felt to be kissed at the small of your back, to have your shoulders stroked and kneaded while someone sucked on your neck.

The heavy, heated weight of his erection slid along the curve of my rear end, and I rubbed against him. He slipped into me just a little, and I gasped with delight at the sensation. He began to withdraw.

"No." I arched my back, taking him in more deeply.

"A minute," he said, voice hoarse. Then he was gone, and I had never felt so cold and alone.

A rustle, a plastic snap, and he returned, urging me onto my side so he could pull me against him. My back to his front, he curved around me. We fitted together just right.

He moved my hair aside and kissed my ear, his hands still fluttering over me, smoothing down my flank, sweeping up to my breasts, teasing and tempting.

I could see nothing. Even though I knew a night-stand sat here, a chair there, not a shadow remained. The windows didn't shine or reveal a lighter shade of midnight. It was as if Malachi and I had been trapped in a sightless universe where sound and scent, taste and touch were heightened.

His kisses became something more as he took small folds of flesh between his teeth and suckled. My skin seemed on fire, shot through with electricity reminiscent of the vanished lightning.

I rubbed against him again, and suddenly I was on my back as he muttered in three languages. He leaned in and kissed me, hard and fast, his hair brushing my face while his erection jutted against my hip. "I don't think I can wait."

"You don't have to."

I urged him closer, drew him to me, opened myself, and let him in. Yet still he hesitated. "If you're not ready."

"Malachi," I groaned. "I'm so ready I may get there without you if you don't shut up."

His laughter caressed my face, warm and sweet. "Well, then," he said. "We can't have that."

He sank into me, slow but sure. Carefully he braced himself, keeping most of his weight off me. I ran my palms over his biceps, which quivered at my touch.

"I won't break," I whispered, wanting to feel that weight as much as I wanted to feel his heat and his hardness within.

He gave me what I wanted, what I needed, pushing into me, pulling out, slowly coming to rest against me until I didn't know where one of us ended and the other began.

Try as I might, I couldn't see him—not a flicker of movement, not a glint of a reflection in his eyes. Because of that, it seemed as if I were dreaming, as if he were a fantasy, a phantom, the mist.

I did things I never would have done in the light, reaching between us and cupping him, stroking and kneading until he said my name like a prayer or maybe a curse. I sucked on his tongue, scraped my teeth across the throbbing vein in his neck, and then grabbed his hips and pulled him even deeper.

I was in control, and I reveled in it, that power almost as arousing as he was.

He kissed my eyebrow, then leaned his cheek against my hair and whispered, "I canna wait any longer." With nothing more than a catch in his breath, I felt him stiffen, pulse, come.

The rhythmic movements brought an answering response in me. I'd said I wouldn't break, but I hadn't counted on shattering. The best I'd hoped for was being able to get through this without fear.

I cried out, and he continued to move, drawing the tension tighter, making it last seemingly forever.

I ended up wrapped in his arms, the quilt over us both as he murmured words I didn't understand while I drifted away.

We awoke a few hours later and made love again; then I left him sleeping and went to check on Oprah. With the storm past, she had crept from beneath the couch and now snored lustily on top of it.

When I returned to my room, I pulled on a nightgown. Even though we'd touched each other in so many ways, I suddenly felt shy. Foolish, but I couldn't help it. I didn't want to wake up naked in his arms and have him stare at me as if he couldn't recall my name.

Did I really think that would happen? *No.* But better safe than sorry.

I crawled into bed, keeping to one side and leaving him on the other, fighting the urge to touch him, hold him, or have him hold me. I didn't need to become attached. Even if he remembered my name when the sun shone, he was still leaving in a few days.

So I lay there staring at the ceiling, and I couldn't fall asleep. Until Malachi turned and drew me against him, pressing his face into my hair.

At first I stiffened, waiting for the poke of his erection. Not that I wouldn't mind another round, unless he was so out of it he didn't know who that round was with.

However, his body was warm, soft, or as soft as a body that hard could be. He murmured, "Claire," against my neck, then "*a chroi.*"

"Malachi?" I said softly, but from the steady, deep rise and fall of his chest he was asleep. Snuggling into his embrace, I followed him there.

I awoke to bright sunlight across the bed. Mal's eyes were open. He smiled and touched my cheek.

"What does *a chroi* mean?"

His smile froze; he snatched his hand back. "Where did you hear that?"

"You murmured it in your sleep, after you said my name. Is it Gaelic?"

"Yes."

He didn't elaborate. I started to wonder if *a chroi* meant "pig face."

"Mal?"

His eyes met mine. "It means . . . 'beautiful one.' "

I laughed. "I'm not beautiful."

"Who told you that?" He sat up, and the covers pooled at his waist.

I found myself distracted by the contrast of his copper skin with the white sheets, not to mention the ripples across his abdomen as he moved. He was the *a chroi.* Much more so than I could ever be.

"Claire?" I lifted my gaze to his face. "Who dared to say you weren't beautiful?"

He seemed awfully angry about it, as if he'd march

right out and punch this person in the nose. Remembering his treatment of Josh, he might.

"I only have to look in the mirror to know the truth. On a good day—a *really* good day—I'm passably pretty." I held up my hand to forestall his arguments. "And that's okay. Once I thought I wanted to be in front of the camera, to be the star. But I wasn't good enough. If I'm honest, I wasn't all that disappointed. I liked running things."

I paused. Maybe that was why being the mayor wasn't the snore fest I'd thought it would be. I was running a lot of things, and I wasn't half-bad at it.

"There's more to beauty than the curve of a cheek or the length of one's hair." Mal began to play with the ribbon that held the neck of my gown closed. "There's loyalty and honor and strength. Caring about people who need you, and not disappointing them. In that regard, you're lovely beyond words."

His eyes met mine as slowly he tugged the ribbon loose until the collar gaped. "You know this covering doesn't cover you very well?"

I glanced down. The silky white material wasn't transparent; however, it did cling like Saran Wrap, revealing the spike of my nipples and the curve of my breasts and belly as if they'd been wrought in plaster.

He cupped me through the material, his dark hand stark against the sheer white. "It only makes me want to take it off you. May I?"

I opened my mouth to say no. It was broad daylight; he'd see every flaw. But suddenly I no longer cared, and wasn't that progress?

"Yes," I whispered, and his eyes widened. He hadn't expected me to agree.

His hand dropped away. "Claire, maybe—"

"I thought you wanted me naked."
"I did. I do."
I reached for the hem.
And the damn doorbell rang.

27

I CONSIDERED IGNORING the bell, but at this hour the summons had to be important.

"I'll be right back." I tugged on my robe as I hurried downstairs.

Oprah wound her body around the newel post, purring so loudly I swear the floor vibrated. She hadn't been so happy to see me in . . . forever.

I glanced through the peephole, and the reason for Oprah's joy became apparent. Grace stood on the porch.

"Claire?" she called. "I know you're there."

I frowned. How could she know?

"Your stairs creak," she said, "and I can see your shadow at the peephole. You might also want to get this window"—she rapped at the glass next to the door, which was covered with a thin white drape—"frosted."

I opened the door.

She looked me up and down. "I woke you?"

"What the hell time is it?"

"Six A.M."

I rubbed my forehead. "What do you think?"

"Sorry." She bent to pick up Oprah, who was snaking through Grace's ankles and yowling for attention. The cat put her nose right up to Grace's and rubbed.

"What is it with you and that cat?" I asked.

"Soul mates," Grace said, and stepped into the house, crowding me backward.

"What's so important that you're ringing my bell at this ungodly hour?"

"Balthazar's still missing."

"Hopefully forever."

Grace set Oprah on the floor. "You need to watch what you say."

"I was joking. You said almost the same thing yesterday."

"I know. But—"

"But what? You're queen of the ha-ha sarcasm, so I can't be?"

"People on your shit list are disappearing, Claire. First Josh, then Balthazar."

"You think I disappeared them?"

"No."

"Then what?"

"Have you seen Cartwright?"

I fought not to betray the truth by glancing upward. "Why?"

Grace made an aggravated sound deep in her throat. "Why do you think? He had altercations with both men right before they disappeared. I have to talk to him. But I went to the lake, and he wasn't there." She scowled. "Though with them, who knows? He might be, and they were just covering for him. They're wiggy around cops."

"They probably have good reason to be."

"I didn't say they didn't, but they're making my life hard. Just makes me want to return the favor."

The steps creaked. Malachi stood at the top, fully dressed. But since his hair was a mess, his clothes were crumpled, and he'd obviously just come out of my room, clothes didn't mean much.

Grace gave me a stoic stare. "Were you going to tell me?"

I shrugged. I wasn't sure what I'd been going to do.

"What did you hear?" Grace asked as Malachi descended the stairs.

"All of it."

"I need to take you to the station."

"Grace—," I began.

She held up her hand. "I know what I'm doing. It won't help him, or you, if I give him special privileges at this stage of the game."

"Me? I thought we'd established that I had nothing to do with this."

"We established that I didn't think you had anything to do with it. But that was before I understood that you'd been playing hide the salami with the chief suspect."

"So?"

"Men who've hurt you, physically and professionally, have disappeared."

She said it slowly, so I'd understand, but I didn't.

"Did you hire him?" Grace asked.

"To sleep with me?"

"To disappear those guys."

"What? No! Why would I do that?"

"You didn't want Josh to disappear?"

I opened my mouth, then shut it again. Had I said as much to Grace at one time? I couldn't recall.

"*I* wanted him to," Grace said.

"Then suspect yourself. I was handling things. I didn't need anyone to *help* me, and I especially didn't need anyone to kill for me."

Her perfectly arched brows lifted. "Who said anything about killing?"

A HALF AN hour later, all three of us walked into the sheriff's department. I'd insisted on coming along, and Grace hadn't argued. I had a feeling I was going to get a turn in the interrogation room as soon as she was done with Malachi.

I glanced at my watch. If she was ever done with Malachi.

I'd left a message for Joyce saying I was at the sheriff's department and she should contact me only in case of an emergency. So far, none had arisen, though I didn't hold out much hope for the rest of the day.

The door to the interrogation room opened at last, and Grace stepped out. She motioned to one of her officers, and he slipped in. Her gaze went straight to me. I knew immediately that something was wrong.

"What is it?" I asked.

"A body's been found."

I'd expected her to say Malachi had confessed. And why had I expected that? I didn't believe he'd killed anyone.

Though while I'd been waiting I had gone over and over the expression on his face right before he'd popped Josh in the nose. Malachi had looked murderous. Then he'd followed Josh, and no one had seen the other man since.

As for Balthazar, he'd disappeared after their altercation, too. Sure, Balthazar had gone into the woods looking for Grace, or so his minion had said, but she had an alibi in the men of her hunting party. If Balthazar had annoyed her and she'd whacked him, someone would have noticed.

I kept hearing the things Mal had said to both men, threatening things when taken in a certain light. I also recalled Mal promising that no one would hurt me again. Wishful thinking, or had he known?

I shook my head to make all the frantic, unproductive thoughts go away.

"Who did they find?" I asked.

"We'll see."

"We?"

"I've got three missing people." Grace held up one finger. "Hiking tourist." She put up a second. "Josh Logan." Then a third. "Balthazar Monahan."

"And?"

"Our emergency personnel would know Balthazar. Which leaves Josh and our bitten tourist, Ryan Freestone. My money's on the latter. But if it's the former, I want you there to identify him."

"Swell," I muttered, and followed her through the parking lot to the funeral home.

The morgue at the hospital wasn't able to provide the type of isolation needed to preserve evidence, so the funeral home doubled as a forensics lab.

"Did you call Bradleyville?" I asked.

Lake Bluff shared a medical examiner with the next closest town. Neither one of us needed a full-time specialist of that magnitude.

"Someone called from the scene. Doc's been there, and he's on his way here."

"Where did they find the body?"

"In a ravine near Brasstown Bald."

Brasstown Bald was the highest peak in these parts. Coincidentally, or maybe not so much, it was part of a larger section of the mountains known as Wolfspen Ridge.

"Who found it?"

"Hiker. It's that time of year."

Another of Grace's officers stood guard at the door—standard procedure for cases like this. Although I couldn't recall the last time there'd been an unexplained death or murder in Lake Bluff.

"Ever have to handle a questionable death before?" I asked.

Grace slid me a look. "*I'm* more than qualified for this, ma'am."

"Are you insinuating that I'm not?"

"You're a goddamn suspect!"

"You're the one who wanted me to come along. If I killed the guy, or asked someone to do it for me, I probably shouldn't be here at all."

Grace stopped. "Hell."

"Oh yeah," I said, and shoved open the door to the temporary lab, "more than qualified."

Before she could stop me I strode to the tarp-shrouded body in the center of the room and yanked it back. It was Josh all right. Although how I could tell for certain through the blood, I couldn't say.

I swayed. Grace was there instantly, pulling the tarp up, then shoving a chair beneath my legs and my head between my knees.

"Girl," she muttered with just enough force to be an insult.

"*You're* a girl," I managed.

"I don't faint at the sight of blood."

"I didn't faint."

"Close enough," she muttered, and the door opened behind us.

"Doc," she greeted him. "Thanks for coming."

I sat up, blinking as black spots threatened to converge in front of my eyes and make the whole world go away.

The medical examiner from Bradleyville, Dr. William Cavet, Doc Bill to everyone who knew him, had been a physician for over fifty years. He'd spent most of them as a GP, back when GP was what they were called. Soon after GPs became FPs and the health insurance system went to hell in a handbasket, he'd become the ME.

"You okay?" He shot me a quick glance from beneath bushy white eyebrows that reminded me of woolly caterpillars.

I was dizzy, as much from the horror as the conflict of emotions. I'd wanted Josh dead, dreamed of it, too, but now that he was, I wasn't sure what to feel.

"Fine." I swallowed thickly as Doc went straight to the tarp and threw it down.

"I've been to the scene." Doc wasted no time. One of the many things I liked about him. "Body was dragged to the edge of a ravine and tossed in."

"I'm going to have to detain your boyfriend," Grace muttered.

"That'll ruin the show."

"I can't let a murderer walk around just so the show can go on."

"Lake Bluff needs the money," I said.

"Do you ever think about anything else, *Mayor*?"

"That's what I was hired to think about, *Sheriff*."

"Children, could you put a sock in it?"

Grace and I scowled at each other but didn't answer.

Doc Bill snapped disposable plastic gloves onto his hands, then began to poke and prod Josh's still form. Soon those gloves were soaked in blood and I had to turn my head.

"There's no need to detain anyone."

"What?" Grace asked.

"Why?" I added.

"See this?" He pointed to Josh's throat, pulling the head back until the wound made a disgusting sucking sound. I bit my lip as the swirling black dots returned.

"What about it?" Grace bent over to get a better look.

"Jagged, more ripped than cleanly cut." He pulled off his gloves and covered Josh again with the tarp. "This man wasn't killed by a human but an animal. Canine most likely. A big one."

Grace and I exchanged glances. We'd been here before.

"Except animals don't usually toss their kills over a cliff," the doctor mused. "Although they might bury them to feed on later."

I made a choked sound, which both of them ignored.

"What *does* toss its kills into a ravine?" Grace asked.

"Man."

"So a canine killed him, then a man tossed him into a hole? Why?"

"An excellent question, Sheriff."

28

THE DOCTOR APPEARED deep in thought, as if he might have an answer to that excellent question if he could only think about it long enough. Then he gave himself a little shake.

"If you'll excuse me," Doc Bill said, "I need to get down to business."

Since his business involved knives, saws, and the removal of various body parts and fluids, I made haste for the door.

Grace lagged behind. "You're sure he was killed by a canine, not a bear or a big cat?"

"I did some training in the recognition of various animal kills."

"That doesn't seem to be common training for a GP," Grace observed.

"At one time I considered moving west, taking a job at Yellowstone. But the wife didn't want to leave Georgia. Now she's gone and I'm too old."

"What brings you to the conclusion that this is a canine kill?" Grace asked.

"Cats use their claws to hold victims steady. Think of a domestic cat with a mouse."

"They play with them," I murmured from my position near the door. Oprah did it all the time. Drove me crazy.

"Exactly," Doc Bill agreed. "Which means a victim would not only have his throat torn but also exhibit scratches, serious ones if we're talking cougar and the like."

I glanced at Grace, suddenly understanding where she was headed with this line of questioning. Malachi's cougar, or even his grizzly, might have been used to kill Josh; then Malachi could have dumped the body in the ravine.

"And bears?" Grace pressed.

"Will swipe at their prey."

"I can see why you don't think this is a bear or cat kill, but what leaves the impression that it's canine?"

"The modus operandi of canines is to knock their victims to the ground and rip out their throats."

Lovely.

"I'm certain when I examine the body I'll find fur consistent with my theory. Has there been any hint of rabies in the area?"

Grace glanced quickly at me, then back at Doc. "Why would you think that?"

"Cats have been known to attack humans. Remember that situation in California where the cougar grabbed a woman right off her bike?" We nodded. "And it wasn't long ago that a mother was killed protecting her child from a bear at Yellowstone. Those animals weren't sick. We don't know what set them off. But canines don't commonly attack unless rabid."

"You have a strong feeling one way or another about what type of canine we're dealing with here?" Grace asked.

Doc Bill chewed on his lip as he stared at the corpse. "I'd be inclined to say 'wolf,' except there hasn't been one in these mountains since before I was born."

"That may have changed," Grace said. "We had a tourist attacked by what he swears was a wolf."

"Really?" Though the older man's body stayed in the same relaxed position, I got the impression he was suddenly very interested. "I'd like to take a look at this tourist."

Grace winced. Doc noticed. "He died?"

"Not exactly."

"*What* exactly?"

"He—uh—got up and left the hospital in the middle of the night, and he hasn't been seen since."

I expected a shocked reaction from Doc. Instead he continued to gnaw on his lip and stare at dead Josh.

"What about his wounds?"

"Sir?" Grace asked.

"Had they healed?"

Grace and I exchanged glances again.

"It appeared that way on the security tape," Grace said, "but they're notoriously fuzzy."

"Damn," Doc murmured.

"You seem to know something about . . ." Grace spread her hands. "Whatever this is."

"I haven't seen anything like it since I was in Germany."

"When were you in Germany?" I asked.

"Nineteen forty-four, forty-five."

"You were in the war?" He didn't look that old.

"Lied about my age. Dumbest thing I ever did."

"What happened?" Grace asked.

"We won," the doctor answered drily.

Grace's mouth curved; she always appreciated well-timed sarcasm. "I meant, what did you see there that reminded you of—?" She waved vaguely in the direction of the body.

"It was so long ago, sometimes I'm able to convince myself I imagined it."

He paused, rubbing between his eyes as if a headache pounded. I didn't think we were going to like what he had to say, but then, I hadn't liked much of what anyone had said lately.

Doc dropped his hand. "I was a paratrooper."

"Like *Band of Brothers*?"

"Pretty much. They dumped us behind the lines in France while the others came in from the sea. I wouldn't have wanted to have been them, though floating through the air between the bombs and the gunfire wasn't exactly my idea of a good time."

"I bet not."

"Once we landed, we were supposed to meet up with our unit and head east, liberating towns as we went. I'm not going to go over how long it took or how many we lost in the air and on the ground, but eventually we crossed into Germany."

"And then?" Grace asked.

"Then some weird things started to happen. There were wolves everywhere. Hundreds of them."

"Why is that so weird?" I asked. "Isn't the Black Forest—home of Grimms' fairy tales and a whole lot of wolves—in Germany?"

"Problem is, we weren't in the Black Forest and these wolves weren't exactly wolves."

"How can wolves not be wolves?"

"These were smarter than the average beast. They herded us, stalked us, followed us for miles and miles. They seemed to know what we were going to do, as if they'd been listening to our conversations and understanding them. And when they killed us . . . some of us didn't stay dead."

I glanced at Josh, then quickly away. "You know how crazy that sounds?"

"Why do you think I never told anyone about it before?"

"When you say they didn't stay dead . . . ," I began.

"They were attacked, throats ripped out, and then they healed all their wounds and walked away."

That sounded far too familiar.

"You never saw them again?" I asked.

He went silent, staring at his feet.

"Doc?" Grace pressed.

"I saw them again." He lifted his head. "As wolves."

I discovered I'd inched away from the door and closer to Grace and Doc Bill. I was having a hard time catching my breath.

"Doc," I managed. "What are you saying?"

"I think he's saying that his friends were bitten by wolves, then they healed their wounds and became wolves themselves," Grace said, as if she were reciting the Miranda warning. "Is that right?"

"That's right," the doctor agreed. Then he pulled a shiny scalpel from his bag and stabbed Josh in the chest.

I gave a little shriek and stumbled back. Grace took a step forward, hand on her weapon, but she didn't draw it. Instead, she laid her other hand on Doc Bill's shoulder. "What the hell?" she asked quietly.

"I've been carrying that scalpel around for sixty years," he explained. "Pure silver."

"That'll kill them?"

"Yep."

"What *them* are you talking about?" I asked.

"What kills on four legs, then disposes of the corpse on two?" Doc asked.

"A man and his dog?"

"Claire," Grace said quietly. "You know what he means."

I did? Maybe. But I didn't want to say so.

Doc had no such problem. "They say Hitler ordered a werewolf army," he murmured. "And Mengele gave him one."

"Mengele," I repeated. "Isn't that the guy—?"

"They called him the Angel of Death. He experimented on those incarcerated in the camps."

We'd heard about the camps before. From Malachi.

From the expression on Grace's face, she remembered that, too.

I couldn't help it; a laugh escaped me, just one. "This is insane."

I waited for Grace to agree with me. Instead, she and the doc exchanged a glance that made me the outsider.

"It's not?" I asked.

Grace let her hand slip from her gun as the doctor removed his pure silver scalpel from the body.

"Every culture has a shape-shifter legend," Grace said.

"Legends are make-believe."

"Not always. Sometimes they're the only way to pass on the truth."

"You believe this?" I demanded.

"I've been considering a lot of strange things since our mauled tourist jumped out a hospital window and disappeared."

That had bothered me, too, but I hadn't made the leap to werewolf.

"There's also the little matter of the swastika at the scene," Grace pointed out.

I'd forgotten about that. In light of Doc's revelations,

I liked the finding of that rune less now than I'd liked it then.

"You found a swastika?" Doc Bill asked.

"A rune." At his confused expression I elaborated. "A talisman. Icelandic in origin, as is the swastika. Before the Nazis got hold of it, the symbol was used for protection and rebirth."

"It might have been used for that *after* they got ahold of it, too," Grace muttered. At my quizzical expression she continued, "If Hitler ordered a werewolf army and Mengele gave him one, perhaps the swastika has something to do with it."

"I'm not following."

"Talismans are kept now for luck, but they were once considered magic."

"Still not getting it."

"Knowing Hitler, he didn't plan to stop at one army."

"Right," Doc agreed. "Once Mengele found the formula, or whatever the hell he was up to, they could have turned the entire Nazi army, as well as every other army they conquered, into something that was very hard to kill."

I got a chill, even though Hitler and his pal Mengele had been dead a long, long time.

"So maybe the swastika wasn't just a symbol they appropriated because they liked the way it looked on their flag," Grace said. "Maybe it had something to do with the changing of the man into the beast. Rebirth, then protection from all enemies." Grace glanced at me and shrugged. "It could happen."

Now I rubbed my eyes. "You two are giving me a major headache."

"I've done a bit of research into magic and shape-shifting myself," Grace said.

I dropped my hand and stared at her. Sure, her

great-grandmother had been a medicine woman, but I'd figured they were discussing herbs and roots, and maybe they had been, along with other things.

"Every culture has a shape-shifter legend," Grace repeated. "Most of the Native American tribes believe they were descended from some sort of animal."

"Believing and being are two different things."

"I'm just saying the shape-shifter legends aren't new. They've been in place since long before the Nazis showed up, so maybe they just appropriated one."

"You're saying we've got a Nazi werewolf running around?" And wouldn't that just be special?

"I have no idea." Grace turned to the doctor. "How do we recognize a werewolf?"

"If you shoot them with silver, they'll explode, in both forms."

"Anything marginally less violent?" I asked.

"In wolf form, a werewolf retains its human eyes."

I started, remembering. "I saw that."

"What?" Grace turned to me. "Where?"

"In . . . a—well, a crystal ball."

"You saw a wolf with human eyes in a crystal ball?"

"I was getting my fortune told. A wolf appeared in the center of the crystal with a bunch of shadows and mist all around. Then Edana, the fortune-teller, said, 'Beware the devil who is a shape-shifter.'"

"Always good advice," Grace muttered. "Did the eyes of that wolf match the eyes of our missing tourist, or anyone else you might know?"

"Too small." I made the shape of the crystal ball with my hands. "I could see the whites but not a color. Not really."

"You saw a werewolf," Doc said. "Wolves, normal ones, don't have whites around their irises. Only people do."

We went silent for several moments, pondering that.

"Let's take stock," Grace said. "The rune was found where the tourist was attacked. He became the beneficiary of miraculous healing and disappeared into the mountains. In theory, he was reborn a werewolf, and now we need to kill him. With silver."

How the hell was I going to explain silver bullets and exploding wolves to . . . everyone?

"Isn't there a way to cure him?" I asked.

"Not that I'm aware of." Doc fixed both Grace and me with a somber gaze. "I don't think you're seeing the entire picture."

"I think we're seeing it fine," Grace said. "Our missing tourist is a werewolf."

"He might be." Doc pressed his lips together as if he didn't want to impart any more bad news, but why stop now? "He probably is. But there's one question you haven't asked yet."

Grace lifted her brows. "What's that?"

"*Who* bit *him*?"

29

"CRAP," I MUTTERED.

"Shit," Grace said more succinctly.

"Exactly," the doctor agreed.

"Wait a second." Grace held up one finger. "Who said anything about biting?"

"Yeah," I agreed, seeing her point. "If the rune's magic, isn't it razzle-dazzle he's a werewolf?"

"Didn't work that way in Germany. Biting was needed. And I didn't see any runes back then. Not that I hung around to search."

"That doesn't mean the rune can't be the cause of the change here."

"True, but then why bother to bite your tourist at all?"

He had a point.

Doc held out his hand. "May I see that rune?"

I checked my right pocket, then my left. My eyes widened. "It's gone."

"That's evidence," Grace said. "I wouldn't have let you keep it if I'd known you were going to lose it."

"Really, and here I was thinking you'd definitely handed it to me so I could do just that."

Grace scowled at my sarcasm, but I didn't care. I couldn't believe I'd misplaced evidence. I was queen of the idiots. Where *was* that dunce cap?

"I had it . . ." I thought back. "At the Gypsy camp. I showed it to the ticket taker and . . ."

Malachi. The big burly bouncer. Hell.

"A few others," I finished.

"Did you leave it there?"

"No. I'm sure of it."

"They steal, you know." We both looked at Doc. "Gypsies. They can't help it."

I sighed. Not him, too.

Grace's lips tightened. "Someone *might* have taken the rune at the lake. *Someone* might also have taken it at your house."

The way Grace put the emphasis on "someone," I knew what someone she meant, and for an instant my heart stuttered.

What if Malachi had slept with me to get his hands on that rune? He had wanted to keep it when I'd shown him the wood chip at his camp, although he hadn't seemed desperate to.

Then I remembered. He'd been taken in for questioning.

"Did you find it on him at the station?" I asked.

Grace's brow creased. "No."

I spread my hands.

"He could have hidden it before he came downstairs this morning."

"If the rune's still at my house, then he didn't steal it."

She couldn't argue with that.

"What I'd like to know," I said, "is how Mengele

made his first werewolf. Maybe the whole rune thing started with him."

"Not necessarily."

"You *said* Hitler ordered him to make a werewolf army."

"That doesn't preclude him making the army from another werewolf," Doc said. "In fact, Hitler was fascinated with wolves and werewolves. His name, Adolf, can be translated as 'Noble Wolf.'"

"You're saying Hitler was a werewolf?"

"He had the personality for it. Once bitten, humans become possessed by the demon lycanthropy. They're no longer quite sane."

"Hit that nail on the head," I muttered. "But Hitler died of cyanide poisoning."

"And a gunshot to the noggin, or so they say. But maybe he died of silver poisoning."

"Is that a euphemism for explosion on contact with a silver bullet?" I asked.

"Considering his cronies dumped gas on him and the new missus, then torched them before the Russians arrived, it's hard to say."

"Does it really matter if Hitler was a werewolf and birthed his own army?" Grace asked. "That army and its descendants are still running around screwing up our life now, and we need to do something about it."

"She's right," Doc agreed, "because soon, if not already, there'll be more than one or two werewolves in these mountains."

"How you figure?"

"The Gypsy woman was right to call them the devil. Werewolves enjoy killing as well as making more of their own. If you don't nip this in the bud, the entire town, the entire state, perhaps the country, will be overrun."

I couldn't believe we were talking about this. Worse than that, I kind of believed it.

"I need to get some silver bullets." Grace glanced at me. "You think they've got them on the Internet?"

"Aren't you jumping the gun?" I lowered my gaze to her weapon, then back to her face. "So to speak. You can't go around blasting wolves with silver bullets. They'll put you in a room with bars on the windows. Wolves, especially around here, *have* to be endangered."

"It isn't a wolf," she said, her mouth set into a stubborn line.

"According to you, it's a person who's morphed into a wolf. You think that explanation will get you in less trouble after you shoot it?"

"If I see a wolf with people eyes and it's coming for me with dripping fangs, I'm not going to wait around to become one, too. I don't care if they put me in a cell."

There was just no talking to her sometimes.

Doc Bill twirled his silver scalpel between two fingers. "A werewolf in human form will be burned at the touch of silver."

"That's handy," Grace said.

"You're going to go around sticking people with silver just to see if they smoke?" I demanded.

"If need be."

"Grace!" I smacked myself in the forehead. "Listen to yourself."

She ignored me. "Thanks for everything, Doc. I'll be in touch."

With a nod at Doc Bill, she left.

"Uh, thanks," I said, and followed.

Dead or not, I didn't want to be in the same room with Josh any longer than I had to.

I caught up with Grace halfway across the parking lot. "Hey." I grabbed her arm. "Where you going?"

"To talk to our suspect."

"But . . ." I frowned. "He isn't a suspect anymore. Josh was killed by a wolf, or near enough."

"What if Cartwright is the wolf?"

I blinked. What if he was?

"I pulled him in because people who'd hurt you were disappearing. That still makes him my prime suspect."

"You really think we have a werewolf running around the forest?"

"Yes." She met my eyes. "I do."

Grace stalked off, and I was left to hurry after her again. "Let's say, for argument's sake, we do," I said. "Why did the werewolf kill Josh instead of making him a werewolf, too, like he did with Ryan Freestone?"

"Once we figure out who he is, we'll ask him."

I was tempted to smack myself in the head again, but I'd only make my impending headache worse.

Malachi glanced up at our entrance, and his welcoming expression turned concerned. "What happened?"

Grace opened her mouth, then shut it again, stumped. How did one ask a man if he turned furry and killed people? Typically, Grace figured it out. "What do you know about werewolves?"

Malachi's eyebrows drew together. "I'm sorry. What?"

"Grace—," I began, but she silenced me with a slash of her hand.

"Werewolves. Men or women become evil creepy things and kill. Ever heard of it?"

"We have legends, like all cultures. Stories to tell around the campfire, used to scare children into staying out of the woods."

Which reminded me . . .

"Why aren't there any children in your caravan?"

"Yeah," Grace said. "Why aren't there?"

"You think we'd drag them across the country and back again? Anyone who chooses to have a family finds a relative to watch over their children while they're away." His dark eyes burned. "Did you think we ate them?"

Grace didn't dignify that question with an answer. "We've had a few wolf attacks in the area."

"A few?" Malachi glanced at me. "I'd heard about only one." Understanding lit his face. "Ah, another to-day then."

Grace didn't confirm or deny. "There hasn't been a wolf in these mountains for centuries, and you insist you don't have a wolf in your caravan."

"We don't. You've seen for yourself all the animals we possess."

"You could have hidden it."

"It isn't that simple to hide a wild animal. However, you aren't really looking for a wolf but a werewolf."

"I'll take either one."

He didn't appear concerned that the sheriff had lost her mind; he didn't even seem to think she had.

"All our problems seemed to start when you showed up," Grace continued.

"We came for the festival, along with a thousand other people you don't know."

"You told us yourself that Hitler incarcerated the Gypsies in the camps. Now we've just discovered that Mengele was making a werewolf army in those camps."

Mal's face went still.

"Coincidence?" Grace asked. "I don't think so."

"My people aren't werewolves, Sheriff."

"Then you won't mind if I search your camp," Grace said.

"That would be fine." Malachi stood. "Shall we?"

"I'll need to talk to everyone in your group. Privately."

"All right."

"Good." Grace indicated I should join her in the hall. Once there she began to pace, muttering, "Gotta find something silver."

I sighed. "Fine. Do you have an earring . . . ?" The word made me pause, then laugh.

Grace stopped pacing. "Have you flipped out?"

"Mal isn't a werewolf." I grinned like a fool.

"How you figure?"

"His crucifix earring."

"I don't think the crucifix thing works on a werewolf, just vampires."

"He's still got silver stuck right through his ear, and he isn't on fire."

Her lips tightened; then she shrugged. "I guess that'll get him off the hook. For now."

A shuffle at the end of the hall caused us to turn. At the sight of Doc, we tensed.

"Is there a problem?" I asked.

His face crumpled into lines of confusion. "Problem?"

"With Josh?" I clarified. All I needed was for him to be a newfangled werewolf that was resistant to silver.

Wouldn't that be special? Running from Josh the werewolf for the rest of my life?

"Oh no. He's deader than dead."

"Which is the best kind of dead," Grace said. "How can I help you, Doc?"

"I remembered my good-luck charm." He reached into his pocket and held up a shiny silver bullet.

"Those of us who reached Berlin had them made the day we arrived."

"I can't take that," Grace said. "Then you won't have one."

Doc put his free hand back into his other pocket and drew out a second. "Ever since I left Germany I've never left home without a few."

"Thanks." Grace accepted the offering. "This will come in handy."

Doc Bill left; Grace continued to stare at the silver bullet.

"How will that come in handy?" I asked. "You wouldn't actually use ammunition that's over sixty years old, would you?"

"Not in a gun, but—"

She tossed the thing at me. I had no choice but to catch it or let it hit me in the nose.

Grace lifted her eyebrows. "Nothing smoking. Guess you're clean."

"You thought I was—?"

"I'm going to think everyone is," Grace said, "until proven otherwise."

30

THE REST OF the day was taken up with searching the Gypsy camp and interrogating the residents. They weren't happy about it, but since Mal ordered them to cooperate, they did. Nevertheless, I heard a lot of muttering in both Rom and Gaelic that didn't sound complimentary.

Grace brought along several of her officers, whom she told as little as possible. Since everyone knew there was a wolf loose and no one trusted the Gypsies, the camp and surrounding area were searched thoroughly without complaint.

They found no secret wolf hideaway, no evidence of a canine of any type. Just the same animals that had always resided in the menagerie.

Once that was established, Grace sent everyone back to town but me and handled the questioning herself, with only Malachi present. Another smart move. How was she going to explain tossing a silver bullet at person after person? With him there, she didn't have to. I got the impression his people were a little scared of him.

What I really wanted to know was what Grace was going to do if one of them caught the bullet and began to burn.

While she quizzed yet another performer, I wandered off. I'd been ordered to keep an eye on things, though what I was supposed to be keeping an eye out for I wasn't sure.

Did Grace think the werewolf would just walk into camp and let us shoot it? And if it did, what would we shoot it with? A single sixty-year-old bullet that didn't fit in any of our guns?

Even though I'd been the only one—left alive anyway—to see a werewolf, and despite Doc Bill's claims and Grace's acceptance, I was still having a hard time believing it.

I stood outside the snake enclosure, which was slightly different from the other menagerie wagons. Since a snake could slither right out between the bars, one wall was made of glass.

Squinting against the glare of the dying sun, I counted snakes. There appeared to be a new one. Well, Malachi had said Sabina picked them up wherever she went. What a strange girl.

The sudden rise and fall of angry male voices drew my attention, and I followed the sound to the largest, most elaborate sleeping wagon in the clearing. Painted on the side was the same strange full, red moon I'd seen on Edana's cards. A hidden moon, whatever it was, must mean something special to the Rom.

Mal and Hogarth stood in front of the tableau arguing in two languages. Grace had to have finished her questioning. I should get back, but I found myself rooted to the spot by the tension that vibrated in the air. I'd never seen any of the Gypsies behave with anything other than respect toward Malachi—until now.

The big man leaned down and put his face near Mal's, spitting out something in Romani before finishing with, "You must do it, *ruvanush,* or all of us will continue to suffer."

"You think I don't know that?" Mal said, the words so anguished I took a step toward him.

The men glanced up. Mal's lips tightened, and he shot a glare at Hogarth, who returned that glare first at him, then at me, before stalking into the trees.

"I'm sorry," I said. "I didn't mean to interrupt."

Mal crossed the short distance, stopping when our bodies were only a whisper apart. He reached out and captured a strand of my hair, rubbing it between his fingers. "Fire and ice," he said. "You're so damn beautiful."

When he looked at me like that, I actually felt beautiful. In his eyes, maybe I was.

"Claire!"

I turned, and Mal let go of my hair, stepping back. As Grace approached, she flicked her hand in Mal's direction, as if casting a spell. Even though I knew what she'd been doing for the past several hours, I still started when something small and shiny flew toward Mal's face.

Mal snatched the bullet out of the air with a speed that blurred his fingers. Then he handed it back to Grace with a sardonic tilt of one brow. "Sorry to disappoint, Sheriff."

She shrugged and accepted the offering. "Can't blame me."

"I don't." With a dip of his head that made his silver earring sway, he left.

"Grace," I began, but she held up her hand.

"Not a single person burned at the touch of silver. I was desperate."

"You sound upset."

"I'm back at square one. I can't exactly question everyone in town." Her shoulders lifted and lowered on a sigh. "I'm tempted to cancel the festival."

"You can't!"

Her eyes met mine. "Oh, I think I can."

"But that'll kill Lake Bluff."

"You think a ravening werewolf won't? We've got so many people here now, the place is like a freaking buffet. No wonder the beast showed up."

"Listen to yourself." I threw up my hands. "You're planning on canceling our main source of income because you think there's a werewolf. You tell the merchants and townspeople that and I can guarantee we'll both be out of a job come Election Day."

"I don't give a rat's ass. Besides, I don't have to say 'werewolf'; 'rabid wolf' will do the trick just as well."

"You can't force people to leave, Grace."

"I know." Her shoulders slumped. "I was just hoping to make things easier, but nothing ever is. We may as well go."

I glanced toward what I assumed to be Mal's wagon, but he was gone.

"Are you staying for the show?" Grace asked.

I thought about it, then shook my head. I wanted to do more research on the rune, along with the whole Hitler werewolf army angle. Besides, I wasn't getting a very warm and fuzzy feeling from any of the Gypsies but Mal. I never had really, except for Sabina, and I hadn't seen her all day.

I followed Grace to where she'd parked her squad car next to my vehicle. Before coming here, I'd retrieved my car, checking the entire house for a trace of the missing rune. I didn't find it.

"I'm going to leave a few men here," she said. "Can't hurt."

The Gypsies bustled about, getting ready for tonight's show. Customers began to trickle in.

"You going home?" I asked.

"Yeah."

We said our good-byes and she pulled away. I sat in my car a few minutes, pathetically waiting to see if Malachi would reappear. I could stay and watch the performance, but after last night and today, I didn't think I'd make it through without falling asleep.

I called the office, but Joyce either wasn't in or wasn't answering. I guess it was kind of late. I dialed her house and got the same response. Maybe she was on her way here. I could wait, or I could assume that if there were a problem, she'd have called me. That's what cell phones were for. I started the car and headed for home.

As I turned off the gravel path from the lake and started up the winding hill toward town, the sun died, spreading shadowy tendrils across the road. Grace was long gone; not even an echo of her taillights flickered in the distance.

Two dozen cars passed me going in the opposite direction, and then the highway was deserted. The last vestiges of light filtered through the pines, making dust motes dance across the windshield.

Everything was so quiet. No wind, not a single birdcall. The air had that still, close feeling that comes right before a tornado. I pressed my foot harder on the accelerator. I just wanted to get home and lock the door behind me.

A dark shape shot in front of the car; I barely had time to brace myself before I hit it. I slammed on the brakes, yanked the wheel to the right, and stopped with a jerk that threw me forward so fast my seat belt caught with a sharp click. Whatever I'd hit hadn't been big enough to cause my air bag to deploy, or maybe I just hadn't hit it hard enough.

I released the catch and jumped out.

A large, black wolf lay beneath the right bumper of the car. Blood darkened the pavement, and his neck was twisted at an impossible angle.

I inched closer, and the beast opened his eyes. "Balthazar," I whispered.

The animal jerked his neck, and the resulting *crack* made me take a single step backward. He shook himself, and blood flew from his fur, pattering against the pavement and the front of the car like rain.

I dived inside. The thunk of the automatic locks made me feel safe for the single instant it took the wolf to land on the hood.

I didn't have time to think, let alone react, though I don't know what I would have done. The wolf with Balthazar's eyes lunged, smacking his snout against the windshield, leaving a smudge of blood and gore across the glass. I yelped and cringed against my seat.

"He can't get in," I assured myself, though the tremor in my voice did not inspire confidence. "Windshields are a lot harder to break than we think."

I reached for the ignition and Balthazar struck again. The glass shattered.

His snout was through, snarling, slavering; his claws scraped against the front of the hood as he fought for purchase. I sat frozen, horrified and fascinated. I'd always known Balthazar had it in for me.

I straightened. I hadn't planned to let him best me in an election; I wasn't going to let him best me in . . . whatever this was.

I snapped on my seat belt and started the car; then I stepped on the gas. The vehicle lurched forward, bringing the wolf dangerously close. I stomped on the brakes, and he flew backward, glass spraying all over the hood. His rump hit the slick surface and slid off the front.

I didn't wait. I slammed my foot onto the accelerator and ran over him.

My front tires rose and fell with a sickening thud; then my back tires did the same.

"Brakes. Reverse." I completed the tasks as fast as I could. Nevertheless, when I glanced over my shoulder, Balthazar was already climbing to his feet.

I hit him once more, ran over him again.

He got up.

"What I could really use is a solid silver car."

Balthazar, the wolf, stood poised in the glare of my headlights. I could keep running over him all night, and it wouldn't do any good. He meant to kill me.

I reached for my cell phone, but I was afraid to take my eyes off the wolf for even an instant. He charged; so did I. A game of chicken.

An instant before impact, there was a sharp crack, and the wolf exploded. I ran over him anyway. I couldn't stop.

I was terrified my car would blow up, too. I didn't pause until I was several yards beyond the fire. Then I peered into my rearview mirror and watched him burn.

Someone had shot him. Someone who knew enough about werewolves to buy a silver bullet and a gun to use it.

My eyes scanned the forest, but no one was there.

31

"YOU'RE SURE IT was Balthazar?" Grace asked.

I'd hurried home, leaving the flaming corpse where it had fallen. I could have called Grace from the car and waited for her to join me, but the idea of sitting on that dark lonely road with Lord only knew what watching me from the woods was too much.

"Believe me, Grace, I've seen the man often enough to recognize his eyes, even in the face of a wolf."

"Well, that's one less missing person." I could hear her getting into the squad car. "And one less headache for you."

"Hey!" I protested. "I wouldn't wish that on anyone."

"I know. But I still find it strange that the dead and undead are all on your shit list."

"Not all. I never met Ryan Freestone."

"Good point. So we're down to two werewolves at least. Unless . . ." She trailed off. I could hear the distant hum of her tires against the pavement.

"Unless?"

"Unless Balthazar was the original werewolf. He was awfully hairy and a huge pain in the behind."

"You think that might be true?"

"It would certainly make things tidier." She sighed. "So probably not. Life is never that easy."

I heard her stop; a car door opened; then footsteps crunched on gravel. "I'm shining a big spotlight right where you said. Nothing on fire, but . . ." *Crunch. Crunch.* "A few ashes. Ground's scuffed. Someone was here."

"Obviously, Grace. *I* didn't shoot him."

"I'm going to pull my car off the road. Try to track this guy. I'll call you later."

"Hold on. Whoever shot Balthazar could be as nutty as . . . well, someone who's nuts."

"Seems pretty sane to me. Shoot werewolf with silver. Kaboom. I wish I'd done it."

"Be careful. If he's on the up-and-up, why didn't he stick around for the band, the parade, the salutations?"

"Got me. Now stay inside, and if you hear or see anything hinky, call nine-one-one."

"So one of your officers can become wolf bait?" I asked, but she was already gone.

I'd run home because it felt safer than the car, especially now that my windshield was history. But standing in my kitchen, staring at the sliding glass, I didn't feel so safe anymore.

But where could I go? I didn't think there was any place, anywhere, that was going to be safe from what was out there.

I checked all the doors, all the windows—not that a lock would help, but it wouldn't hurt. Then I got to work.

On the Internet I found all sorts of strange things. As Grace had said, there were shape-shifter legends all over the place. Shamans told of transforming into their spirit animals. Some carried talismans that contained the essence of their other nature. I wished, not for the first time, that I hadn't lost that rune.

Even the Cherokee had a transformation legend, although theirs involved a panther. The Ojibwe told tales of the Weendigo, a werewolf cannibal, and witchie wolves, invisible wolves that guarded the resting places of warriors.

The Navajo believed in skinwalkers, both witch and werewolf, who donned the skin of an animal and became one.

In Haiti they shared the legend of the *lougaro*, a shape-shifting sorcerer who traveled through the night drinking the blood of children. They also told tales of the Egbo, a leopard society from deepest Africa, which was used to keep the slaves in line by actually turning into leopards on occasion.

When I searched for incidents of miraculous healing, I got a lot of religious Web sites. Made sense.

There was also one site of conspiracy theories where incidents of miraculous healing were proof of aliens, Satan, and complicated government plots.

When I searched for sightings of wolves where wolves weren't supposed to be, I found a Web page on exotic pets. Their theory was that people who had raised wolves from infancy had dumped them when they became too difficult to control.

I was also sent to a Web site on cryptozoology, which studied legendary animals—like Bigfoot. They thought there were werewolves all over the place.

Next, I typed *Gypsies* into the search engine. I got back a helluva lot.

I made my way to a promising Web site, run by an anthropologist in California writing a book about the legends and folktales of the Rom. She asked for any new tales to be sent to her at an e-mail address provided. A table of contents for the book listed the titles of the chapters she'd already written.

One in particular interested me—"Strigoi de lup"—because *loupe* meant "wolf" in some language or another, so it followed that *lup* might be just that in Romani. Wouldn't hurt to ask.

I clicked on the e-mail link, composed my question, and hit *send*. A creak on the staircase made me tilt my head, my ears crackling as I strained to listen.

While I doubted a werewolf would creep quietly up my stairs—I had firsthand experience that a werewolf would just crash through the window—nevertheless, I was nervous.

I grabbed the phone, stuffed it into my pocket, then glanced around my office for a weapon of some sort.

"Where's a silver candlestick when you need one?" I muttered, though I'd never been able to figure out exactly when such a thing would be needed. Now I knew.

I picked up a crystal paperweight. Beggars couldn't be choosers.

Creeping into the hall, I cursed my father's thrifty nature. After years of nagging, I could no longer leave a room without shutting off a light, so the stairwell was as dark as the first floor below it. Shadows swirled. To me, they all looked like wolves.

I was just turning back to the office when another creak made me hurry forward, skirting as close to the wall as I could, hoping if I couldn't see them, they couldn't see me.

Yeah, that always worked.

Reaching the landing, I peered down the steps.

They were empty.

A *scritch* from the other direction made me spin.

Oprah sat in the middle of the carpet, blinking solemnly.

Duh. The cat. How could I have forgotten? In my defense, I *had* been thinking of a hundred other things.

Suddenly Oprah's gaze shifted behind me, and she hissed, then scampered away. I had a really bad feeling something was coming up those stairs. Perhaps something I couldn't see but Oprah sensed.

I wanted to follow the cat to whatever hiding place she'd run to, but I'd let fear drive me from Atlanta. I would not let fear stalk me here.

I spun around to discover Malachi halfway up the steps. I let out the breath I'd been holding in a noisy rush.

The relief I felt not to discover a slavering, snarling man-wolf disappeared as my head went light with delayed reaction.

"Are you crazy?" I held up the paperweight and waved it around. "I could have killed you!"

He approached cautiously. "I don't think that would have killed me."

"Think again," I muttered.

Right now the adrenaline rush was so high, I thought I might fly. I would definitely have caused some damage if I'd put that energy into my pitching arm.

"How did you get in?"

"Did you think any lock could keep me out?"

"You couldn't knock? Ring the bell?"

"I didn't want to wake you."

"Only frighten me half to death." The paperweight dropped from my suddenly limp fingers, and I swayed.

"Claire!" He took the remaining steps at a run, catching me around the waist and dragging me away from the edge.

"I'm okay."

"You're not. What happened?"

"Besides your breaking into my house and scaring the shit out of me?"

"Yes." He stared into my face, frowning. "Besides that."

How did he know? Had he read my mind? Or had he been in the forest earlier with a gun?

No. If Malachi had shot Balthazar, he would have told me so. He knew what Grace suspected, and he hadn't been shocked by it. I told him everything.

When I was through, he carried me to my room, then kicked the door shut behind us. He set me gently on the bed, turned the bedside lamp on low, then lay at my side.

"I could have lost you," he whispered.

"You believe me?"

"I've seen so many things, *a stor,* so many. A man who turns into a beast?" He lifted one shoulder. "I'm certain it could happen." Malachi gathered me into his arms. "I should never have let you out of my sight."

Oddly, his need to protect me didn't make me want to shriek and break free as it had when my father had tried it. Because something had changed in me? Or because I'd gone out in the big bad world and realized I needed protecting? Perhaps it had happened when I'd come home to be safe and discovered I wasn't.

"You can't be with me every minute," I said. Soon he wouldn't be here at all.

The thought made my throat clench. Oh boy. I hadn't gone and fallen in love with him, had I? That would be stupid. Of course, in matters of men, "stupid" seemed to characterize me.

Malachi's dark eyes stared into mine as if he knew my thoughts. I just wanted him to kiss me, to make me forget.

Did I lean toward him? Did I pucker up? Regardless, he took my face in his big, hard, dark hands and pressed his lips to mine.

He tasted me as if he never had before, nibbling gently, sucking my bottom lip into his mouth, then sweeping his tongue across my teeth. His fingers tangled in my hair; mine tangled in his. My thumb brushed against his earring, and it swung to and fro, catching the lamplight and reflecting sparkles across the ceiling like falling stars.

I tugged at his blousy white shirt until it came loose from his black pants, then ran my hands all over his warm, smooth skin. Maybe my near-death experience had made me bold, or maybe he just did, because I reached between us and cupped him, rubbing my thumb down the length of his erection until he grabbed my wrist. "Keep that up and we'll be done afore we start."

He left me to kick off his boots, lose the pants and socks, then stood at the end of the bed hesitantly. "May I undress you, *a chroi*?"

His voice was so quiet; his eyes fell as if he expected me to say no, to continue to hide my body from him as if I were ashamed. But I didn't ever plan to be ashamed again.

"Yes," I whispered.

His gaze lifted, both hope and wariness alight in his eyes. "You're sure?"

"Completely."

He sank down on the bed and reached for the buttons of my blouse, opening each one so slowly I wanted to help him. Now that I'd agreed to making love in the light, I wanted it to happen. I wanted nothing to stop us, especially a last-minute panic attack.

When the last fastening opened and my blouse fell away, the heat of his gaze was a caress. He trailed one finger down the center of my stomach, then hooked it in my slacks and flicked the single button at the waistband. He drew the zipper lower, the sound loud in the pulsing silence.

My pants descended, the slither of cloth on skin making me shudder with both reaction and anticipation. Then he bent his dark head and kissed me, hot and eager against the thin nylon of my panties.

I arched, and his mouth became hard, demanding; his beard, rough at the end of the day, added another sensation against the most intimate part of me. My body tightened, and he retreated, hooking his fingers in my underwear and tossing them with the rest of our clothes on the floor.

The only item of clothing that remained was my front-clasp white cotton bra. I wished momentarily that I'd worn sexy underwear, but it was a foolish wish since I didn't own any. I'd never been the type. But perhaps, with him, I could be.

I figured he'd flip the catch, release my breasts, indulge in a little foreplay, and since my body was already singing from the slow, sensual assault of his hands and his mouth, anything he wanted right now was fine with me.

So when he covered my body with his, slipping gently inside, I merely sighed and welcomed him in.

The lamp splashed golden light across his sleek skin; his pupils expanded, blending into the black of his irises. He appeared almost otherworldly. I might have been frightened except this was Malachi, a man who'd been nothing but honest and gentle with me. He'd brought me out of the cold, scary place that had been my life, and despite the strange things going on all around us, I felt stronger, saner, happier, because of him.

His thrusts slowed, as if he wanted to make this last forever. I indulged my need to touch him, running my fingers through his hair, along his face, then spreading my palms across his chest, shoulders, and down the long expanse of his back. I showed him a better rhythm, a little faster, a little deeper, and soon we were both gasping on the edge of the world.

"Claire." He nuzzled my breasts, then seemed to notice for the first time that my bra was still in place.

Shifting his weight, he used one hand to crunch the clasp at the center. The plastic scratched my skin, the sensation sharp, even as the bra slid open, and his hand smoothed over me, cupping me almost reverently, watching himself touch me, the bronze shade of his hand stark against my moon-pale skin.

His fingertip scraped my birthmark, and he tilted his head so the lamplight caught in his eyes and caused a flare at the center like a flashbulb.

Then he lowered his mouth, touched his lips to the mark, and whispered, "It's you."

Though muffled against my skin, his voice sounded anguished, but before I could ask what was wrong, he thrust again, and I forgot everything as the orgasm carried us away.

But it wasn't over quickly; instead he continued to thrust, face now buried against my neck, his hair cascading over my face, the water and earth scent of him filling my senses even as he filled my body again and again with himself.

He pushed me toward the edge, then reached between us and forced me there again with a combination of his fingers and his lips and his tongue. The second time I came crying his name, and when the tremors died away, I barely registered him turning off the lamp and tucking me against him beneath the quilt before I fell asleep.

When I awoke well before the sun did, he was gone, and I wondered for just an instant if he'd been there at all. But I could smell him in the room, on the sheets, on me.

I stretched, my body a little sore, but a sore I wouldn't mind experiencing again and again.

Though I would have liked to remain in bed dreaming a while longer, worry plucked at the edges of my mind.

Grace hadn't called, so as soon as I was dressed I called her, despite the lack of sun on the horizon.

No answer. I tried her cell and her office with the same result. What would I do if something had happened to her?

I grabbed shoes I could use to tramp around the woods should any tramping be needed, but when I headed for the stairs, my computer chimed softly to signal an incoming message.

I hesitated, then decided it could be Grace e-mailing me a progress report rather than waking me. As soon as I jiggled my mouse and my computer sprang to life, so did the disappointment.

Not Grace. Instead, the anthropologist had replied to my e-mail:

Ms. Kennedy,
Thank you for your interest in my book. Copies will be available through my Web site for $29.99. To answer your question, a strigoi de lup *is a Romanian sorcerer. Usually a pretty young woman in a white dress, she is said to lead the wolves. In some legends she does this by becoming one beneath the light of the moon. She protects her identity by killing anyone who sees her in that form and talks about it.*

An interesting legend, but we hadn't had a Romanian sorcerer in these parts in . . . forever.

I made a copy of the e-mail, tucked it into my pocket, and headed out the door.

32

DAWN SPREAD ACROSS Lake Bluff as I drove to Grace's house. Considering the state of my windshield, I'd backed my dad's Ford Focus out of the garage. It smelled like him—cigarettes, mint Life Savers, and Old Spice.

"Hey, Dad," I whispered, and patted the dash.

The longer I stayed here, the more our past disagreements seemed just that—the past. I could see now why he'd loved his job, this place, the people, so much, and I was sorry I hadn't stuck around and at least given the job a try. I wasn't all that bad at it. In fact, I was better at being the mayor than I'd ever been at anything else.

"I'm here now," I said, and for just a minute I felt as if he'd heard me.

Mist still shrouded the tips of the mountains, pink and gold and orange swirling through the wash of green and blue.

Grace's windows were dark; I wasn't surprised. She was the kind of person who got up at the last minute, drank a single cup of coffee in the shower, and ran out the door with wet hair.

I had an odd sense of déjà vu as I climbed the porch steps, rang the bell, then waited vainly for her to answer. I glanced through the glass on each side, saw nothing, and headed around back. However, this time when I knocked, the door swung open.

"Grace?" I stepped into the kitchen. The house was as silent as a tomb.

The cliché made my skin crawl, so I hit the lights and shouted, "Grace!"

The table was covered with guns and ammo, the boxes from a specialty gun shop in Tennessee that boasted "made-to-order anything." Places like that gave me the willies, but I guess, in this case, it was lucky for us they existed.

Grace must have dropped a bundle to get this stuff here so quickly. The truly interesting thing was that they had to have had the bullets ready-made to have sent so many, so fast. Which only made me think we were a little slow on the uptake in regard to the existence of werewolves.

It wasn't like Grace to leave loaded weapons where anyone could find them, just as it wasn't like Grace to leave her back door open if she wasn't at home. It really, really wasn't like Grace to do both at the same time.

I picked up one of the guns, a pistol with a safety that I made certain was on, and slowly made my way through the house.

She wasn't on the first floor—dead or alive—so I headed up the stairs. The bathroom was empty and as dry and cool as a midwinter Sunday. Grace hadn't taken a shower and gone to work, absentmindedly leaving all her guns and ammo behind and forgetting to lock the door. Besides, the squad car was right outside.

On the one hand, the car made me relax. She'd returned here after following the mysterious shooter into the woods last night. On the other hand, the car made me really nervous. Where was she?

"Grace!" My voice was both angry and frightened— a combination that was becoming too familiar lately.

She wasn't in her bedroom; either the bed hadn't been slept in or she'd made it, tucking in the corners as anally as a sergeant major.

I remembered how I'd found her the last time and pulled out my cell, hitting the speed dial for hers. The distant *brrrring* drew me out of her room and toward the second flight of stairs that led to her dad's former attic lair.

Well, I had wanted to see what she'd done with the place.

I climbed the winding staircase, my eyes on the dark circle at the top. Suddenly I wasn't so sure I should go up there, but what choice did I have? Grace might be hurt, or worse.

I reached the landing. The knob turned in my hand, the door swinging open with a head-splitting shriek. I felt around for the light, flicked the switch, but nothing happened. Luckily, the sun was up just high enough to push golden tendrils through the single window and illuminate the books and the beakers, the test tubes and the toads.

Make that toad. In an aquarium. I didn't think it was a pet since it was as dead as Balthazar, though a lot less crispy.

Crystals lay scattered about; dream catchers hung from the ceiling. I didn't think they were of Cherokee origin, but whatever. The thing that bothered me the most was the swastika-marked rune atop her worktable.

"Lucy, you've got some 'splainin' to do." I scooped up the rune—I couldn't tell if it were the one I'd "lost" or another one entirely—then thundered back down two flights of stairs and out the back door to find Grace emerging once again from the forest wearing nothing but a snow-white robe. However, this time that meant a whole lot more to me than it had last time.

I lifted the gun. "*Strigoi de lup*, I presume?"

Instead of being concerned, she snorted and strode toward me. "Gibberish will get you a smack in the head before I've had coffee."

"Grace." I put both palms around the grip of the gun to steady it. "You're a werewolf."

"Am not," she returned, then stopped, contemplating my face. "But you think I am. Tell me this, genius. If I'm a werewolf, how did I manage to toss a silver bullet at fifty Gypsies, or load the damn guns without frying my fingers off?"

"I only have Doc's word that silver causes burns in human form."

"You'll just have to trust me."

"What the hell are you up to, Grace?"

"Nothing that affects this."

"No?" I displayed the rune between my thumb and forefinger.

She growled with annoyance and snatched the gun out of my hand. Lucky for her I hadn't removed the safety.

"Don't be an ass." She stalked into the house, calling over her shoulder, "Come on. We need to talk."

Since she was right, I followed her inside.

"You first," she said, as she measured coffee grounds into the basket. "What are you doing here at this time of the morning, and why do you think I'm a werewolf?"

I handed her the copy of the anthropologist's e-mail. We sat at the table, and when she was done reading, she handed it to me. "I'm not Romanian."

"I've seen you coming out of the woods twice dressed in a white robe and nothing else."

"I'm Cherokee. I like to commune with nature."

"Why don't I believe that?"

Her lips tilted. "Yesterday you were arguing with me about the existence of werewolves, today you think I am one?"

"I saw that wolf with Balthazar's eyes. Seeing goes a long way toward believing."

"Well, until you see me sprout a tail and fangs, would you mind not shooting me?"

"I wouldn't have shot you," I said.

"Damn straight, with the safety on."

I should have known she'd notice that.

"What's with the dead toad?" I asked.

"He was Gramma's."

"How old is that thing?"

Her green eyes met mine over her second cup of coffee. "You don't want to know." She took a sip, then set the mug down, revealing a slash of dirt across her wrist.

"What happened?"

She turned her hand over; it was filthy. "I fell."

Grace had been voted least likely to fall in high school. Grace was . . . graceful, almost freakishly so.

She lifted one foot onto her knee. The sole was scratched. "I should know better than to walk around in the woods barefoot. Stepped on a stone. Winced, tripped. Bam." She spread her hands. Both of them were in need of a good scrubbing.

"You should get cleaned up."

"I will. Then we'll head to the camp." She studied

me for a minute. "I've been thinking that maybe silver doesn't hurt them at all."

"Sure hurt Balthazar."

"If that was a silver bullet."

"From Doc's eyewitness testimony, I'd say that was a silver bullet."

"What if silver doesn't hurt them in human form?"

I thought about Mal's earring, the testing Grace had done of the Gypsies. "That could be a problem."

"Or maybe our culprit is superwerewolf," Grace continued. "Able to resist silver, wolfsbane, and pentagrams."

At my curious glance she continued. "I did a little research, too. Wolfsbane, or monskshood, is said to drive off werewolves. Which makes sense because it's extremely poisonous."

"And the pentagram?"

"There are quite a few different beliefs about those. A few state that the symbol will repel a werewolf like a crucifix repels a vampire."

"And the others?"

"That a pentagram is actually the mark of a werewolf. You didn't happen to see a tattoo on Cartwright's chest or his palm or any other part of his body?"

"Why are you so set on believing the werewolf is a Gypsy?"

"Our troubles started when they showed up. They travel with animals. Who's to say they don't have one more than they're admitting—one that isn't an animal all the time? The rune was found near their camp. They insisted on complete privacy on 'their land' in the days leading up to the appearance of said wolf. And that the Gypsies were in the camps where Mengele made werewolves is just too big of a coincidence to ignore."

"Not *these* Gypsies."

"Not necessarily." Grace shrugged. "If they're werewolves, they live forever."

"You've been thinking about this a lot."

"It's what I do. So, any pentagram on Cartwright?"

"No. And I saw pretty much all of him."

Grace lifted her brows. "Is he as good as he looks?"

"Better."

"Just your luck he could be a murderous, blood-drinking beast."

"Yeah, wouldn't that figure. But . . ." I paused, biting my lip.

"You don't think he is."

"Doc said once humans are infected they become different. Evil. Mal's one of the kindest men I've ever known."

"Unless he's breaking someone's nose."

He had seemed pretty different while dealing with Josh, as well as Balthazar. But I still couldn't resolve "murderous beast" with Malachi Cartwright.

"Getting back to pentagrams," Grace continued, "they can be used to conjure good or evil. One point ascendant for good, two points up welcomes the devil."

"If I ever see one, I'll be sure and remember that little cheat. Now, as long as we're talking about symbols, why don't you tell me how you got your hands on this one?" I tapped the rune that lay between us on the table.

"I found it in the woods last night."

"In the dark, with all the prehistoric trees and creepy crawlies, you happened to stumble upon this little ole thing."

Her eyes narrowed. "You say that as if you don't believe me."

"I don't."

"You think I stole this from you and . . . what? Turned myself into a *strig de* whatever?"

"It's just weird, is all."

"What isn't lately?"

"You know you could tell me anything and it wouldn't matter," I said.

"I could tell you I'm a ravening beast under the moon? That I killed Balthazar, Josh, and tourist man, and it wouldn't matter to you?"

"Well, maybe it would matter, but I'd still love you, and I'd still be your friend."

"But you wouldn't turn your back on me."

"Hell, Grace, I don't do that now."

Suddenly we were grinning at each other like fools.

"Well, thanks," she said. "That's probably the nicest thing anyone's ever said to me."

She definitely needed to meet more people.

"Why don't you tell me exactly what happened last night?"

"Okay." Grace thought for a minute. "After you called, I went to the scene, found the stirred dirt and ashes, and followed an iffy trail."

"What kind of trail?"

Her eyes met mine. "Wolf tracks only."

"No shoes?"

"No."

"Weird." Last time I checked, wolves couldn't fire guns. So who had shot Balthazar and why hadn't they left any tracks?

"Very," Grace agreed. "It took me several hours to finish because it was dark and the signs weren't strong, but eventually the pitter-patter of wolfy feet led me back to the camp."

"What camp?"

"What camp do you think?"

"Summer camp?" I offered hopefully. Grace stared

at me until I was forced to admit, "Balthazar, the wolf, headed out from the Gypsy camp."

"As near as I can tell."

"And the rune?"

"Underneath the same tree as last time, which, by the way, is exactly where his trail ended."

"There's something hinky about that tree."

"You think?" Grace asked. "Even if lover boy isn't the original source of the werewolf, he knows more than he's saying."

Malachi had lied; I don't know why I was disappointed. I'd thought he was different, but he was still a man. Maybe.

"We searched that place from top to bottom yesterday," I pointed out. "Not a wolf in sight."

"That was before the show. Everyone and their kid sister was out there last night."

"Which means anyone could have done whatever it takes to create a werewolf out in those woods, and it wasn't necessarily a Gypsy."

"Theoretically, yes."

"But you don't think it was just anyone."

"We've got a lot of circumstantial evidence, but it all points to the Gypsies. Which just makes me suspicious as hell of a frame job, but who'd want to frame them? The two main suspects on my 'pissed off at the Gypsy king' list are dead."

"Which brings us right back to the Gypsies."

"Exactly. So let's head out there." Grace stood. "I'll be ready in a few minutes."

GRACE WAS TRUE to her word, returning ten minutes later in her uniform, with her hair braided into a long, wet tail down the center of her back.

"Ever hear of a hair dryer?" I asked.

"They give me split ends."

"Running around with wet hair is going to give you pneumonia."

"You know darn well wet hair has nothing to do with getting sick."

"So they say." But I'd never been convinced.

The drive to the lake passed in silence until Grace turned onto a narrow hunting trail a good half mile from the Gypsy camp.

"What are you doing?" I asked.

"We wanna find out anything, we need to go about this a little quieter than usual."

"Sneak up and spy on them you mean?"

"Yep. If you've had an attack of conscience, you can wait here."

I didn't like the idea of spying, but since I liked the idea of marauding werewolves even less, I followed Grace into the woods.

A heavy bank of clouds drifted over the sun. Shadows danced through the leaves, making me glance to the right, then the left, on more than one occasion, fearing I'd seen something more solid than a flicker flitting between the trees.

"I'm getting a bad feeling," Grace murmured.

I had the same feeling, but I kept it to myself. What good would talking about it do? I'd only become more spooked.

We reached a slight incline. Grace dropped to her stomach and peered over the edge. I did the same. We lay on a rise that sloped down into the trampled, grassy area used for parking. Not a soul was in sight there or near the surrounding wagons.

I consulted my watch. Early, but there should still be someone hanging about.

"Bad feeling getting badder," Grace said.

We waited a few more seconds; then Grace got to her feet and headed down, hand on her weapon—one of those I'd seen on the kitchen table, loaded with silver.

When we reached the edge of the camp Grace paused, putting her finger to her lips. Then she closed her eyes, took a deep breath, and held it as she cocked her head.

Moments later she released the breath and opened her eyes. As always, the flash of green against her dusky cheekbones surprised me. "No one's here."

I tended to agree with her, but— "How do you know?"

"Deserted places have a . . . well . . ." She looked away. "An aura."

"An aura," I repeated. "Is that like a musty smell?"

"Hell!" She stalked toward the animal wagons. I hurried after.

We rounded the corner at the same time, then stared at a whole lot of empty.

"This is not good," Grace said.

"Understatement. Where could they be?"

"Where do you think?" She swept her arm toward the trees and nearly clocked me in the nose. "We're going to need Animal Control." She began to pace, thinking out loud. "Tranquilizer guns. If that grizzly or that cougar gets near town—"

She didn't have to finish. She didn't have to tell me to hurry. I headed back the way we'd come, scrambling up the incline and over the top with Grace on my heels.

As if by mutual agreement, we stopped, turned— and hit the dirt as if our legs had been swept out from under us.

Animals slipped from the trees and into the Gypsy camp.

Grace drew her weapon, but there were too many of them for it to do us any good if they suddenly heard or smelled or sensed us up here and decided to attack. In fact, there were a lot more of them than there should be.

Grace flicked a glance at me, eyebrows furrowed. She was having the same double-vision problem that I was.

Out of the trees lumbered two grizzlies, two cougars, two zebras—was there an ark around here we weren't aware of?

Multiple animals continued to appear. More than two of each in the categories of monkeys, snakes, and birds but also more than what I'd tallied the first day.

To my amazement, the cougars weren't tearing apart the zebras. The grizzlies weren't eating everything. They appeared to be one big, happy family, and they all seemed to be waiting for something. Then Malachi stepped out of the trees.

I tensed. Just because the grizzlies were trained, or at least one of them was, didn't mean Malachi might not be mistaken for breakfast.

But he walked among them unafraid, touching certain animals on the head, the shoulder, the tail. He even leaned down and brushed his fingers across the back of a snake. Straightening, Malachi opened his arms as if welcoming them.

Mist spread from his fingertips, swirling across the assembled throng. Clouds formed above those he'd touched, and the sun sparkled through the haze, seeming to rain diamonds onto the backs of the chosen ones.

They shimmered, and then they shifted.

One second a great lumbering grizzly bear gaped at the sky; the next a naked Hogarth straightened from four legs to two. A cougar became Molly; a zebra turned into the lithe young woman with the streak of white through her dark, dark hair. Two monkeys morphed into slightly hairy older men—one I recognized as the snarly ticket taker. Another became Edana, the fortune-teller, which kind of explained her joke with the paw. The snake grew and grew, writhing, expanding; then, in the blink of an eye, Sabina stood in its place.

"Oh boy," Grace breathed.

I couldn't speak at all. I could only stare at Malachi while the mist swirled around him.

The good news? He wasn't an animal.

The bad news? I doubted he was entirely human, either.

33

Y OU CAN COME down now." Malachi looked up. "No one will hurt you."

The people and animals wandered off to their respective wagons, except for Sabina, who stared at us, too. Snakes trailed over her bare feet, and one twined up her ankle.

"Sabina!" Mal barked.

She lifted the snakes into her hands, tossing several around her neck and over her shoulders before heading toward their enclosure.

Mal started toward us. I guess running wasn't an option.

Grace and I climbed to our feet. She kept her gun in her hand, though she did point it at the ground.

He stopped in front of us, casting a quick, almost guilty glance in my direction.

"When were you going to tell me?" I asked.

"I just did."

"You *told* me nothing. We snuck in and watched."

"He knew we were here," Grace said.

"How?"

"He can change men and women into beasts and back again. You think he isn't aware of everything that goes on around him?"

"Is that true?" I asked.

"I can't change them *into* beasts; I can only change them back again."

"They're shape-shifters?" Grace asked.

"Of a kind."

"Maybe you should start at the beginning," I said.

"Maybe I should." He swept out his hand in a "be my guest" gesture. "Let's take this inside."

Moments later Grace and I sat in Mal's wagon. His bed was made, probably because he'd spent the majority of the night in mine, then the rest of it doing whatever he'd been doing in the woods with the others.

His clothes spilled out of drawers built beneath his bed. A single table was covered with books and papers; the titles reminded me of the ones I'd found in Grace's attic. A lot on the paranormal—spells, magic, curses.

"What are you?" I asked.

"A . . . Well, there really isn't a word for it in English. I . . . can do things."

Grace leaned forward. "Magic?"

"Yes."

"Why?"

"Because I'm Rom."

"All Gypsies, I mean Rom, can do magic?" I guess that was a stupid question, since we'd just seen half of them change from an animal into a person.

"No. Only the pure."

My eyes narrowed. Terms like "pure" and "master race" really set my teeth on edge lately.

"Pure in what way?" I asked.

"Pure Rom blood. Not intermingled with the *gadje*."

"I'd think that would be pretty hard to do in this day and age."

"We aren't exactly from this day and age."

My head was starting to hurt. I rubbed my eyes and let Grace take over.

"You time-traveled?" she asked.

He actually had the guts to laugh. "No. I was born in 1754."

"Sure you were, pal."

His eyebrows lifted. "You saw a grizzly become a man, but I couldn't be born two hundred and fifty years ago?"

Grace bit her lip. "Fine. Whatever. Go on."

"There was a *chovhani,* a witch, and she—" He glanced at me, frowned, then looked away. "She loved me, but I could not love her back."

Had that been a hint? Did it matter? Any future I might have dreamed of was lost. He was a magician? A warlock? A sorcerer? I wasn't up on the terminology. Regardless, he was something "other" and his people were shape-shifters. How's that for a good excuse not to commit?

"You pissed off a witch," Grace said. "Nice job. Let me guess, she cursed your ass."

"And the rest of me, as well."

Grace's lips twitched; I didn't find any of this funny.

"How is that possible?" I asked.

"Easy enough," Grace murmured. "With the right spell and a little bit of power."

"A lot of power," Mal corrected. "She had so much more than me."

"Should have told her what she wanted to hear," Grace said. "Saved yourself centuries of trouble."

"I couldn't tell her that I loved her if it wasn't the truth."

Grace snorted. "He's definitely from a different century."

"Where is this witch?" I asked.

"Dead."

"Yet you're still alive."

He dipped his head, though his eyes had gone dark and haunted.

Grace stared at him with a speculative expression. "She cursed you to immortal wandering?"

"Yes."

"And what about your people?"

"We were a *kumpa'nia*. A caravan and a family. I would not leave them behind to be with her." He glanced at me again. "Just to touch her was forbidden. But she was beautiful, and I was weak."

"Sounds like you were human," Grace said.

Mal's lips twisted, both a grimace and a smile. "She made them *jel'sutho'edrin*, companion animals, bound to me. They cannot leave me, ever, and neither can I leave them." His words and manner became more formal, more old-world, the longer he spoke of the past. "If it wouldn't have been for my own magic, I would have been completely alone, without human companionship, for eternity."

"But you were able to change them back?"

"My magic can only hold them in human form for a few days at a time."

"They take turns," I said.

"Yes."

"How did they become different animals?" Grace asked. "I'd think it would be easier to curse them all to be one thing."

"The spell gave them a choice of which animal they

wanted to become. Most chose a beast they resembled in life—like Hogarth and Moses, brothers and twins. Many husbands and wives, like Molly and Jared, chose the same animal."

"Molly is the cougar you called Mary?"

" 'Molly' is an Irish nickname for 'Mary.' She prefers to be called the English form of her name when in her animal shape." He shrugged. "Some do, to remind both themselves and the others that they are two natured."

As if anyone would forget.

"Where's your horse?"

"Far away in the forest. He doesn't care to be around so many animals at once."

"He's not cursed?"

"No, Benjamin's truly a horse." Malachi shrugged. "I like them."

One thing was bugging me. Well, more than one thing, but— "Why would Sabina choose to become a snake?"

"Her arm. Snakes have no need of them."

"Wouldn't an infirmity like that be healed by shape-shifting?" Grace asked.

"This is a curse, Sheriff, not a blessing."

"Why would anyone else choose to be a snake?" I wondered.

"They didn't."

"But—" I glanced through his single window in the direction of the snake wagon.

"Those are also truly snakes. As one herself, most of the time, Sabina has an affinity with them. She always did, even before the curse."

"Why can't she talk?"

He looked out the window, too. "She hasn't spoken since she became two natured."

The guilt in his voice was reflected on his face.

Sympathy flooded me, but I bit back any words of comfort. He wasn't the man I'd thought he was, and I wasn't exactly sure what to do with that.

"I tested every one of you with silver," Grace said. "But no one reacted."

"Silver has no effect on this curse."

"What does?"

Malachi spread his hands. "I have no idea."

"Where's the wolf?" I asked.

Confusion flickered across his features. "There isn't one."

"Don't start lying now, Cartwright," Grace said. "It'll put a quick end to my happy mood."

"You have a happy mood?" he muttered, and her eyes narrowed. "I *meant,* we have no wolf in the menagerie."

"Then what bit my tourist?" Grace asked.

"A wolf."

"Cartwright, I swear—"

"There *is* a wolf, but the animal isn't one of us. Some have sensed it, smelled it, even seen it from afar, but no one's been able to get close."

"I followed the tracks of the wolf that attacked Claire back to your camp." Grace showed him the rune. "I found this under the same tree as the last one, right where the trail ended. I think someone's using this rune to either create werewolves or become one."

"I've never heard of such a thing."

"Which doesn't make it impossible."

"Why would my people bother? They're already shape-shifters."

"Don't ask me," Grace said. "I'm figuring this out as I go."

"The wolf seems attracted to our caravan," Malachi murmured. "Perhaps because we're made up of others who shape-shift. We'll leave immediately." I started, but he didn't even glance my way. "We can lead it away from here, into the mountains where there aren't any people."

"And then?" Grace asked.

Malachi stood and went to the window, staring at the distant peaks. "Then we will do what must be done."

"I'll go with you," Grace said.

"No." He didn't even turn around.

"I'm a tracker, a hunter, and I've got plenty of silver bullets."

"You're needed here. What if the beast eludes us and returns? What if it's made more of its kind and sprinkled them throughout your town?"

"Hell," Grace muttered.

"Yes, it will be."

"You seem to know an awful lot about werewolves."

"I know a lot about everything. I'm two hundred and fifty-three years old. Now, if you'll excuse me, I need to get my people moving."

Grace and I headed for the exit. Once there, she paused. "You'll let me know what happens?"

"Of course."

She stepped outside. I stayed inside and closed the door. Grace was smart enough not to pound on it and ask what I was doing. She knew I had to say good-bye.

I turned and he was right there; his breath stirred my hair. I stared at his throat, watched the muscles flex and release as he swallowed, resisted the urge to lean forward and press my mouth to the shallow well above his collarbone.

"Will I ever see you again?" I asked.

"That wouldn't be a good idea."

"And last night was?"

"I couldn't help myself."

"Because I'm so irresistible? Please—"

He grasped my forearms, drawing me onto my toes as he kissed me. He tasted of cinnamon and sunshine; he smelled like the ocean at dawn. I'd never been kissed with such passion, such desperation and just a hint of sadness. I couldn't help but kiss him back.

I wanted to touch him, but he clutched me so tightly, both holding me near yet keeping me away, I couldn't lift my arms past my own hips. Two weeks ago, being held like this would have frightened me. Now I only wanted it to go on and on.

Outside, the call of one of the Gypsies rose above the shuffle of the wind, and Malachi tore his mouth from mine. His eyes darker than midnight, I could see myself reflected in their depths. A tiny version of me trapped there for eternity.

I raised my hand, and he released my arm so I could cup his face. He hadn't shaved, and his beard scraped my palm. "Isn't there any way to break the curse?"

He flinched, as if I'd struck him instead of caressed him, and backed up, shaking his head mutely.

"I could go with you."

His eyes widened, and he found his voice. "No!"

He turned sharply, leaving me to stand near the door all alone. "Because I'm *gadje*?"

"My people will never accept you, and I can't be parted from them any more than they can be parted from me." His head bent between slumped shoulders. "I'll never die, Claire, and you will."

"Dying is a long time from now."

"Dying is often closer than you think."

I remembered Edana's prediction—I might die, or not, soon—and shivered.

"This isn't love," he murmured. "It's only been a week."

He was right. The new and exciting emotions I'd experienced had merely been leftover satisfaction from a terrific night of sex. Malachi knew better.

His good-bye seemed rehearsed. How many times in the past two-plus centuries had a woman fallen in love with him because he'd made her come?

More than I wanted to know about.

34

G RACE WAITED IN the car. She glanced at my face and started to drive.

"Tonight's the bonfire," she said.

I nodded. Grace knew as well as I did the schedule for the festival. It hadn't changed in the last forty years; I doubted it would change in the next forty. Unless Lake Bluff grew too poor to have the festival.

"I made some calls," Grace continued. "Logan's campaign manager agreed to keep the specifics of Logan's death under wraps for the time being."

"How'd you get him to agree to that?"

"Threatened to feed the media the truth about his golden boy. Works every time."

Interesting. Even though he was dead, they didn't want it touted on the national news that Josh Logan had been a rapist.

"We can still go public once this is over," Grace said. "But right now I'd like to keep the media frenzy out of town—even though the idea of feeding a few journalists to the werewolf does have its appeal. No offense."

"None taken," I said. A lot of people held the same opinion, including me, about certain reporters. "I'd rather let this drop. Josh can't hurt anyone anymore. I want to forget."

Grace glanced at me searchingly, her brow creased with worry. "You don't have to decide now."

"I *have* decided. That part of my life is as dead as Josh." I hoped.

While I should be happy that I didn't have to tell the world my private horror, right now I couldn't manage to feel happy about anything.

"I also talked to Doc Bill," Grace continued. "The fur found on Josh's body tested positive for wolf."

"We figured that."

"It's always good to have data to back up a theory." Grace bit her lip. "I'm not sure what to do about Balthazar."

"What is there to do?" I asked. "Sweep up what's left of him and put it in an urn?"

"That might be a little hard to explain."

"What isn't lately?"

"He's listed as a missing person; it might be best to allow everyone to continue to think that. I'm not sure how to account for the explosion, let alone the tail. I've got the same issue with Freestone, even though no one's actually seen him get furry."

"Freestone may be long gone."

"And if he's a werewolf—"

"We know he is."

"Yeah." Grace sighed. "So if he's hightailed it to the mountains or, worse, to a big city—"

"There are going to be a lot more werewolves soon."

"I wish I knew what to do about that, too. Would be nice if there were some sort of army you could call to take care of this."

"Wouldn't it, though?"

"I'm going to have to go after him."

"I know."

Silence fell, broken only by the hum of the tires against the pavement.

"Parade tomorrow at ten." Grace went back to listing things I already knew. "Picnic at noon, followed by fireworks just after sundown. Then the eclipse and we're home free."

As long as the werewolf, or wolves, followed Malachi's wagons out of town.

"Make sure everyone's got silver bullets," I blurted.

Grace turned in to her driveway. "It's one little werewolf. Maybe two. What could happen?"

I hated it when people said things like that.

I'd left my dad's car at Grace's, so I drove directly to work, where I discovered an empty office. Since Balthazar had . . . disappeared, and his editorial diatribes, too, the number of people requesting appointments had dwindled.

I glanced at my watch. Joyce should be here, but she wasn't.

A quick perusal of her desk revealed she had been here, not too long ago. Where was she now?

The ladies' room was empty, as was the break room. I continued searching, asking anyone who milled about town hall if they'd seen her, tracking Joyce like Grace tracked wolves, through a building instead of the forest. I found Joyce forty-five minutes later in the bowels of the basement. I hadn't been there since I was a kid, and with good reason.

Once I'd come to work with my father and begun exploring. I'd crept down the dark, dank cement staircase then as I did now, feeling chills wind up my spine as cobwebs drifted across my face and clung to my hair.

When I was ten, I hadn't lasted more than a few minutes on the ground level before I'd thundered back up and burst through the door, slamming it behind me. I'd heard strange things in that basement. I heard them again now.

Scratchings and scramblings—mice, no doubt. I didn't like them, but they weren't enough to make me run before I found out what in hell Joyce could be doing down here. I figured that all the times she'd gone missing, this was where she'd been. Considering what was going on in Lake Bluff, I needed to know what she was up to.

The lighting was dim—several bulbs were burnt out. My shadow trailed ahead of me across the cement floor, making me jump every time that I saw it.

The corridors twisted and turned. The basement was mainly used for storage and maintenance. Cardboard boxes, rusted filing cabinets, brooms, mops, and fuse boxes abounded.

In the distance I heard a low growl, and I paused. Maybe I shouldn't be down here after all.

Somewhere ahead lay an old storm cellar door, leading to the outside. Town hall was the tornado shelter for most of downtown Lake Bluff. People could get in from the street if need be, or out if they became trapped once the tornado knocked the building down. That also meant that anyone, or anything, might be hiding here.

I reached for my cell phone, thinking I'd get Grace to come and hold my hand.

"No service," I muttered. Should have known.

The odd growling noise increased, sounding more mechanical than feral. Maybe the air-conditioning was about to blow up.

I continued on, one hand trailing along the damp,

cool wall of the basement. I turned a corner and there she was, hunched over a desk like a crone.

"Joyce?" I murmured, and she shrieked, the sound bouncing off the close cement walls and making my hair stand on end.

She whirled, the stark bulb overhead flaring across her face, making it ghostly white, even as her eyes appeared completely black.

I skittered back, heart pounding from both the sight and the sound of her, if not the sharp, shiny knife in her fist.

"Claire! You scared the crap out of me."

She moved forward out of the light, and she was just Joyce again, though she still had the knife.

"Wh-what are you doing with that?"

"This?" She frowned at her hand, then reached back to the desk and held up an envelope, slitting it. "Opening mail. What did you think I was doing?"

For an instant I'd thought she'd been performing bizarre rituals right beneath my nose, but the desk was merely covered with letters. Nevertheless, I checked to see if she had a swastika-bearing rune anywhere close. She didn't.

Joyce glanced at the paper she'd withdrawn from the envelope, scowled, and fed both of them to the shredder next to the desk. The machine growled, low, deep, and almost as menacing as a wolf.

"Why aren't you doing this upstairs?" I asked.

She didn't answer, just kept opening envelopes and feeding the junk to the machine.

"Joyce? Is there something going on that I should know about?"

More than there already was, that is. I didn't think Joyce was aware of the werewolf problem, and I didn't plan on telling her. She'd think I was crazy, or she'd want to do something to help. I had enough on my plate worrying about Grace and myself; I didn't need Joyce deciding to hunt the woods as her father had done and winding up wolf bait like Balthazar.

The very thought made me physically ill and brought home just how desperate our situation was. If we didn't stop this thing haunting our town, soon people I knew, people I loved, would no longer be people.

Joyce bit her lip, as if she was trying to keep the words from spilling out. What was she hiding?

"You're not selling mail-order porn, are you?" My voice rose, thinking of the field day Balthazar—well, not Balthazar, but someone from the paper—would have with that scandal.

"What?" She glanced up, then laughed. "Oh, the Cleavers. No. I'm just taking care of stuff."

"What kind of stuff?" I asked warily, thinking of Granny and her still.

"Well, I guess you had to find out sometime."

"Joyce, you're scaring me." Considering what had been going on lately, that was saying a lot.

"I'm doing the extra work whenever I get a few minutes."

"What extra?"

"There's a lot more to running Lake Bluff than I've let on. I didn't want you to break and run before you found your stride."

I stared at her for several minutes as I processed that info. "Let me get this straight—you're working down here so I don't find out the job's harder than I think and take off like a chickenshit loser for greener pastures?"

"Pretty much," Joyce agreed, and opened another envelope.

"I thought you had more confidence in me than that."

"I do. But why push my luck? I certainly didn't want Balthazar in charge."

"You won't have to worry about that," I muttered.

She cast me a quick suspicious glance, but she didn't ask how I could be so certain.

"This is ridiculous." I waved at the pile on the desk. "Bring everything upstairs, and I'll help."

"You know, I kind of like it down here. No phone. No one dropping in to whine."

I could see her point. "You want to stay?"

"Maybe just a few hours a day."

"I should still be helping. I don't mind work."

"Once the festival is over, I'll give you a list." Her face took on a wary expression.

"What?"

"There are a few more meetings you have to chair."

I groaned. "Isn't the council bad enough?"

She smiled. "Nothing as bad as them, though Hoyt left a message."

"I suppose they thought up a bunch of new business."

"Of course. But he also wanted to make sure you were planning on going to the legion with them after the next meeting."

"Me?"

Joyce smiled. "Yep."

"Huh."

"Yeah. You've been anointed, girl. Congrats."

All the way back to my office, I floated. Although I wasn't happy to discover there was more work to being the mayor than I'd thought, it did explain a lot about my dad's obsession. Still I was thrilled that the council had accepted me as one of them so quickly. Those old coots weren't easy to get along with. I doubted they ever would be, even after several pitchers of Bud Light.

My office and the waiting area were still empty. Ya-hoo. Joyce arrived momentarily.

"Anything else come up this morning?" I asked.

Joyce shook her head, already preoccupied with the mound of paper in her in-box.

"Hold my calls," I said.

Once behind my desk, I stared at my blotter. I should get to work, help out Joyce, but instead my mind went directly to the nights I'd spent with Mal. I relived every touch, every word. Would I be reliving it for the rest of my life?

I turned to my computer, but instead of answering e-mail, I spent the next ten minutes finding a translation site for Gaelic.

"*A ghrá*," I murmured, typing it into the translator.

My love, my dear.

I frowned. He'd said that meant "pixie."

I leaned forward, thinking hard on the other words he'd murmured.

"*A stor.*"

My darling.

He'd never actually told me what that one meant; however—

"*A chroi*," I said as I typed.

My heart, my heart's beloved.

A little more personal than "beautiful one," which had been nice enough, but why lie?

Because those words were endearments. If he'd

touched me and whispered, "My heart," I'd have known what he kept in his.

What other words had he lied about?

I frowned as I tried to recall, but the only Gaelic he'd used had been that.

I remembered asking him to translate something else. *Ruvanush.* The title his people had used for him. Romani for leader, an elder.

Or so he said.

I managed to find a site that translated the Romani language, and it only took me forty-five minutes.

"*R-u-v-a-n-u-s-h.*" I stared at the word. "Is that spelled right?"

Shrugging, I hit *enter*. If it weren't, the thing would spit the word back as unidentifiable.

But it didn't.

I jumped to my feet and ran out of the office, ignoring Joyce as she shouted my name. Seconds later I was in the car, headed for the lake at a speed certain to get me a jail cell if anyone caught me. But I had to get to Malachi, and I had to get there quick.

Because in the language of the Rom, *ruvanush* meant "werewolf."

35

I HIT THE speed dial for every phone Grace owned with one hand as I drove hell-bent with the other.

"She's on patrol," said her dispatcher.

I reached voice mail on both her home and cell phones.

"Meet me at the lake," I said. I left out the part about the *ruvanush*. Time enough to explain that when she arrived.

Malachi's people had been calling him *werewolf* right under our noses. Not that anyone would know what the heck it meant, or bother to find out.

Until me.

What would he say when I confronted him? For all I knew, he followed the path of the *strigoi de lup* and killed anyone who knew the truth.

Except why hadn't he killed me? From what I'd read online and heard from Doc, werewolves were evil. They were unable, or perhaps unwilling, to keep their murderous natures at bay. Yet Malachi had been nothing but gentle and patient with me. He'd never hurt me; in fact, he'd healed me.

If he was a werewolf, how had he been able to remain in human form night after night? Unless only the approaching full moon brought out his beast. What then was the excuse of the other guys?

And how had Malachi managed to keep from burning when Grace had thrown the silver bullet at him? How was it possible that he wore a silver earring?

Either *werewolf* was a nickname or perhaps the test of silver was worthless.

The sun filtered through the trees, throwing dappled shadows across the front of my car and sparking blinding flashes off the windshield. When I shot over the last rut and slid into the clearing, I was left blinking as much from the reflections as the sight that greeted me.

"When they say they're leaving, they don't fool around." I got out of the car.

If it hadn't been for the trampled grass, both in the parking lot and at the base of the lake, as well as the indentations where the performance ring had been, I would have thought I'd imagined the Gypsies.

I strode back to my vehicle. They were traveling in wagons drawn by horses; they couldn't have gone far.

I reached for the door handle just as a shiver of movement appeared in the window glass. I began to turn and—

Bam! Out went the lights.

I AWOKE TO a darkness so complete I was disoriented. The throbbing agony in my head didn't help.

I lay on a cool, smooth surface. Not the ground. Not home. Where had I been? Where was I now? Who in hell had hit me?

I remained still; the pain wouldn't permit anything else. I must have slipped back into unconsciousness, because I awoke again—minutes, hours, days later, I had no idea. But I could sit up without wanting to shriek. I still couldn't see my hand in front of my face, even though I sensed the movement.

Crawling across the floor, I swept one arm out and struck something thin, metal, with a space between it and another just the same. Bars.

I shoved my arm through all the way to the shoulder and swung it around. Nothing but air.

I began to get nervous that I was not in a cage but outside of it, which would mean I was sticking my arm inside—to be torn off by Lord knew what—and I skittered back, smacking hard against a solid wall about six feet away.

Running my palms over the surface, I reached a corner and slid down another solid wall. I was inside a menagerie wagon from the feel of it, which meant there should be a door on the far side.

I managed to get to my feet, then shuffle across, arms still waving in front of me. The idea of running smack into Hogarth—in either form—almost made me go back to the corner and cringe. But I was done cringing. It felt so much better not to.

I stumbled into something and waited for the inhuman roar. Nothing happened.

Lowering myself to my knees, I reached out, then snatched my hands back.

That had felt like a body. But the skin had been warm.

Not dead then, or not dead for long.

I needed to know who it was. Biting my lip, I reached out again.

Long, silky hair, strong blade of a nose, full lips. I

knew the truth even before my fingertip brushed his earring.

"Mal?" I patted his cheeks. No response.

"Mal!" I put my hand on his chest. He was breathing. Unconscious, but how? Clocked in the head like me? He was immortal—although we hadn't really gone into details on that. Technically, "immortal" meant unkillable. It might not preclude getting knocked out.

But why had someone knocked us out and locked us in a cage? Where could we be that was large enough to house a menagerie wagon yet small enough to close off completely from any source of light?

Malachi moaned and began to move. I reached out to help, then inched back. I'd come looking for him because I'd discovered his people called him werewolf and we had a werewolf stalking our town. Now I was locked in a cage with him and the full moon was . . .

Well, depending on how long we'd been here, it could be full and rising any minute now.

I skittered to the far wall and listened. Groan, shuffle, curse. Still, silent, then—

"Claire?"

I didn't answer, couldn't move, tried not to breathe, but it was useless.

"I know you're here," he said quietly. "I can see pretty well in the dark."

"S-stay where y-you are." I sounded terrified, and that wasn't good. Animals sensed fear.

"How did you find out?" he asked.

"Find out what?"

"That I'm a werewolf."

I hadn't expected him to admit it. But then, he'd never behaved as I'd expected.

"*Ruvanush*," I said.

"Who translated for you?"

"Internet."

He sighed. "They've been told not to call me that, but after a few centuries, it's hard to stop. And before you, no one was around enough to notice. Before you, no one cared."

Though my chest hurt, probably from my heart breaking, anger began to trickle through the pain. Sure, I'd hoped I was wrong, that *ruvanush* was some sort of nickname. But it wasn't, and I had to deal with that, and with him.

"No one *cared* that there were people missing from their town? No one *noticed* that there were suddenly wolves where wolves weren't supposed to be?"

"There weren't."

"What do you mean there weren't? You haven't killed or bitten people in other places? Why is Lake Bluff special?"

"Wait a second; I haven't attacked anyone here."

"Then how do you explain werewolf tourist, werewolf Balthazar, and dead Josh?"

"It wasn't me."

"When you shift, do you even know what you've done?"

I couldn't believe I was having this conversation, but lately that happened a lot.

"I'd better explain exactly what kind of werewolf I am."

"There are *kinds*?"

"Hundreds. Thousands. I don't know for sure."

"You weren't made by Mengele for Hitler's werewolf army?"

I sensed a swift movement in the dark and reared back, my head smacking against the wagon wall, making me see stars in the ever-present darkness. But he hadn't moved toward me; his voice still came from the other side of the cage.

"How did you find out about that, anyway?"

"The doctor who examined Josh was in the war. He saw them."

"I've been a werewolf longer than that. Remember, I was cursed over two and a half centuries ago."

"That was true?"

"You think I lied?"

"Mal, you've been lying to me since we met." I sounded so defeated I wanted to smack myself for letting him know how much he'd hurt me.

"I didn't lie outright; I just didn't tell you everything."

"A lie just the same." I rubbed my eyes, which ached from the strain of trying to see in the dark. "Never mind that now. Finish what you started."

"I didn't go anywhere near Germany during World War Two. We traveled throughout Europe performing, but we heard about the camps, knew that others of our kind were being incarcerated and used in Mengele's sick experiments."

"Do you know how? Why?"

"We're magic, Claire. You think Mengele could construct a werewolf army without using supernatural means?"

"I don't know how he made a werewolf army at all." And I wasn't sure I wanted to.

"Lycanthropy is a virus, passed through the saliva like other viruses, which is why biting infects the victims. Although eating the flesh will only make them dead. Mengele mutated viruses and combined what he discovered with the blood of the pure Rom to create a werewolf."

"Where do people come up with this stuff?" I muttered.

"Evil people perform unbelievable atrocities. Werewolves weren't the only things Mengele made."

"What else?"

"Anything you can imagine, and a lot you couldn't. Beings that should only live in nightmares, but now they walk this Earth."

"Now?" My voice wavered.

"He released his creations before the Allies found his lab."

"Why did Mengele bother to make a werewolf? According to you, they've been around a long time. Wouldn't it have been easier to nab a few and proceed from there?"

"I don't know what he was thinking. Maybe he could exert some sort of control over the wolves he created. We'll never know since he destroyed his records."

"What happened to him?"

"Escaped Germany under a false name. Lived the rest of his life in South America. Died of a stroke in Brazil in the seventies."

"That sucks."

"You don't think he should be dead?"

"I think he should have been hung, drawn and quartered," I muttered. "Not allowed to live any kind of life. Did you ever hear any rumors about Hitler being a werewolf?"

"There were always rumors. When people are beyond evil, and they thwart many attempts to kill them, tales like that will spread."

"If you're not one of Mengele's wolves, what are you? Why doesn't silver affect you? Does silver work at all?"

"On wolves infected with the virus, yes. For me, no.

I was cursed by a witch. She called on the moon to make me a beast, and I became one."

"And then?"

"I killed her."

His voice was cool, detached, terrifying coming out of a darkness so complete I could see nothing, yet he could see me.

"You said you hadn't killed anyone."

"I said I hadn't killed anyone *here*."

I shivered. "You chose to be a wolf?"

"That was chosen for me."

"Why a wolf?"

"Her name was Rhiannon."

"Stevie Nicks complex?" I asked, before I remembered that this Rhiannon would have been born centuries before Stevie ever heard the name and wrote a song and twirled and twirled her skirt as she sang.

I guess it was true that in times of panic the mind goes to its happy place. Or maybe I was just so upset, I could only think in gibberish.

"She'd been named after the Celtic goddess of the moon, and she worshipped it as we did."

"I still don't see where the wolf comes in."

"Rhiannon was the Celtic counterpart of Diana and Artemis."

"I got a C in mythology."

"Goddesses of the hunt, they command the moon and the night. Patrons of the wilderness and the werewolf."

That made a little more sense.

"If I was a wolf, she thought she could control me, but—" He broke off.

"It's a little hard to control someone when you're dead."

"In truth," Malachi continued, "though she was

mi'zak, wicked, she had great power. It's understandable that she might think she could control the wolves;
she did command the moon."

A short bark of laughter escaped me. "She did not."

"On the night she cursed me, Rhiannon lifted her
arms, and the moon went red."

"I don't understand."

"You've never seen a hidden moon?"

I suddenly recalled the card Edana had shown me—
the moon flaring red, a hidden moon.

"A total eclipse," Malachi continued. "They're very
rare."

I suddenly understood that Malachi hadn't just
stumbled into town on a whim; he'd come here for a
reason.

"What happens to you when there's a full eclipse?"
I asked.

"The moon takes my soul, and I become an evil,
murderous, uncontrollable beast."

"The moon can't take your soul, Malachi, any more
than Rhiannon caused that eclipse. You *have* learned
something in two hundred–odd years, haven't you?"

"I learned that on the night Rhiannon hid the moon,
astronomically speaking, there shouldn't have been an
eclipse."

Hmm. I didn't like the sound of that.

"The Rom believe that Alako, our god of the moon,
takes our souls at death."

"You're not dead."

"I was. When she cursed me, when the moon went
red as blood, life left my body, and I was reborn as a
wolf."

"You're saying you can only shape-shift during a
total lunar eclipse?"

"Yes."

"Then who—?"

"I don't know!" His voice rose with frustration. "There is no wolf in my caravan. I was sentenced to be alone—the only wolf when wolves are pack creatures. Even though my people are cursed to remain with me, they're different animals, and they blame me for an eternity of wandering. They respect me as their leader; they fear me as the *ruvanush,* but they hate me, too."

"Where are they?" I asked. "You said they couldn't be away from you."

"Not more than a mile or two, at most, five. As animals, they need to roam."

"What happens if they get too far away?"

"They feel as if they're walking on hot coals. Their heads ring; their chests erupt in agony. No one's tried it more than once or twice."

"If the werewolf isn't a Gypsy, then why the rune?"

"I don't know. Rebirth points to shape-shifter. The swastika brings us back to the Nazis, and since we know they were creating werewolves with the blood of the Rom . . ."

"It's too much of a coincidence that you all wound up here on the eve of an eclipse."

"Yes."

"Someone's up to something and we don't know what it is."

He hesitated as if he meant to say more, then sighed and merely repeated, "Yes."

"Something that has to do with you?"

"I wasn't sure, but since I woke up in a cage—"

"Probably."

He didn't bother to comment.

"You said there wasn't a cure."

"There isn't."

The lights came on with a *thunk.*

"But there is," said a woman's voice I'd never heard before.

When my eyes adjusted to the sudden light and I saw who'd turned them on, I understood why the voice was so unfamiliar.

"Sabina?"

36

THE GYPSY GIRL stood near a door that revealed a small slice of the outside world—dark sky and a full, silver moon.

I glanced uneasily at Malachi, who sat in one corner of the cage, back pressed to the wall. How long had we been here? Was it still the night before the eclipse or was it the night of? Either way, I had a very bad feeling I'd been stuck in here with him for a reason. One I was not going to like.

Sabina let the door slide closed and walked toward us across the long, empty expanse of what appeared to be a warehouse. I'd been here before.

"We're behind the *Gazette,*" I said. "Where they load the trucks."

Sabina smiled and suddenly she didn't seem so sweet and helpless anymore; I doubted she ever had been.

"Balthazar was kind enough to give me his key before . . ." She paused. "Well, just before."

Before he'd turned into a wolf? Before he'd exploded and turned into ash? Did it really matter?

"How is it that you can suddenly talk?" I asked.

"I could always talk; I chose not to. When you're mute, people think you're deaf, too. You find out all sorts of things."

"You haven't talked for centuries?" I found that hard to believe.

"Not to anyone I couldn't trust."

"Edana," Mal muttered, and the way he said it made me glad I wasn't her.

"Let me out of here," I demanded.

"No."

"Sabina," Mal began. "You know what's going to happen in a few minutes."

I glanced at him uneasily. "A few minutes?"

"I feel the eclipse coming."

Ah, hell.

Sabina just stood on the other side of the double bars, staring at us.

"Sabina!" Mal said more loudly.

Her gaze met his. "You have to do it, *ruvanush*. It's the only way."

"I won't."

"But you will." Her lips curved. "You won't be able to help yourself."

"Do what?" I asked.

"He hasn't told you? And here I figured he'd spill his guts so you'd understand why he had to kill you. If it was me, I wouldn't care. I'd do what had to be done; I always do. But him——" She cast a disgusted glance at Malachi. "Over two hundred years looking for you, then he refuses to kill you."

"I——I don't understand. How could he have been looking for me for two hundred years? *I'm* not immortal."

Sabina made a *tsk*ing sound and shook her head.

"Didn't tell her that either, *ruvanush*? Shame on you. At least she should know why you fucked her."

I winced. I had liked Sabina so much better as a mute.

"And why she let you."

Malachi's head dropped between his knees, and his hair fell over his face.

"What's she talking about?"

He didn't answer. However, Sabina couldn't seem to shut up. "Have you been plagued by mist lately?"

"There's always mist. . . ." I waved my hand. "Because of the mountains."

"Or the *ruvanush*. The mist is his magic."

I frowned, remembering the vapor shooting from Mal's fingers when he'd changed half his band from animal to human, and how it had wandered through my dreams of a mystery lover.

"He didn't have time to court you," Sabina said. "He had to make you want him. He's become quite good at it. Usually the women come to him. But not you."

Had Malachi been playing me all along? Why should he be any different?

"The mist is a part of him," Sabina said. "It carries his scent, his essence, so that when you met him, he seemed familiar and safe."

I wanted to hit something, or someone.

"He had to see if you were the one who could end his curse," Sabina continued, "and ours, too."

I cast Malachi an evil glare. Liar, liar, pants on fire.

"Claire—," he began, but I looked away.

"How would he know if I was the one?"

"You have a birthmark." It wasn't a question.

In my mind's eye I saw Mal leaning over me, buried inside of me, kissing the mark, and whispering, "It's you."

I *had* wanted him much faster than I should have. Me, who hadn't wanted anyone since Atlanta. I hadn't wondered why; I'd just been happy that I had.

"He probably had you begging him to take what he'd been after all along."

I swallowed thickly, mortified to realize she was right.

"Is this true?" I asked. "You seduced me with the mist? You slept with me to see if I bore a mark?"

And then told all of his people that I had? My mortification deepened.

"He had to."

I rounded on Sabina, fists clenched. "I didn't ask you!"

She giggled, put her fingers to her lips, and made the motion of turning a lock, then throwing away the key.

"You knew what had happened to me"—I turned back to Mal—"yet you raped me, too?"

His head came up. "I wouldn't."

"If the sex is not given freely, that's exactly what you did."

"I stopped using magic days ago. Before I ever—"

"What? Touched me, kissed me, went down on me?"

"Made love to you."

"Love?" I laughed. "Right."

"I stopped," he insisted. "I was never inside of you because of magic."

"You were inside my head. You made me want you."

"That was before I knew—" He broke off.

"Knew what?"

"That I'd rather stay like this forever than hurt you."

"Asshole," Sabina muttered. "You try crawling on your belly for two centuries."

"There has to be another way!" Mal shouted. "I'm not going to hurt her."

Sabina just smiled.

Mal hit the bars and the cage rattled. "Let me out!"

"No."

"What does my birthmark have to do with anything?" I asked.

Sabina turned her attention to me, and Mal gave up trying to convince her, though from the way he continued to stare in her direction, he hadn't given up trying something.

"In every generation, one female descendant of the witch who cursed us bears that mark."

I didn't recall any witches on my family tree, but that didn't mean they weren't there.

"Rhiannon had many children, with many different men. Her descendants spread all over the globe. We traced them as best we could, but the records from that time aren't that good. We've been trying to find one who bears the mark for hundreds of years."

I glanced at Mal, who still glared at Sabina. "He's been seducing women for centuries to get a look at their breasts?"

Sabina shrugged, which I took as a yes.

I don't know why the thought of Mal screwing his way through the centuries bothered me. It wasn't as if we were going to get married and live happily ever after.

"You've never found a single descendant who bears the mark until me?"

"Poor timing appears to be a hallmark of the curse."

"Sabina," Mal murmured. "Why are you doing this? You were such a sweet child. Now you're almost . . . evil." He said the last word as if it were a revelation.

"Took you long enough to catch on, *ruvanush*." Sabina tossed the swastika-marked rune into the air.

"I don't understand," I said. "You're a snake."

"As long as I have this, I can become a wolf." She

stopped tossing the rune and rolled it between her fingers. "I am reborn."

"How does it work?" I asked.

"Under the moon I hold the rune; I say an incantation, and I become a wolf."

"That's it?"

She shrugged. "I feed the swastika with the blood of the pure."

"Feed it." My lip curled.

"Trace the outline."

"So it isn't red paint."

She merely raised an eyebrow. There *had* always been something creepy about that rune.

"How long have you been moonlighting as a werewolf?"

"A week." She stretched sinuously, still more snakelike than canine. "God, I love it."

"Why now? Why here?"

"The tree."

We'd kind of figured that, too.

"To make a rune of such power, I needed a tree that was as old as these hills, one that had stood the test of fire beneath the moon."

I remembered the long black lightning mark on the trunk.

"I wasn't sure it would work, but there's power there—the storm, the earth and sky. Magic. Now everything's going to be all right."

For her, anyway. My life appeared kind of dim.

"Once I was a wolf, I wanted to make more like me. I was so tired of being alone."

"You haven't been alone," Mal said. "You've been with people who loved you."

"No one was *like* me. I was a snake among mammals. You know I never had sex until I was a wolf?"

Too much information! I wanted to slap my hands over my ears.

"Not Josh."

"No. He was too much of a pig to give the gift of eternal life. I was walking along; he stopped his car, picked me up. I told him I lived down a deserted dead-end road. . . . I would have made him like me, but he grabbed me before I could change and tried to—" Her eyes darkened.

"I know," I said, sympathetic for a moment.

"I shifted and I killed him; then I drank his blood to make certain he'd never rise again."

My sympathy didn't last very long. Josh hadn't deserved that, although there'd been times I'd imagined much worse.

Sabina scowled at Mal. "Once you put an end to my curse by doing what you have to do, then I can be a wolf whenever I want to."

"Why would you want to be a wolf?" I asked.

"I'm tired of being weak. I want to run free and have everyone fear me."

"But your arm—"

"What about it?"

"I didn't think becoming a werewolf would cure it."

"So I limp a little. I'm still so much stronger than any human." She tossed the rune one last time into the air, then slid it into her pocket.

" 'Beware the devil who is a shape-shifter,' " I murmured. "Edana meant you. She showed me the wolf in her crystal ball, but it was too small to recognize the eyes."

Although it had held up its paw, I'd figured the thing was hunting. It never occurred to me the wolf might have a crippled appendage—in both forms.

"I knew she was up to something. Crazy old bat."

"Pot. Kettle," I pointed out.

"Sticks and stones." Sabina started for the door. "Pretty soon I'll have everything I want, and you'll be dead."

I cast a wary glance at Mal. He was breathing heavily. Sweat rolled down his face as he fought the battle with himself.

"I'll just leave you two alone. I really don't want to watch." Her eyes met mine. "I liked you, Claire. You were nice to me."

"Then let me out of here!"

"I didn't like you that much," she said, and opened the door.

Moonlight spilled in. The silver flash washed over her face, and she breathed it in like ambrosia.

"When the Earth completely blocks the sun's light from the moon, he'll shift." She turned back, and though her face lay in shadow, her eyes glowed. "The legends say that as he drinks the life of the one who made him beneath the hidden moon, he'll return to the form he once knew, and the curse will be broken."

"I didn't make him."

"Close enough."

Sabina reached into her pocket and removed the rune; then as she slipped out of her clothes, she chanted in the language of the Rom. When she was completely naked, she lifted the talisman, and the fading glow of the moon shimmered over her like a waterfall. She fell in a heap.

I glanced at Mal, but he was having problems of his own, curled into a ball, clutching his stomach as if in agony. Writhing, twisting, fighting the change. I didn't know how long he could keep that up, but I doubted it would be long enough.

When I returned my gaze to Sabina, a silvery glow

outlined her body, undulating, changing, re-forming human into animal. Between one blink and the next, a black wolf rose from the ground where the woman had been. The sleek beast stared at me with human eyes. Then Sabina slipped out the open door, leaving me alone with my fate.

37

I TURNED TO check on Malachi and reared back with a cry. He was right next to me, and I hadn't even heard him move. His fingers crushed my wrist as he yanked me to him.

Bones shifted beneath the surface; his nose and mouth merged outward. But it wasn't the physical changes that frightened me so badly I couldn't think, let alone breathe; it was the change in his eyes. Looking into them, I saw an entirely different being from the one who'd been there before.

"I've waited aeons for this," he murmured, his voice much lower, a growl that rumbled from his chest like an earthquake, skating across my skin like ice.

Leaning over, he pressed his nose to my hair and inhaled. "It's you," he said, and then he licked my neck.

I began to struggle, but that only made him laugh. "The more you fight, the faster your blood rushes through your veins. You flush. I can smell the fear."

He traced his teeth where his tongue had been. Then he ran a fingertip, which seemed to have sprouted a claw, from my jaw to my collarbone and with a downward slice, cut my shirt wide open. My bra lay in two identical halves, my breasts spilling upward like a sacrifice. There wasn't a scratch on me. I got the feeling he'd done this before.

His breath warmed my icy skin. He brushed his lips just above my heart, gently, almost reverently, and then he whispered, "Claire," in a voice so broken my heart seemed to thump once and then stop. "You have to run." He pressed his cheek to my skin. "I want to do such terrible things."

He'd released my wrist to wrap his arms around my waist, and I couldn't help but run my hand over his hair. "Shh," I murmured. "I'm here."

"You can't stay." He shoved me away, skittered into the shadowy corner of the cage. I glanced at the doorway as a shadow slid toward the moon.

"I'm trapped," I said. "Just like you."

"Oh, God." His voice wavered between man and beast. "It's coming. I'll kill you, Claire. I'll drink your blood as your life fades. I'd rather be dead, but I won't be able to stop myself."

"That won't be you." I swallowed, pushing aside the images his words conjured. "You can't blame yourself. I won't blame you. I won't hate you." I'd be dead, but that was beside the point.

For whatever reason he'd done what he'd done, he'd healed me. He'd given me back myself. What I'd begun to feel for him over the past few days had been more than I'd ever felt for anyone. If I was going to die soon, I wanted him to know the truth.

"I love you, Mal."

"What?" His voice sounded more human than animal.

"I love you; I know you love me."

"I—" He broke off, shoving a misshapen hand through his seemingly longer hair.

I inched closer. "You were willing to curse yourself to an eternity as a monster, and all of your people, too, for me."

"I couldn't— I can't—" He moaned, a growl of pain from his soul. "But I will."

"Focus on me, not the moon, not that thing whispering inside of you."

"Claire," he snarled. "You have to stay away."

"No." I suddenly knew with a clarity I'd never felt before what I had to do to save him and therefore myself. "I have to be near you."

"The smell of your blood makes me want you."

"I want you, too." I let my fingers trail over his hand. There was fur there; his nails had lengthened even more.

"I'll hurt you."

"Love is stronger than hate. Hate made you like this. She didn't love you."

"I couldn't love her. I couldn't love anyone. She said I wasn't capable of it, and that made me a beast."

"You love me; that makes you a man."

I hoped I was right, that he did love me. That love would be enough to fight what hate had done to him.

In that instant, the Earth moved between the sun and the moon, and the warehouse went eerily red, like a wash of blood across the sky. Malachi jerked out of my grasp; a horrific howl split the night, so close, so loud, my ears rebelled. Then the shriek of rending cloth seemed to sizzle along my nerve endings. It took everything I had not to cower in a corner as far away from what Mal might become as I could get.

But I stayed put. If he was going to kill me, he could do it over there as easily as he could do it right here. I couldn't escape, and in truth, I didn't want to. I would *not* let that witch win.

Murmuring his name, I reached out to cup his still-changing face. He growled, but at least he didn't bite me, then slowly I leaned forward, and I kissed him.

His skin felt as if snakes were writhing beneath my fingertips. At the touch of my mouth against his, everything stilled, and I knew that what I was doing was right.

I lifted my lips and whispered, "Kiss me back."

I waited, hoping, praying, near to begging, and at last, when he pressed his lips to mine with the fervor I craved, his mouth had re-formed into that of a man.

I kissed him, held him, murmured to him as the Earth shadowed the moon. Thankfully this eclipse would be one of the shortest ever recorded—in the vicinity of twenty minutes. If it had been one of the longer ones—where the moon could be hidden for hours—I don't know what I would have done, except died.

Malachi broke away, breathing heavily; when he spoke, his voice was again a growl, and despair pulled on me like the tide.

"I can't do this. The lust is calling the beast."

"Not lust." I tangled my fingers in his hair, which was only hair, not fur, beautiful, black and curling over my wrists in a wave. "Love. Tell me you love me, Mal."

"I—I—"

The rest of the words were drowned out in a bestial

roar. He knocked me onto my back, leaping on top of me and tearing at my clothes.

Closing my eyes, I concentrated on the good times when this gentle man had touched me and made me whole. I wouldn't let this be hate; between us there would only be love.

"Mal," I whispered, and pressed my mouth to his cheek, felt the bone shift beneath my lips. "Love me. Just love me."

He quieted; his hands went from hurtful to helpful, removing my clothes until I was as naked as he. We kissed, our tongues tangling together as our bodies did, too, and when I ran my palms over his back, urging him without words to make what we felt true, there was nothing left of the animal, neither within nor without.

He came into me murmuring my name. I wrapped myself around him, holding him close, opening myself, giving him all that I had.

His body was granite-hard, straining against me, striving for completion. I traced my fingers over his cheekbones, his neck, his chest, terrified I'd feel him shifting, catching my breath with wonder when he did not.

Suddenly the light changed, the pulsing red fading toward silver as the eclipse neared an end. Mal stiffened, groaned, and threw back his head.

I had an instant of total terror, thinking he'd shift while he was still inside me and then—

My mind rebelled at the image.

But instead of something horrible, something wonderful happened. He gathered me close, holding me as the orgasm took me, spreading from where we joined outward, until I tingled even to my toes.

"I love you, Claire," he said in a voice that was purely human. "I'll love you until the day that I die."

On the final word I felt him pulse and come, giving himself to me as no one else ever had before.

And in that instant, the moon burst free of every shadow.

38

WE LAY ENTWINED, staring at that bright, round moon.

"I'm cursed to become a beast beneath the hidden moon," Mal said. "In over two hundred years, I've never been able to resist its pull."

I turned his face to mine. "You were never in love before."

"No." He kissed me. "Never."

"Sabina actually did us a favor by locking us in here."

His face darkened. "I'm going to kill her."

"I don't think you're going to find her."

"I will."

The lights went on with a click, and we scrambled up, Malachi shielding me with his body.

I dived for my clothes, even as I glanced around his shoulders at the man and woman who approached.

The man was tall, far too thin, and older than anyone I'd seen standing. His hair had faded from blond to white, but his blue eyes were sharp and a little frightening. Or maybe it was just the arsenal he carried with him. Two pistols, one on each hip, a shotgun over his shoulder, a rifle cradled in his emaciated arms, bandoliers of bullets slung across his scrawny chest.

Who was this guy?

The woman was also tall, made even more so by black spike-heeled boots. She was both curvy and slim, blond and unbelievably gorgeous. Her jeans were designer, her cobalt blue blouse silk. When she reached up to shove her hair out of the way, I caught a glimpse of a pentagram tattooed on the palm of her hand.

"She's a werewolf," I blurted.

The woman's perfectly plucked eyebrows lifted. "Been doing your research."

"You aren't going to deny it?"

"No. But I'm also not an evil blood-drinking beast. This"—she lifted her hand, revealing a pentagram with one point ascendant—"cures them."

"Them who?"

"Werewolves. Like him." She pointed at Mal, then frowned. "Why aren't you furry and why isn't she dead?"

"If you don't mind," Mal said, "I'll be puttin' on some clothes before you tell me just who in hell you are."

"Be our guest," the old man murmured, the German accent I hadn't noticed when he first spoke deepening so I couldn't help but notice it now.

Mal and I managed to cover ourselves with what was left of our clothes. My shirt was sliced, but I was able to tie it over my breasts so I wasn't flashing anyone. He made a kilt from his pants but gave up on the shirt.

"You think you could let us out?" I asked.

"Perhaps you, but not him. Not yet," the woman answered.

I crossed my arms over my chest. "I'll stay with Mal."

"Suit yourself. Now tell us what happened."

"And who might we be talkin' to?"

The two exchanged glances; the old man nodded, so the woman began. "This is Edward Mandenauer, leader of a group called the Jäger-Suchers, or Hunter-Searchers. I'm Elise Hanover. We hunt monsters." She contemplated us both with an amused expression. "You don't seem surprised."

"After what I've seen lately," I said, "not much surprises me."

She dipped her chin. "In World War Two there was a project begun by the Nazis."

"Mengele, werewolf army." I waved my hand. "Fast-forward."

"You know about it?" She glanced at Mandenauer, who scowled at me so ferociously I got kind of scared.

"We have a doctor who served in the war; he saw things. And Mal's been around awhile."

"So we hear." Mandenauer eyed Malachi as if he wanted to take him apart and see how he worked.

"*How* did you hear?"

The old man's gaze switched to me. "I've been in town for more than one day."

A light went on in my brain. "You shot Balthazar."

He shrugged. "Someone had to."

"You couldn't tell us you were here? Clue us in on what was happening?"

"We do our best to complete our job and disappear. The less people know about monsters, the better."

"There'd be a panic," Elise explained.

"Oh, let's not have that," I muttered. "Much better for me to be locked in a cage with a werewolf."

"But you aren't," she said, "and I have to wonder why."

I opened my mouth, then shut it again as my face heated. How could I tell them that sex had saved me?

Well, not sex—I reached for Mal's hand and squeezed it tightly—love.

"He was cursed by a witch to become a beast," I said.

"Another curse," Elise muttered. "I hate those things."

"There've been others?"

"Several. Each one has to be broken differently, and no one's ever kind enough to leave instructions."

"Instructions on breaking a curse would kind of negate its being a curse, don't you think?"

Elise's lips curved. "You've got a point. So how did you break this one?"

"I was cursed because I could not love," Malachi said. "Claire showed me I loved her, and when I turned that love into . . ."—he searched for a word—"something tangible as I fought the call of the moon, the curse was broken."

"Tangible love," Elise repeated; then her brows lifted. "You did her during the eclipse?"

"If you want to be crude," I said.

"Sometimes I can't help myself." She paused, mouth pursing as she considered what we'd done. "Because he couldn't love, he became a beast, but loving made him human and able to resist the curse, and in resisting it was broken."

"That's the theory," I agreed.

"Pretty dangerous theory. What if it hadn't worked?"

"I knew it would work." I met Malachi's eyes, and

in his I saw a reflection of the love in my own. "I never had a doubt."

"Which might be *why* it worked," Elise said slowly. "Faith is pretty powerful, too."

"Hmmph," Mandenauer muttered. "Touch him anyway, Elise."

"Touch him?" I repeated.

"Werewolves can . . . feel one another," Elise explained. "If my skin touches his in human form, I'll know."

She held up her tattooed palm like a crossing guard miming, *Stop*. "Your hand please?"

Mal hesitated.

"You wanna get out of there in the next fifty years?"

He narrowed his eyes but moved forward. When they both reached out, they managed to brush fingertips between the space meant to separate man and beast.

Nothing happened.

Elise dropped her arm and moved back. "He's clean."

"You're certain?"

"Old man," she said impatiently, "have I ever been wrong?"

"Not yet," he grumbled. "What about her?"

"Me?"

"For all we know, he bit and infected you during one of your . . ."—his lip curled—"tangible love episodes."

"I wasn't like other werewolves," Mal said. "I didn't carry the virus. I never infected anyone, and I couldn't be killed with silver."

"How strange," Elise murmured. "Other curses have changed the makeup of the person, their very DNA, turning them into a true lycanthrope. I'd like to do some tests on you."

"What good would that do now, since he's cured?" I asked.

Elise shrugged. "I prefer to cover all my bases."

I could understand that.

Mandenauer was scowling at Malachi so ferociously I got worried he'd shoot him with silver just to see if he was telling the truth.

"What would kill you?" Mandenauer demanded.

"Nothing."

"There is always something," Mandenauer said.

"I was cursed to immortal wandering, to become a beast beneath the hidden moon. If I could be killed with silver, I wasn't very immortal, was I?"

"I've never heard of a witch with such power."

"I doubt there's ever been one again."

"Her power didn't preclude your killing her," I pointed out.

"Cursing someone in a fit of anger often backfires on the one doing the cursing," Elise said.

"Over two hundred years ago, I never knew when an eclipse might occur." A shadow passed over Mal's face. "The not knowing was a curse, as well. I tried to kill myself, to have others kill me, but nothing worked."

I could imagine how it had been when he'd first been cursed, uncertain each time the sun fell if that night he might become a wolf and kill the innocent. No wonder he'd entertained the notion of killing me. Over two hundred years of that would make anyone desperate.

"I do not like this whisper of immortality," Mandenauer murmured. "If there are more monsters out there that are unkillable, the world as we know it will end."

"Cheer up," Elise said. "You always figure out a way to kill them. It's what you do."

"True." Mandenauer's morose countenance lightened. He waved a skeletal hand in my direction. "Touch her anyway."

Elise glanced at me. "You mind?"

I held out my hand; we brushed fingers and Elise stepped back. "Zip."

"Can we get out now?"

Mandenauer lowered his head in an imperial nod.

Before Elise could unlatch the enclosure, Grace came through the open doorway.

She stopped dead at the sight of Mal and me in the menagerie wagon. One glance at Mandenauer and his weapons, and she drew hers. "Put your hands up, slowly."

Mandenauer snorted and ignored her.

Elise slid in front of him, arms spread wide in surrender. "We come in peace."

Grace scowled. "Then peacefully put up your freaking hands."

She caught sight of the pentagram, and her fingers tightened on the gun. "Who are you, and why did you put them in a cage?"

"Grace, it wasn't them," I said. "They came to help."

Despite Mandenauer's ferocious scowls and muttered complaints of "need-to-know basis" and, my personal favorite, "if you tell them, eventually you have to kill them," I told Grace everything.

When I was done, she scowled at Elise. "Why did you come to Lake Bluff? Did we just get lucky on your 'help the hicks' tour?"

"You called the CDC about rabies, asked about mutations in the virus."

Grace blinked. "So?"

"Calls like that get routed to us."

"You're a little Big Brother, aren't you?"

"You have no idea," Elise murmured.

"I don't think I like that." Grace seemed to have taken an intense dislike to Elise, and I wasn't sure why.

"I don't think we care."

Elise didn't appear to have a lot of warm, fuzzy feelings for Grace, either. Stranger and stranger.

"My people," Mal said. "Are they—?"

"Fine." Grace turned away from Elise with obvious relief. "They're at the lake, and every single one of them is human."

"They weren't human?" Edward said in a voice that made my skin prickle.

Oops. Guess I'd left out that little detail.

"It appears they were in on this whole kidnapping deal." Grace pointed at the menagerie wagon. "They wanted to be cured."

Mal's face went still, but I could see how much that hurt him. He was their leader; they'd been together for centuries, yet they'd gone against his orders.

I could understand why. They weren't in love with me. To them, I was the means to an end, the ancestress of the one who'd turned them into beasts. However, that didn't mean I'd forgive them for locking me in a cage with a soon-to-be werewolf.

"Tell us everything," Edward said. "Immediately."

As I filled them in, Elise's eyes became round with excitement. "I've never heard of a curse like this."

"You'll need to check them all," Mandenauer continued. "Make sure they're truly cured."

"You some kind of scientist or something?" Grace asked.

"Virologist," Elise said shortly. "Doctorate in viruses."

"Must be why you're such a laugh riot."

Elise's lips twitched, but she managed to control her amusement. "I'll head to the lake, sir."

She nodded to Malachi and me, then unlocked the cage and left.

We climbed out. I wanted a shower badly. Even though this menagerie wagon had been as clean as the others—suspiciously so now that I considered it; what kind of animals lived in immaculate cages?—I still felt kind of gamy.

"How many wolves do you think the woman made?" Mandenauer asked.

"I don't know." I glanced at Grace.

"Two that we know of—one's dead; one isn't."

"Probably more than two," Mal said. "There were nights I heard a whole chorus in the mountains."

"But won't they be human now, like the Gypsies?"

Mandenauer shook his head. "The curse is broken, but from what you told me, Sabina made others like her by biting them, so whatever magic she produced gave her the lycanthropy virus. They won't be cured so simply." He chambered a round in his shotgun and walked out the door.

"That's one scary old man," Grace commented.

Since I had to agree, I didn't answer.

"I need to get back to work." Grace put her hand on my arm. "You all right?"

I nodded and suddenly we were hugging, Grace holding on so tightly I couldn't breathe. "You scared the living hell out of me, Claire. When those idiots at the lake told me what they'd done . . ."

I understood. The Gypsies had been turned back into people, and they'd believed that had happened because Malachi had killed me and broken the curse.

Poor Grace. She'd had to drive all the way here thinking I was not only dead but horrifically so. Yet she'd come, as fast as she could, for me.

"I thought I'd never see you again," she said.

"Now you won't be able to get rid of me."

Leaning back, she peered into my face. "You're staying?"

"I think we might."

Her eyebrows lifted and she glanced at Mal, then back at me. "I'll talk to you tomorrow."

As soon as she disappeared out the door, Mal said, "We?"

My heart stuttered. "I thought that's what this was all about. *We.* If you don't want to stay, I'll go with you." Although that wouldn't be easy. I belonged in Lake Bluff, almost as much as I belonged with him. "Your people—"

Mal's hands landed on my shoulders, and he turned me around. "Not only is the curse broken, but so is my loyalty to them. They betrayed me." His fingers tightened, and he kissed my brow. "I think I've done enough wandering for several lifetimes."

"Probably because you've *been* wandering for several lifetimes."

"I never had a home." His hands slid down my arms, then rested at my waist. His thumbs stroked my stomach, and the skin danced at his touch. He froze, frowning.

"What?"

He placed one palm flat against my belly, and heat pulsed.

"Mal?" I murmured as his eyes lifted to mine. His had gone wide with wonder. "What is it?"

"A child."

"What?" I seemed to be stuck on that word.

"You're pregnant."

"How can you know that?"

"I'm magic, remember?"

"Still?"

"Just because the curse is broken doesn't mean I'm any less a pure Rom."

"A baby," I said, stunned. "Can shape-shifters have children?"

"In two hundred and fifty years, none of my people ever have."

"Then—"

"I was cured before . . ." His voice trailed off, and I could have sworn he blushed.

I remembered what had happened and in what order. The moon went from red to silver; he'd said he loved me; and then he came. Talk about timing. There had to be more than a little magic in that.

"Is that all right with you then? A baby?"

So many things were changing; I wasn't sure what to think. After all I'd been through, I was lucky I *could* think.

"I thought I'd be cursed to wander forever," Mal said, "that I'd never have a wife, a child, a home. I never dared to dream of any of them until I met you."

Suddenly the future became clear.

"Marry me?" I asked.

"Isn't that supposed to be my line, as they say?"

"It's the twenty-first century."

"And in this century women ask men to marry them?"

"Sometimes."

His lips curved. "I think I'm going to like it here."

"Is that a yes?"

He placed his palm against my stomach again; I laid my hand over his. Beneath them, I could have sworn something fluttered.

"That's a yes."

Don't miss the next novel in this sensational series
from *USA Today* bestselling author

LORI HANDELAND

THUNDER MOON

ISBN: 0-312-94918-9

COMING SOON IN JANUARY 2008
FROM ST. MARTIN'S PAPERBACKS